THE LIZARD IN THE CUP

A flicker of pink caught his eye beside the path and was still. He stopped and saw a little lizard, two inches long only, spread-eagled on a whitish stone; it was the colour of smoked salmon, and had the same slightly translucent look; at the ends of its wide-spread claws were tiny pads; a spiny little crest ran down its nape. Pibble stared at it, still as the drooping angel of Mrs. Davidson's monument. It rustled and flicked into a cranny.

Not merely interesting – uncanny. The samimithi. You drink the homely milk out of the familiar cup – an action so ordinary that you never even think of questions about trust or danger – and in the last inch you find this creature. And then you die.

Pure superstition of course.

Also by Peter Dickinson
in Hamlyn Paperbacks

Death of a Unicorn
Hindsight
King and Joker
The Last House Party

THE LIZARD IN THE CUP

Peter Dickinson

Hamlyn Paperbacks

A Hamlyn Paperback

Published by Arrow Books Limited
17-21 Conway Street, London W1P 6JD

A division of the Hutchinson Publishing Group

London Melbourne Sydney Auckland
Johannesburg and agencies throughout
the world

First published in Great Britain
by Hodder & Stoughton Ltd 1972
Panther edition 1974
Hamlyn Paperbacks edition 1985

© Peter Dickinson 1972

Printed and bound in Great Britain by
Anchor Brendon Limited, Tiptree, Essex

ISBN 0 09 941830 4

THE LIZARD IN THE CUP

Chapter One

'We could always have him murdered for you,' said Pibble.

'Rub him out?' cried Buck Budweiser, bouncing in his wheel-chair with excitement. 'There's creative thinking! There's a cata-lytic concept!'

He may have been right, but the catalysis never took place. The process was interrupted by a noise from outside the room.

The room was called the Tank, partly because it was where they were supposed to think, or rather Think, but mainly because of the window. This was the typical whim of an architect com-missioned to build a Mediterranean villa for an enormously rich man; a huge sheet of glass composed the end wall of the room, and the bottom third of it was actually submerged in the waters of the bay, so that you could watch the ripple-refracted sunlight moving in monotonously repetitive patterns across the wide green band, and small fish nosing for scraps thrown from the terrace above. You felt that if the glass broke the whole villa would begin to founder. A couple of hours earlier a servant in a frogman's uniform had provided an added distraction by swim-ming across and skimming the algae from the glass with a rubber spatula; though the frog footman was gone, Pibble still had spent most of his time gazing at the window. It was the easiest way of not staring at the girl.

Now, beyond the glass, the noise of the outboard motor which had buzzed and purred through the last hour of the discussion began to get louder, rising as the boat neared to a yammer which drowned talk. The glossy machine bounced into view, driven by an orange-haired woman who waved her free hand to the watch-ers. The white arch of the wake, brilliant in the afternoon sun, hid the taut rope. Now came the water-skier, swinging at an angle to the path of the speedboat and straight towards the window, his portly but still muscular bulk balancing into the fresh curve, his mottled red face grinning with effort; they watched him tilt like a motor-cyclist to bring himself round and miss the house, and then the butterfly-wing of spray forced out from under the slanting ski flapped against the glass and blotted out sea and sky.

'He's certainly a good target,' said Dave Warren as the noise of the motor died with a couple of coughs and the ripple-patterns resettled from their jagged hysteria.

George Palangalos snapped his pencil down on the table beside him. It was a small sound, but as effective as a gavel.

'This is nonsense,' he said in his soft and toneless voice. 'We have talked ourselves into stupidity. Let us call it a day.'

'Hey, but . . .' said Buck.

'Let it go,' said Dave. 'He'll be in in five minutes, and if he wants us to kick it around he can tell us.'

George began to select documents from the piles that littered the table. Dave gathered the rest, rattled them into neatness and slid them into a fat briefcase. Pibble pushed his chair back and sat still, simply waiting. He felt as though he had been all afternoon in a temporary limbo, half-real, as everything in the villa was half-real until the arrival of its master gave it meaning and its inmates flesh and purpose. The curious dull silence of the others made him guess that they had something of the same feeling – though of course they were used to it.

Certainly the discussion had been half-real, however intense and intricate it had become. Pibble was glad to relax from his role of Mafia representative into his true persona, the elderly ex-policeman who had been snatched from the luxury hotel on Corfu, just over the horizon, at the whim of the manic millionaire who had been paying for the Pibbles' holiday. He looked at the others again and decided that the documents ought to have included a cast-list – with Shavian stage-directions maybe, explaining at unwieldy length how the actors ought to look and speak:

MR. HOCHHEIM, played by George Palangalos.

Paul Hochheim is the President of a New England bank, Stubbs of Boston, but he has the appearance of a middle-aged Greek businessman. He is well below middle height and wears his silvery hair cut short. Although he is tanned to a careful brown there is still a greyness about him, as though colour were continually being drained out of him; into his eyes, perhaps, which are black, quick and brilliant. His mouth is almost lipless and moves very little when he speaks. This trait, with his leathery skin and darting eyes, gives him an inhuman look, almost reptilian. He speaks good English, but cautiously, like a man in thin shoes picking his way along a muddy path. He is not prepossessing, but quite impressive.

MR. BARNEY GROD, played by Dave Warren.

Grod is a senior official of the powerful Hucksters' Union, that perpetual target of campaigning journalists. However he appears to be a handsome young man, large and strong. If he were to exercise himself less conscientiously he would have a pot belly. His face is noble, broad-browed and framed by dark ringlets, for he wears his hair almost down to his shoulders; but despite this symbol of emancipated youth he gives the general impression of being staid, hard-working, clever and humourless. If he has a character to match his striking appearance, it is well-concealed. He is Central European by birth, reared and educated in England, but he speaks with the mid-Atlantic accent of the entertainment world, so naturally that you might think he was born between wave and wave.

THE MAN FROM THE MAFIA, played by James Pibble.

The inappropriateness of his appearance and accent for the part are regretted, but the actor is a stand-in for a Mr. Hal Adamson, who has had a regrettable accident in Minneapolis.

KO-ZEE-TOURS INC., played by Mr. Buck Budweiser.

Ko-Zee-Tours are a one-man outfit, and that one man appears to be only half a man, for his legs are negligible and end in child-size shoes that have never known wear. He is in his late thirties, but nearly bald. He is so restlessly excitable that he always seems to be on the point of breaking into sweat, despite the air-conditioning. He is very American, and sounds it. His face is round and eager, as if longing for adventures which his shiny wheelchair denies him. Perhaps it is this urge that makes him so good at his work, so perceptive of the longings of the job-imprisoned hordes. He sounds like a fool and an innocent quite often, but is neither.

DOCTOR ONESIPHORUS TROTTER, played by Doctor Titus Trotter.

Dr. O. Trotter is Minister of Tourism in the Southward Islands. He is a yellowish black man, stooped and hesitant. Half the government of the islands are his cousins, and he despises all of them. Having grown up on an island where only a few colonial officials were white, he became colour-conscious comparatively late in life, and defends himself against suspected prejudice by talking in a comic-Babu lingo he has invented for himself.

An Anonymous Guerrilla, played by Tony d'Agniello.

The islands have developed fast enough to boast their own revolutionary movement. Yes ... well ... yes ... oh, pull yourself together man. The guerrilla is beautiful, a beautiful mongrel, negro and Spanish (or Italian, to judge by the name) and perhaps Chinese, which would account for the angle of her cheek-bones. She holds herself entrancingly badly, in a drooping slouch which she makes look fluid and comfortable. If she stood straight she'd be nearly six foot tall. She is slight but not frail. Her skin is clear brown and her small face has large features – huge brown eyes, a wide mouth, a nose that looks boneless and made for soft nuzzlings. Her hair is not negroid, but long, luxuriant scooped curves of glossy fawn, dyed presumably, but strangely right for her. No, no, of course she doesn't look like a guerilla, but she manages to sound like one in the little she says, catching the jargon exactly. She has brains, then ...

Pibble decided that in this limbo of waiting no one was paying any attention to anyone else, and so he would not be noticed if he continued to look at her. But she turned and smiled at him, understanding his thought and enjoying his enjoyment of her as though that were perfectly natural. He managed to smile back in a strained sort of way.

Then the door at the back of the Tank banged open and they were all made real.

'Hi,' shouted Mr. Thanatos, 'how did you all make out with my game?'

He swept his free arm down a line of switches and the lights in the room blazed on. He stood in the glare, huge in his garish gold bathrobe, grinning with the animal spirits of ski-ing. His other arm was round the orange-haired woman's waist but Pibble could see that the pose was habitual, adopted with any woman who stood that close to him, and implied no intimacy. He could also see that the woman was not so sure.

'Your game was a draw,' said George Palangalos. 'No score. There is nothing they can do.'

'Oh, crap!' said Mr. Thanatos. 'They're sore and they're going to lose a pile of money. They'll try something.'

'Rub you out, Jim says,' put in Buck.

Mr. Thanatos glanced at him with a look of dismissive irritation, as if he'd made a joke in taste too poor even for this permissive household.

'Crap to that too,' he said. 'Come in and say hello, honey. You know George, I guess. That roman-emperor type is Dave Warren, my secretary. The darkie is Doc Trotter, who's going to run some hotels for me. The grey runt is Jim Pibble, who's just an old pal. The guy in the chair is Buck Budweiser, who's an ace at suckering folk to spend their money in my hotels. Tony d'Agniello's my girl. And this is Zoe Palangalos, men — George's brand-new wife. She's a great girl — came straight off the ferry looking like a peach, drove my boat for me for an hour and didn't hit any rocks and still looks like a peach. How's that?'

Greetings were grunted, murmurs of meeting muttered. Zoe fidgeted with the orange edifice of her coiffure — Pibble wondered what industrial resin she used to cement it into place so that it would retain its shape through the hurtling and spray of the speedboat. She smiled at George and put out her hand to him, though still clutched to her host's side.

'Ullo darlink,' she said. 'You work ard?'

George drew his hand down the side of his face so that dry skin rustled on dry skin.

'We saw you driving the boat,' he said. 'Did you have a comfortable trip?'

Her shrug was exaggerated, implying that no journey could be comfortable for a creature so delicate as herself. The gesture was comically inappropriate, she was such a robust-looking little woman.

'You finish your work?' she said. 'Now we are playink?'

George took the excuse to shift the conversation away from her.

'I think that part's finished,' he said. 'There's nothing they can do. They are fixed, Thanassi.'

'Except . . .' began Buck.

'That is nonsense,' interrupted George.

'Now wait a minute,' said Dave slowly. 'I thought it was nonsense at first, but I've been thinking. I reckon we ought to run it through the machine a bit.'

'Businessmen do not murder businessmen,' said George. There was a faint snap of anger in his words, as though the mere idea were blasphemy, but his face showed no emotion at all.

'Oo is murderink oo?' cried Zoe in frilly alarm. 'You George?'

The black eyes stilled her. Mr. Thanatos let go of her waist and she stood for a moment as if she were waiting for the next gentleman to clutch her to him, that being evidently the custom of the house.

'It's a crappy idea,' said Mr. Thanatos.

'Oo? Oo? Oo?' cried Zoe. The repeated hoot sounded like the beginnings of hysteria. Mr. Thanatos turned to her, very gently by his standards.

'Listen, honey,' he said, 'and then you won't have to ask questions. The government of the Southward Islands – that's in the West Indies – decided to develop one of their islands, called Hog's Cay, for tourism, and first off they got hold of a very respectable bank called Stubbs of Boston to raise the money. Stubbs got a group of guys together, and they were very tough guys indeed. The Hucksters' Union – you've heard of them? And the Mafia, because Stubbs looks like an old Boston Club, all colonels and professors, but in fact it's got a lot of Mafia money behind it. So this was all set up. There was a pile of money behind it anyhow, but the Mafia were interested in more than that; they had their eyes on this island less than two hundred miles from the States, with a government they thought they could push around. They'd have had a law-proof depot for their drugs trade. And they'd have set up Hog's Cay like Vegas ten times over. Then I happened along, sort of. I hit it off with the President of the Southward Islands, who's a great guy, a real big man, only he keeps his head in the clouds so he doesn't see what's happening round his ankles. I sort of showed him, and he sacked half his government and gave me the concession. Right? Now these other guys are still there, and they're sore, and they're all set to lose a packet of money, so it's high odds they'll try to get back at me. I want to know what, so I got some friends together and set up a War Game . . . ah, come on, you've heard of War Games . . . It's like this: some government wants to guess what's going to happen next in the Middle East, for instance, so they get hold of a group of guys who know about this and that and they say to them now you're Egypt and you're Israel, and you're Palestine and you're Moscow and so on, and the guys play it like it was real. That's what we've been doing here. Right?'

Zoe nodded. Pibble wasn't quite sure how many of the actual

words she'd understood, but Mr. Thanatos had focussed his moral energies into his explanation, and perhaps had rammed it home like that.

'So they are killink you?' she said, like a child who has got the sum right at last.

'Ah, crap!' shouted Mr. Thanatos, unfocussing and becoming once more a crackling mass of unrelated forces, like a thundercloud. 'Let's hear your thinking, Dave.'

Dave's great brow was furrowed with thought and worry.

'First,' he said, 'George is right that businessmen do not kill businessmen, but that's because they have nothing to gain by it. If Ford bumps off the head of General Motors, it does not result in Ford selling any more cars . . .'

'Fewer,' said Buck.

'But you're different. Your Organization is you, like Onassis is Onassis.'

'And Howard Hughes is Howard Hughes,' said Buck. 'And look what happened to him a couple of years back.'

'So George's point won't wash. Second, you've got a good hunch. We've all seen it working. And this time your hunch is they'll try something; we've been sweating all day to figure what, and they've got no options, only this.

'Third, another reason why businessmen don't murder businessmen is that they aren't equipped for it. They wouldn't know where to begin. But this lot aren't like that. The Hucksters aren't squeamish – they've settled some of their own policy disputes with a gun. And the Mafia still have the men.'

'New Jersey is a long way away,' said George.

'But Sicily's only just across the Adriatic,' said Buck.

'That Mafia is quite different,' said George.

'They've been getting closer, haven't they, Jim?' said Buck.

'I believe so,' said Pibble.

'What's your view, Jim?' said Thanatos. 'Christ, I wish we had Hal Adamson here.'

Pibble didn't wince at this reasonable wish.

'I agree with George, almost,' he said. 'I think it's incredible that they'd try anything of the sort. A hundred to one against, say. But it's still just worth thinking about, for that hundredth chance.'

Thanatos snorted.

'We haven't heard from you, Doc,' he said.

'It would work,' said the negro in his church-organ bass. 'The President told my cousin Onesiphorus "You are Minister of Tourism, so get us an industry." And now he and all my other cousins would be riding about in Rollses if you had not intervened. Your death would be popular with the Trotter clan. Our President is not a good judge of my cousins – there are better ones to be had. Some of them will be back in his government soon, and with you disposed of there will be no tourist industry unless they let these other people come back. With proper safeguards, naturally – proper unworkable safeguards.'

He laughed.

'Honey?'

Tony d'Agniello stirred uneasily before answering in her soft, slurred accents. 'It's getting violent out there in the world,' she said. 'Rougher every year. More dead.'

She spoke almost like a medium, as though another spirit were talking through her mask. The effect was chilling enough to make it difficult for the next person to break the curse-held silence.

'Ah, Christ!' shouted Mr. Thanatos. 'Let's have a drink.'

He hurled himself to the bookcase, clawed at the spines of a uniform edition of the novels of D. H. Lawrence and prodded his finger against the switches thus exposed. To his left a panel slid open at floor level and with a faint hum a trolley sidled into the room, laden with the paraphernalia of booze; but before it had quite cleared the panel it halted, juddered and sidled back. The panel closed.

'Ah, screw it!' shouted Mr. Thanatos. This time he worked the switch with his thumb and held it down, pressing fiercely as though he were prodding at the robot's electric jugular. The committee which had been meditating the unreal question of his life or death woke from the trance of boredom and became the eager audience of his duel with this gadget. The trolley, as if now certain of its function, darted into the room, stopped with a jolt that rattled the cans, then darted back. The third time it did not emerge at all; the panel slid silently open and shut, and that was all.

'Screw everything!' hissed Mr. Thanatos, and proceeded to do so. Perhaps he was trying to unstick the quavering circuits by operating the switches near-by. A steel storm-shutter chuntered across the outside of the big window, shutting out the day; the lights dimmed and a projector whirred into life, throwing on to the side wall a picture of a yellow hand with enormous finger-nails caressing a white breast; the lights changed to mauve; a blast of roasting air drove through the room, followed by a wind off winter mountains; the pictures on the walls replaced them-selves like postcards on a souvenir rack, Van Goghs flickering out of sight to be succeeded by autumnal Renoirs, succeeded in turn by gaunt Dubuffets; the atmosphere became a scotch mist of Chanel; Sinatra crooned.

'Srew everybody?' shouted Mr. Thanatos and turned the chaos off, carefully, switch by switch, until the steel panel slid back and let the dying daylight in.

'I don't know why I come to Greece,' he snarled, plunging into a vast armchair. 'No one here knows how to connect one wire to another. Get Serafino. Come and comfort me, honey.'

Pibble noticed Zoe Palangalos twitch, but it was Tony d'Agniello who got up and slouched across the room, smiling at her childish old lover. She nestled into the chair beside him. George picked up a telephone and said a few words in Greek.

'Watch this,' said Dave Warren, as though he were a guide at a quaint local custom. 'Serafino'll fix it, and that'll make Thanassi sorer than ever.'

A dark, plump man in a white coat came in, smiling with a servant's detachment, as though it were merely his duty to smile. He pressed the switch that had baffled his master; while the panel was still sliding open he rapped it with the toe of his glistening shoe; the trolley sidled out, but before it could hesitate Serafino nudged it with his knee, and stamped hard on the floor behind it as soon as it was clear of the opening. It hummed sedately to its proper terminus and stopped. The panel closed.

'Sorry,' said Serafino. 'Is the air condition. No like when room too cold.'

With a harlequin gesture of chilliness, arms huddled across his chest, he smiled himself out.

'Screw him, also,' said Mr. Thanatos with a world-weary grimace. 'Make me a drink, Dave, and tell me what to do.'

Dave sloshed and rattled at the trolley, still frowning.

'You're staying on? 'he said at last.

'This weather? Sure. Even if I *knew* a couple of punks with sub-machineguns were laying for me, that wouldn't stop me ski-ing. I'll go anywhere you like as soon as the weather breaks. It's sure to next week, or the week after. It never lasts long into November.'

'O.K., that's a fixed point,' said Dave. 'We could have looked after you better in London or Paris, but ... I reckon Jim's got the right approach. He said a hundred to one. Shall we take those odds?'

'O.K.'

'Right. You stake a week and that gives you two years.'

'I'm stupid today. Try again.'

'You behave for a week as if the hoodlums are out there. If we're right, then that buys you the rest of your life. If we're wrong, then you've wasted a week of your life. I reckon you can expect to live more than a couple of years more, doing what you damn well fancy, so it's a good bet at those odds.'

'O.K. I get you. So how do I behave?'

'Jim's the expert,' said Dave, as he carried a pint-size silver mug of bloody Mary over to his master.

Pibble quivered. Still, in a way, it was true. Or at least he was less inexpert than anyone else in the room. He cleared his throat, but was interrupted.

'I'm still ski-ing,' said Mr. Thanatos, 'and not in my bullet-proof vest, neither. That's what I come for – that and the local girls.'

He pinched Tony's thigh to make sure she appreciated the insult. She snatched up his hand and bit it. Good humour started to seep back into him.

Buck perhaps noticed the change as he wheeled himself back from the trolley, cradling his martini between his tiny thighs.

'You'll be O.K. inside the fence,' he said, beaming. 'You stay here, and hire some professionals, and they can't touch you.'

'New York offices are open now,' said Dave. 'I'll get on to Whatmore at Pinkerton's and have him send some good men out. And, too, he's got Mafia contacts – he might be able to check that end whether they're showing any interest in this place, or you.'

'Jim?' said Thanatos patiently.

'The first thing you ought to do is contact the local police. They . . .'

'No cops,' said Thanatos. Behind the two words came the whole force of his soul, now focussed again. This mattered. Mattered more than his hypothetical murder.

Pibble didn't like it at all, nor the stillness of the rest of the group, waiting to see how he'd take it. He turned to the trolley and found a bottle of Whitbread's, much too chilled for his taste. When he turned back with the icy glass in his hand the faces round Mr. Thanatos were still forcing themselves into naturalness. Only Doctor Trotter, who was standing over by the window teasing Zoe's broken English with his pidgin, seemed unaware that a new and nastier wind was blowing.

'You still want to help, Jim?' said Mr. Thanatos. There was a question in his hot small eyes, and it wasn't Who's been paying for a holiday you could never have afforded? It was Who do you trust? Where are your loyalties? Who is your friend?

'I suppose so,' said Pibble. 'I was going back tomorrow. I'll have to ring up Mary . . .'

Mr. Thanatos cackled.

'I like you, Jim,' he said. 'Now tell me what to do.'

Pibble found it hard to collect his thoughts as he stood in front of the armchair and watched Tony d'Agniello's long fingers moving in small caresses through the fuzz of fur that showed on the rich man's chest where his gold robe opened in a vee. It was impossible not to feel jealous – jealous in a different fashion from how he might have felt if she'd been curled up against heavy, handsome Dave instead of this gross old bear.

'How long have they known you'd be coming here now?' he said.

'A week, ten days. I didn't know myself. Buck was here already, doing a job for me, but the rest of us came out almost as sudden as you.'

'All right,' said Pibble. 'I think Buck's right and you should stay inside the fence for a couple of days. It looked quite good to me . . .'

'Cost twenty pounds a yard,' said Dave. 'We've got guards on it, and three dogs. We can arm the men.'

'You said a couple of days, only?' said Buck. He sounded as though that spoilt the fun.

'Suppose we treat the threat as real,' explained Pibble. 'There are three serious possibilities. First, that the enemy have an ally inside the house, who might, for instance, poison you. Second that they will try a commando-style attack, probably from the sea. Third that they will send a couple of professional gunmen to the island and try to ambush you. Shall we take them in that order – which is actually the order of improbability.'

'We've hired a new gardener,' said Dave. 'And there's a room-maid I've not seen before.'

'Pay them off,' said Mr. Thanatos. 'We can grow weeds and sleep in dirty linen.'

'O.K.,' said Dave. 'The mouth of the bay's narrower than it looks. We can get *Tisiphone* round.'

'Until a sou'wester blows up,' said Mr. Thanatos. 'I'm not having my new boat smashed for a crappy idea like this.'

'If a sou'wester blows up there won't be any ski-ing and you can go to Paris,' said Dave. 'A raid's a lot to lay on, isn't it, Jim?'

'Yes. That's why I said it was improbable. You'd need a boat, a crew, someone who knew the water . . . The best bet is gunmen on the island. I think we could check that in a couple of days.'

'It's a hell of a lot of island,' said Dave. 'Guerrillas hid out for months here in the war.'

'It isn't like that,' said Pibble. 'When a professional lays on a job like this – usually it's a bank raid – the first thing he plots is his getaway. He won't tackle it unless there's an escape route. Here he'll have a powerful boat at a safe anchorage, and another over at Zakynthos probably. He will pretend to be a tourist, which will give him a reason for wandering about in unlikely places, and my bet is that he wouldn't seem to have any connection with the getaway boat, which would have arrived separately. He'd be staying at one of the hotels, or just conceivably in a tent. So what we've got to do is check the hotels, have a look at the new arrivals if possible, and check the safe moorings. If we draw blank in both, I think Thanassi will be safe out on the rest of the island. The odds would have risen, and he'd be staking a hundred years against his week, which isn't such a good bet.'

'We have come here to work,' said George. 'Not to play foolish detective games.'

'O.K., O.K., we'll let you off,' said Mr. Thanatos. 'Dave, too. What's your Greek like, Jim?'

'Puerile,' said Pibble sadly.

'Hell. Buck can check the hotels – he's only got to show his card and they'll give him every document in the building – line all the guests up for him and throw out the ones he picks on. O.K., Buck?'

'Fine.'

'Zoe can check the harbour for you,' said George. 'This is a stupid game, but she will enjoy it. She likes boats, and making friends with strangers. It will amuse her while I do my boring work.'

'That's great,' said Mr. Thanatos, beaming. 'She can find a few pretty girls for me while she's at it. Then Jim can do the rest of the island, seeing he thinks it's so easy.'

'What does it consist of?' said Pibble.

'Nothing except a bunch of phoneys out at the South Bay villas, the other side of the town,' said Dave. 'Some of them have jetties, and they all speak English.'

'Is that all?' said Pibble, surprised.

'Most of these islands are like that,' said Dave. 'They look as if you could land anywhere, and so you can; but the minute a wind blows up you've lost your boat. Even those South Bay villas are dangerous in a west wind, and this place is hell in a sou'wester. The rest of it's rocks and cliffs and a few beaches.'

'Then we should be able to do it in two days, quite easily,' said Pibble. 'After that you'll have your professional bodyguards here, and they can keep an eye on the likely places in case something turns up after we've checked. I don't think there are any other precautions we can take with the men we've got, and even if there were I don't think there'd be any percentage in taking them.'

'Don't forget the monastery,' said Mr. Thanatos.

'Hell, they wouldn't try up there,' said Buck.

'Best anchorage on the island,' said Mr. Thanatos. 'And those two old lushes would do anything for a few hundred drachs. They know more about smuggling than they do about praying. If they get their souls past St. Peter it'll be as contraband. You go and look them over. Jim. Look the whole place over. It's worth the visit.'

'What's your interest, baby?' said Miss d'Agniello, tweaking a hair out of the mat on his chest. 'I don't see you getting to be a monk.'

Thanatos clutched her to him and his grating laugh shook the Dubuffets.

Chapter Two

'*Yasas, pater,*' mouthed Pibble carefully. It was not the meeting he had rehearsed, but the greeting would have to do. The monk peered down from the tree. His beard was a dirty yellowish grey and covered almost all his face, except for the bloodshot brown eyes and the blue lips. The unkempt hair and the blue colouring, all framed by the silvery olive leaves, gave him the look of some hitherto unclassified ape; but the long black garments and the decrepit riding-boots were human enough, even perched among the branches.

'*Kalos orisate,*' said the monk, deep and formal. He studied Pibble for a while and then said '*Englesos?*'

'Yes,' said Pibble. 'I mean *ney*.'

The blue lips smiled sweetly at him, and then spoke a long sentence. Pibble shrugged helplessly.

'*Then sas kataleveno,*' he said, ashamed as always that the one sentence of the language he was really practised in expressed his incomprehension of all the rest.

The monk smiled again, and pointed to where a number of baskets were propped against each other by the foot of the tree. They were shaped like flower-pots, two large ones and four small ones; one of the large ones had a layer of glossy black olives in the bottom; Pibble picked it up and heft it towards the monk, who began to descend gruntingly from his perch. He had only one hand to hold on by, because the other hand was clutching a section of his black garment in front of him as if it had been an apron. It took a bit of manoeuvring before both men were in a position where he could tip the olives he had picked into the basket. He balanced himself, let go of the branch he was holding, and used both hands to shake the fruit out of the apron. He had almost finished when he slipped.

Pibble would not claim to have caught him; but he undoubtedly broke his fall. Part of it, anyway, for the monk must have managed to clutch at a branch and slow his descent, or Pibble would have been more crushed than he was. The man was large, and well-fleshed, and his garments smelt like a cow-byre.

Pibble lay on his back; the monk lay on his front, spreadeagled across Pibble; the basket, its base caught in a crotch, rained olives on them. In a few seconds the monk grunted, stirred, and hauled himself upright by the tree-trunk, where he stood, cursing. Pibble was slightly winded, but the monk made no effort to help him up. Suddenly the big face tilted to ask a brief apology of the sky for the bad language, and then smiled down at Pibble.

'O.K.?' he asked.

'O.K.,' wheezed Pibble, and sat up. The monk picked up one of the smaller baskets, knelt, and began to gather the fallen olives, so Pibble took another one and did the same. There were two sorts, the glossy, almost plum-like ones, soft and showing white flesh where the fall had broken the skin, and little raisin-like objects, shrivelled and hard. He showed one of the latter to the monk, who said '*Ohi*' and jerked his eyebrows up, so Pibble left them lying.

An hour later he was up a tree himself, and ludicrously happy. This was his sixth visit to Greece, and though he loved the country almost as much as Mary, his total failure to learn the language had left him each time more discontented; he still lacked the knowledge and confidence to do more than order easy drinks in tavernas too primitive for the waiters to speak English. On one's first holiday in any foreign country what matters is landscape and buildings and beaches and food; the inhabitants, apart from bringing the food and driving the excursion coaches and arguing drunkenly under your window in the small hours, seem to have no more relevance than the mysterious small figures in the corner of a Poussin landscape; but at each fresh visit they matter more – as in the Poussin, where one comes to realize that the landscape would be nothing without the figures, and starts to wonder what the man's heroic gesture means, and why he is wearing his helmet for what otherwise appears to be an amorous assignation. The inhabitants become steadily more solid, and oneself, the tourist, less so; to them, one finds, one is not a person at all, only part of a crop. There is a tree-like structure in their lives and interrelations, rooted in this soil, putting out leaf and flower – no, the tourist is not the fruit, that is his money; he is only a curious earwig-like creature, crawling from flower to flower, from resort to resort, making them fertile. And even if one were to settle on Hyos – supposing one could afford one of the staring new villas of the South Bay, which Pibble had seen from the ferry – one would still be only a parasite on the tree; mistletoe, or the aptly-named dodder. Pibbles, unless they are very much in need of a rest, make poor tourists; after the first few days they are oppressed by their own functionlessness; if only there were a wall to repoint, a series of petty thefts to be sorted out, roses to prune; but all one is permitted to do is be a bystander, to sit drinking retsina by the quay while the octopi are tossed ashore. One is a ghost-like thing, unreal because one cannot take part in the real life, doubly unreal because one cannot communicate.

But now, up in his tree, Pibble was at least taking part, and had no need to communicate. Picking olives turned out not to be a difficult job, in a technical sense. The black ones were ripe, the green ones were not. The trouble was that it was early in the long season during which olives are gathered, so that there were comparatively few of the black, and those were mostly towards the top of the tree, where they got more sun. The first tree he had done had been properly tended, pruned as one prunes a standard apple to keep it open and airy; but the one to which the monk had now led him was a mess, a tangle of criss-cross twigs through which he had had to force his way until he emerged into the brilliant October sunshine. But it was worthwhile; a lot of olives had ripened up here, the tangle of twigs gave him something to balance his basket and the main branches offered several good footholds. He made a resolution to climb more trees for pleasure; it must be fifty years since he had last done so – and only occasionally since then by way of trade. Last year he'd climbed down a cedar to escape from a burning building, and before that – it must have been 1958 when that tobacco heiress had tried to fake her own kidnapping in a balloon ... He began to wonder whether there was a book in it – must be *natural* for ex-apes to climb trees, subliminally frustrating not to – or would it be more profitable to found a tree-climbing clinic? The Dendropsychists?

He was stretching for a succulent monster olive at the limit of his reach when somebody yelled at him from the ground. He started, rebalanced himself and the basket, and parted the leaves to peer down. The man shouted again. He wore a grey shirt, pale old jeans, and even paler boots; his face was as brown as timber, his eyes dark, and he had trained across his cheeks a sweeping black moustache which gave fire and drama to what would otherwise have been a vacuous countenance. He went on shouting. He gesticulated. He kicked the tree.

'*Pater* ...' said Pibble feebly, and gestured towards where he had last seen the monk, but as his arm was hidden by the leaves the man could not see the gesture, and must have thought that Pibble was claiming an improbable kinship. He blinked, and kicked the tree again. Pibble poked an arm through the screening leaves and pointed up the grove. The man turned and started shouting again, but not at Pibble. The monk appeared in his circle of vision, put his hands on his hips and stood his ground, like a fishwife about to embark on repartee. The stranger, still shouting, gestured fiercely at Pibble. The monk smiled up through the leaves and pointed emphatically towards the ground.

'*Englesos*,' he said to the other man.

Pibble didn't want to come down. There was still plenty to pick up here, and for all his work his little basket was less than half full. But there was nothing for it, so he made his way carefully to earth.

The moment he landed the newcomer rushed over, snatched a handful of olives from the basket and thrust them under Pibble's nose.

'Don't ask me,' said Pibble.

The English phrase was like a bucket of water thrown over a fighting dog. While the man grappled with the knowledge that here was someone it was no use shouting at, the monk began to answer the accusation in his deep, harsh voice; as he did so he pointed with priestly emphasis at various parts of the grove. Without warning the newcomer turned away and rushed down the slope to a yellowish lump of rock that projected among the dark tree-trunks some twenty yards away; when Pibble looked at it properly he saw that it was the butt of a broken column. The man took his stance by it, then paced towards them, shouting the number of the steps as he came, until he stopped well beyond the tree in which Pibble had been perched. He spun round, his body tense with triumph, and barked at the monk. Calmly the monk pointed up the slope and began to count trees from the top. Pibble fidgeted and hoped that he was not going to be called as a witness in a law-suit – that would be partaking in the life-pattern of the inhabitants too intensely.

He was scratching a minor itch near his left nipple when his hand bumped against something bulky and unfamiliar in his shirt-pocket. Thanatos's cigars – this might be a chance to get rid of them. Both Greeks were in full voice as he unscrewed the metal caps and shook the huge weeds half out of their protective metal cylinders; then he stepped forward and offered them to the disputants.

Both stopped in mid-shout. The monk's blue lips smiled. '*Ep-haristo*,' he said as the took one. '*Parakalo*,' said Pibble, knowing what was expected of him, though the conversation didn't usually take place this way round. The other man took his more gingerly, and sniffed at it. The monk bit off the end of his with yellow teeth and spat it out. '*Fotia?*' he said, and the other man produced a box of matches, lit one and held it out. The monk made a clicking noise and took the whole box. He lit a fresh match, warmed the end of the cigar, lit another, repeated the ritual, and finally put the cigar in his mouth and drew at it. Quite a monk-of-the-world, thought Pibble. The stranger imitated the monk, if dubiously, and soon the sweet and civilized reek of Cuban tobacco was drifting through the grove, bringing inappropriate memories of city dinners to mix with the dusty, herby smells of the island air. The stranger turned and politely offered his box of matches to Pibble.

The brown face flickered at the realization that Pibble was not smoking. The man took his cigar out of his mouth and offered it, glistening with saliva, back to Pibble, who shook is head, realized that that would be meaningless to a Greek peasant used to the click-and-eyebrow trick, and pulled out his Collins phrasebook. The only reference to smoke in the index was to do with the funnels of steamers, so he put the book back, tapped his chest and coughed expressively. The stranger stared at him, sniffed warily at the smoke of his cigar and glanced sideways at the monk.

'*Englesos*,' said the monk, puffing confidently. God might permit his olives to be spilt, but He wasn't going to let him be poisoned by such an excellent cigar. The stranger's face cleared, as if he thought it quite reasonable that a non-smoking English-man should be climbing his trees, stealing his olives, carrying two enormous cigars. Even if Pibble had been bilingual, he'd have found it difficult to explain the nuances of gifts from Mr. Thanatos – deliberately useless tokens being his host's notion of tactful generosity. It was fellow-millionaires who had ten-thou-sand-drach notes, pressed into their hands as they left for a walk round the town, non-smoking paupers who were given cigars. Perhaps the reasoning was that it was indelicate to imply that anybody was so poor as to need anything, so if you wished to be generous you had to load them with gifts they didn't need. Also it embarrassed them: Thanatos would enjoy that aspect.

The monk stood in silence, relishing the tobacco, then spoke quietly to the stranger, who answered with perfect placidity. He took the small basket from Pibble. The monk strode up the grove to where the other baskets were and emptied the small ones into one of the big ones; then he stacked the small ones into the other big one and picked that up. It couldn't have weighed much, Pibble reckoned – certainly not as much as the half-hundred-weight or so of the morning's harvest which *he* was left to carry. The stranger watched, clucking at Pibble's efforts to swing the thing up between his shoulders, then took one handle. Together they carried it up to the path.

The gold-coloured gravel and rock of the path dipped just beyond the grove and passed a neat well before rising to another horizon, a ridge screened by more olives, a few cypresses, and a little wood of twisted ilexes. Pibble was puzzled, because he was certain they must be very near the sea – had in fact expected to top the previous ridge and look down on a spread of white walls and pink tiles, with perhaps a cracked bell clanking, and all this silhouetted against calm blue water. But no. Here they were, striding out of yet another close and broken valley. The monk's skirt swished; cicadas squeaked their intolerable endless squeak; one helicopter troubled the enormous air.

It also troubled Pibble; he felt very frivolous having spent an hour learning to pick olives; but at least he'd been told to come, and had wormed his way effectively into the monk's reeking bosom.

The monastery had been hidden by the ilexes, and it was a disappointment. Instead of the interlocking planes of sun-soaked tile and plaster, he saw only a wall topped with a negligible slope of roof. Apart from one large doorway there was no opening in all its length, though it ran in an irregular fashion out of sight behind trees in either direction. It looked old, or at least battered, but uninteresting. Away to the left a couple of workmen were retiling a section of the roof. Between the wood and the wall ran a cleared strip, most of it rank with withering weeds; but by the path someone had scratched the soil enough to produce a few rows of vegetables.

The monk opened the door with a silly little key and stepped inside without looking round. The peasant muttered something to Pibble and lowered his side of the basket. When Pibble did the same, the peasant made flurried gestures with his cigar to show that he was now going to carry the small basket only, and Pibble would have to do the best he could with the big one.

'All right,' said Pibble, 'but you'll have to help me up with it.'

The doubled weight seemed enormous. He nearly let go, stepping through the doorway, and again nearly fell as he followed the peasant on to one of the two flights of stairs that led down from either side of the big landing inside the door. There were windows on the left side of the stairs, letting in a flood of light and a glimpse of dazzling water, but he couldn't gaze out to discover why there seemed to be no tree-tops or roofs beneath him because he had to go down the stairs crabwise, looking away from the windows, to balance the weight on his back, picking his way through the slippery hollows worn by generations of holy soles.

The bottom step led straight into a room where Greek voices were already talking. Pibble lowered his basket carefully on to the nearest of a number of shiny red café tables and looked about him.

The room was a barrel-vaulted chamber, large and plain. It was lit by two glassless windows, each with a central pillar that supported a pretty double arch of carved stone. The tall monk who had brought them was now at the inner end of the room, rattling in a cupboard and talking over his shoulder to another monk. This one was smaller and older; he had swung round from a sloping desk at which he had been painting a picture and was making inquisitive noises. Beside him an even smaller painter worked on, wearing blue jeans, a pink blouse and long dark hair – a hip novice, wondered Pibble. The peasant had put his basket of disputed olives on to another of the incongruous tables and stood sentry over it.

The large monk turned from the cupboard and put glasses, a bottle and a pitcher on to one of the four tables that had been arranged together in a line up at the end of the room, to form a sort of High Table. The pitcher had a piece of sponge jammed into its neck. The small monk licked his lips, which were a shade bluer than the large one's, just as his beard was dirtier and his spectacled eyes more bloodshot. He turned to the visitors.

'*Kalos irthate, Vangeli,*' he said.

'*Kalosti, Papa,*' said Vangelis, standing surly by his basket.

'*Kalos irthate, kirie,*' said the old man to Pibble, so mumblingly that he sounded uncertain whether his visitor was there or not.

'*Kalos sas vrikame, Papa,*' said Pibble, and went sturdily on with a couple of other sentences that he knew reasonably well, from practice: '*Imi Anglos. Legomai James Pibble.*' He never said this without imagining how his hearers would be mentally spelling the syllables into greek: Tzaimz Pimpel.

'*Anglos?*' said the monk with doddering interest. '*I Nancy inai Anglida.*'

With a sigh of boredom the supposed novice looked round. She had large, dark eyes but her other features were small; her skin was smooth, brown, young and very dirty.

'Hello,' she said with nought per cent friendliness in her voice. 'What are you doing here? *Yassou, Vangeli.*'

'*Yassou, Nancy,*' said Vangelis.

By now the large monk had poured five shots of colourless liquid into the tiny glasses; Vangelis darted forward, picked one up, muttered a health and almost drained the glass at a gulp. He glanced over his shoulder, as if to make sure that both Pibble and the basket were still where he'd left them, and poured another colourless liquid from the pitcher into the dregs. The result was a chalky white. Hell, thought Pibble, ouzo. The small monk lurched off his stool while this was going on, and had drained his own glass before Vangelis turned to carry his diluted drink back to his guard-post. The monk refilled his own glass from the bottle, not the pitcher, and wavered back to his desk with a second shot of neat ouzo. The girl swore in English and went to get her own; now that he saw her standing, Pibble realized that she was tiny; but for that experienced young face she might have been a twelve-year-old. As he followed her to the drink-table he was able to see what she had been painting – an icon, the Virgin and Child in the traditional pose, but done with slick modern brush-strokes. She had been copying the design from a postcard pinned to the board, and had finished the background and most of the robes. Only the faces were still blank.

The artist-monk said something in that curious interrogative note which Pibble was so bad at catching; the big monk came round the table and handed over his cigar; the painter took several appreciative puffs at it and then offered it to Nancy, but she had been quick with her own cigarette and, though she didn't light it, had an excuse for refusing. Pibble was glad to see that she hadn't even sipped her ouzo, and in the confusion was able to refrain also. He followed her over to the window.

The big monk repossessed his cigar and took one of several ancient box-files from the shelves by the cupboard, crossed the room again to pick the spectacles off the painter's nose, put them on his own and began to hunt through the papers. The girl swore again, nastily; or at least the old word sounded nasty on her lips.

'I'm afraid we interrupted you,' said Pibble, very stiffly.

'Sorry,' said Nancy, tucking her cigarette back into its case. 'You get into bad habits when nobody understands what you're saying. The trouble is Father Polydore can't paint without his glasses, so he'll drink. And after a couple more drinks he won't be able to paint, even with his glasses. And I can't paint if he doesn't, because then pictures aren't holy and it would be a fraud to sell them to the tourists.'

'I could help myself to another and knock the bottle over,' said Pibble, looking down at his untouched glass. Nancy's, he noticed, was already empty. He was sure she hadn't drunk it.

'There's a dozen more in the cupboard,' said Nancy. 'We're in for a session with Vangelis here.'

Her eyes followed the movement of his hand as he edged his glass over the sill and tipped the liquor out. She must have done the same, but her look was not one of complicity.

'I can't stand the taste,' he said.

'I like it,' she said, 'but I'm off liquor.'

The large monk called, and Vangelis left his post and pulled up a chair opposite the central seat of the High Table. The monk tossed him a sheet of paper. He picked it up and stared at it, rubbing his chin. The monk snatched it back and, holding it at arm's length, started to read it out in a deep, intoning voice.

'Vangelis can't read,' said Nancy, 'let alone legal Greek. What the hell's all this about?'

'I was helping the old man to pick olives, and I was up the tree he'd shown me, picking away, when Vangelis appeared underneath and started bawling me out. It looks as though we've come down here to look at a legal document.'

'You've come down here to blow your tops on ouzo,' said Nancy sourly. 'What kind of a tree was it?'

'Are there different kinds? I suppose there must be. The olives looked just like the other ones but the tree hadn't been pruned for several years.'

'He's a bloody old crook,' said Nancy. 'If it hadn't been pruned, that means that nobody was quite sure who it belonged to, so no one was prepared to do the work. But anyone would pick the fruit if they got a chance, especially if they could get a stranger to do the dirty work. These early olives are worth a mint.'

'They seem pretty engrossed,' said Pibble. 'Will it be rude if we turn our backs on them? I'd like to look at the view.'

'No, it's all right,' she said. 'In fact I'd be glad to keep out of the row. Vangelis is my landlord, sort of – that's to say he lets me live in a hut in his vineyard – and I earn my keep from the Fathers. Anyway, it's worth looking at.'

There was just room for a pair of shoulders between the window's edge and the central pillar. Pibble leaned his elbows on the gold sill and craned out. Faint noises, and the feel of the air, had prepared him for half of what he saw – the sea lolling against the rocks of the deeply indented bay a hundred feet below. But not the other half. Where the cliffs should have plunged sheer there was nothing but building – blue and pink and gold, ornate and plain, arched windows and square, vertical village appliquéed to the rock. He might have been leaning out of the window of a city flat and looking at a complex old tenement across the square, except that where the traffic would have churned there was still water, and the buildings didn't reach to it; on an irregular line, but always at least twenty feet above the surface, they stopped and became natural rock. In places where the cliff sloped back there were quite big areas of roofing, the common rounded tiles of the Mediterranean, or a scree of slates; but mostly the walls went vertically up, pocked with windows, scarred with erratic balconies It was like . . . like the houses of a town pictured in a mediaeval manuscript, all on top of each other? Yes, a bit. No, it was like the combs of wild bees clinging to the cliff.

'Crippen!' he said at last. 'How old is it?'

'Oh, bits of it are very old. There's always been a monastery here, ever since St. Sporophore.'

'I've missed out on him.'

'He was a beautiful youth, a Christian, and one of the pagan emperors wanted to make him his lover. Domitian, I should think.

It's usually Domitian. So he prayed to be made unacceptable to the emperor, and the Virgin Mary came to him in a vision and gave him a beak and covered his body with feathers, which made the emperor cross enough to peg him out on a hill to be eaten by crows. But the crows undid the ropes and picked him up and carried him over the sea and set him down in a cave here, in the cliff, and fed him like Elijah. And that made him so holy that a group of disciples came and formed a . . . a *lavra*, I think the word is . . . and filled up the other caves and then started to build huts on the rock, and the monastery grew out of that. Until about two hundred years ago you couldn't reach it except by being lowered from the top or pulled up from the sea.'

Pibble missed his moment to ask about the harbour, because he was amused by the story and the way Nancy told it, as though all the parts of it were as true as each other.

'Does St. Sporophore have his own day?' he said.

'Of course he does. As a matter of fact it's next Sunday, November the first.'

'But that's All Saints' day, isn't it?'

'Not in the Eastern Church. They have their Ton Panton on the first Sunday after Pentecost. But actually St. Sporophore's day is a bit like All Saints' here, because they do a marathon service for all the other holy men who've lived in the monastery. There've been hundreds of them.'

Pibble looked at the nicked and noduled cliff-scape and thought of the centuries of occupation by bearded, black-robed monastics. He remembered the legend.

'The monks must look quite like crows,' he said. 'I mean, from the other side – if there were one on that balcony there. How many of them are there?'

'Only these two old birds.'

'It's a hell of a lot for them to keep up, isn't it? Or does the government help?'

'Nobody's bothered till just recently. Look, over there, there's a whole patch of roofs fallen in. And round to our right – you can't see it from here, but it's a bit beyond the Catholicon – a strip of cells fell out about twenty years ago, from top to bottom, and now you have to get across to the other side on planks.'

'Someone was mending the wall at the top,' said Pibble.

'Yes, they've come into money. They're probably the richest men on the island – I mean, of the people who really belong here.

Ages ago, in the nineteen-thirties, I think, the government in Athens confiscated a lot of land from the monasteries all over Greece. They used to be huge landowners before that, but then they became poor, and that's one of the reasons why you practically never see a young monk, except in places like Athos. Anyway the government couldn't get rid of all the land at once without playing hell with land prices, so they sold it or gave it away bit by bit. But then there was the war, and other things, and a lot of it was never sold and two years ago this government – you know, the Colonels – passed a decree to give back anything that hadn't been sold to the monasteries. There was quite a lot on Hyos, all in little scattered patches, where people had made wills leaving the monks strips of land here and there. And it had always been a bit unlucky to take monastery land – though not nearly as unlucky as it was to sell it afterwards. I know a family in the town who did that, and within three months the mother had died of apoplexy and the two elder sons drowned fishing in a calm sea. So Father Chrysostom has been going round checking on his property. The first thing he did with the money was to buy these gruesome tables. There used to be fabulous stone benches in here, but he chucked them out. That's a bit of one you can see down there – no, don't bother – it's only when you know what it is that you can see it isn't a rock. He didn't start repairing the monastery until he found he had enough money to be wasteful with it. By the way, I bet you he went picking olives next to Vangelis on purpose, as a way of checking whether he could claim those particular trees. You must have been a godsend to him – he's a cynical old bastard.'

'He knew all about how to light a cigar.'

'He would. Are they your cigars?'

'I was given them – beads for the natives, sort of. I don't smoke.'

'Are you staying at the Aeschylus? You don't look the type.'

'No, I'm staying with a friend.'

'In one of the South Bay villas? I see quite a lot of that gang.'

'No, the other side of the town. Porphyrocolpos, it's called.'

'Buck sent you up here?' she asked.

'Buck Budweiser? No. You've met him?'

'Well ... he's been up here a couple of times in one of those beach-buggy things. He drives me mad, talking all the time, showing off his Greek. He's better at it than I am, though his accent is gruesome. I thought he was alone there.'

'No – Mr. Thanatos is there now.'

'*He's* your friend?'

'Well, sort of.'

She stared at him round the pillar. Her look slowly changed from astonishment to something harder – either that chilliness he'd heard in her first words, or else the prospector's madness which seemed to infect everybody – even a grubby girl who lived in a hut on the hill – at the mention of that gold-loaded name.

'I'm not that type either,' said Pibble. 'I did a job for him once, and I was in Corfu, and he wanted me to talk about another one.'

Her look didn't change. He heard a bumbling noise behind him and Nancy withdrew into the room. He did the same, and found Father Polydore swaying there with the bottle in his hand. He filled their glasses, inaccurately, and tossed the now empty bottle through the window.

'*Epharisto*,' said Nancy and Pibble together, raising their glasses to sip the vile muck.

'Eff off,' said Father Polydore, smiling bluely.

'Some sod of a sailor taught him that,' said Nancy. 'Told him it was the polite thing to say. It's the only English he knows.'

'*Anglico?*' queried Father Polydore.

'Very good,' said Pibble. '*Poli kalo.*'

'He's a bit simple,' said Nancy. 'That's why I'm allowed in here at all. I'm a bit simple too. If I weren't, I'd be living down at the villas, instead of in Vangelis' hut. When he's finished his next glass, try and get him to say something about me, and you'll find he uses the masculine.'

She gave a sharp cry as Father Polydore tottered over to the desks, but stayed where she was. Father Chrysostom looked up from a document he was expounding to Vangelis, got to his feet and strode swiftly round the High Table. Meanwhile Father Polydore had picked up a brush and jabbed vaguely into several paint pots before holding it wavering above Nancy's unfinished icon. Father Chrysostom arrived just in time to slide his document between the brush and the picture, Father Polydore painted a brisk oval on it, and two long eyebrows before Father Chrysostom took the brush out of his hand and led him gently back to the High Table. He took the glasses off his face and put them on

Father Polydore's, and settled him down to continue reading the document to Vangelis while he fished and fussed in the store cupboard. Father Polydore read in a brisk, reedy chant, as though the document were part of a liturgy. Pibble was interested to see that the cupboard was well stocked with bottles and cans, and also held a number of pots and jugs, all carefully covered with little squares of cloth with beads round the edge.

'They're very hygienic, in some ways,' he said.

Nancy was baffled.

'They haven't washed for fifty years,' she said.

'I meant about covering food up.'

'Oh, that's because of the samimithi. Everybody covers food and drink on Hyos. I don't know about the other islands.'

'What's a samimithi?'

'It's a sort of lizard. A gecko. A little pinkish thing with pads on the end of its fingers so that it can run up walls. If it runs across your food you get very ill, and if it drowns in your milk you die.'

'Is it true?'

'I don't know,' she said restlessly. 'I tried to look it up last time I was in Athens, but that was before I'd seen one, and my Greek wasn't very good then – it isn't now – and I thought people were talking about a sort of spider. Anyway, it wasn't in any of the books under that name, but it might have a different name on the mainland. But it isn't in any of the guidebooks either. They usually tell you about things like scorpions.'

Pibble looked at her. She'd spoken in an offhand mutter which at first made him think she was bored with his company; then he sensed that it was something else, perhaps a general fidgetiness and frustration at being prevented from painting . . . She looked, if anything, slightly feverish rather than lethargic.

'It sounds a useful custom for a country with so many flies in it,' he said, and told her about the hotel at Portofino where, years ago, Mary had complained about flies in the hot milk and the waiter had fetched a sieve and sieved out a whole pile of corpses before their eyes and put the milk back in triumph on the table. Nancy might not have been listening.

'Let's go and look at the Catholicon,' she said. 'I'm not allowed in, but you might as well see it.'

She called a brief word to the men at the High Table, who answered without looking up, and led the way out through an archway to the left of the painting-desks. They walked into a narrow passage, with cell-like rooms on their left, between the passage and the sea. In the first one every inch of wall was covered with tatty reproductions of scenes involving the Virgin Mary.

'Father Polydore's pin-ups,' said Nancy. 'Hagiography can be just like pornography. In fact I don't have to paint any different now from when I was doing bra ads in London. Careful here.'

The corridor dipped and curved. It was more like a country lane, accommodating itself to the contours of a hill, than any mason-measured thing. Pibble put out his hand against the inner wall at a steep, dark place to steady himself, and found that it was indeed the rock of a cliff, though all its projections were polished and greasy from a million similar touchings.

'The Catholicon is the main church, isn't it?' he said.

'Yes. There are a lot of little chapels – most of them are caves, really – but the Catholicon is the important one. It's where the monks met for all their day-to-day services.'

'I'm surprised you're allowed into the monastery at all,' he said. 'On Mount Athos . . .'

'I know, I know. Father Polydore's forgotten about all that. I do the backgrounds of his pictures for him, and he does the faces, and that means he can do one a day like he used to twenty years ago. They're still holy, provided he does the faces. Father Chrysostom doesn't care what anyone thinks. It's his monastery and he likes company – that's why he bought those tables. But the island women won't come beyond the gateway at the top – a lot of them say I'm a whore, trying to steal the Fathers' treasure. They don't blame the Fathers; they think it's quite natural for them to want to have their own whore – but really they all know, with another part of their minds, that Father Polydore is only interested in painting and Father Chrysostom is only interested in boys. Last year he had a ghastly German hiker who . . .'

'What treasure?' said Pibble. He thought that Nancy's previous brusque animosity might be easier to cope with than her current brusque frankness.

'There's always treasure,' said Nancy, stopping where a wooden walk spanned an overhung section of cliff to which the monks had been unable to attach masonry. 'Anywhere where people are used to being very poor they always know that there's treasure buried in some old man's orchard, or up in the hills, or down a well. Haven't you noticed?'

'Like a cargo cult?'

'Or the pools. And there sometimes is treasure, really. All these islands were full of pirates for more than a thousand years. Christian pirates. Turks, Russians, all with secret harbours and so on. This was one.'

She leant on the rail of the walk and pointed down at the innocent-looking water. Pibble stood beside her. From here he could see all round the bay. There was no perceptible landing-place. He knew that he ought to be hurrying back to the town to check on the meaning of the helicopter.

'It doesn't look very hospitable,' he said. 'Could they get ashore?'

'If the monks would let them. There are places where you can lower a ladder. Vangelis' aunt told me that usually the monks were the pirates themselves, but Father Chrysostom says that's the sort of lie you'd expect from someone whose second cousin married a communist. I expect that the monks had a sort of arrangement with the pirates, the Christian ones anyway. They were a front.'

Pibble grunted, thinking of Stubbs of Boston.

'You know,' said Nancy, 'selling the pirates food, looking after the loot, taking a small cut, lying to the authorities. It's the only other possible harbour on the island, apart from the main one in the town. And even if the pirates weren't friendly they'd have been pretty safe – I found some brass cannon over at that end there, too. Their only trouble would have been water. The well's down the hill. Anyway, there may have been treasure here once, but my guess is that they spent it on the Catholicon. Come and see.'

She moved off brusquely. The walkaway led into another wrig-gling corridor, and then on to a much more imposing arcade than anything Pibble had yet seen. Stone pillars supported round-topped arches, all carefully carved; the pavement was a pattern of egg-shaped black pebbles set into mortar; the inner wall was of squared stone, and contained two dark-glazed windows and a large painted door. Nancy twisted the handle and leaned her small weight against the wood, like a waif at an orphanage portal. Pibble helped her push the door open.

'You won't be able to see much,' she said in the nervy whisper that agnostics tend to adopt when inspecting religious monuments. 'I'll wait here.'

The church was a dim and incense-reeking cavern lit by two dismal lanterns. At first their reddish flames were all that Pibble could see, but gradually glittering awoke in the gloom, where the light was reflected from glass and gold. The place was as oppressive as a rain-forest; heavy pillars carried round arches, and every flat or curved surface was covered with mosaics and pictures; right above his head he could just see the Christos Pantocrator frowning down from the unnecessary dome. Unnecessary because this was a church hollowed out of the cliff, an extension probably of an existing cave; but the diggers had shaped it as though it needed to stand in the open air, giving it the inner architecture of any other Greek church that had real walls and a real roof. But they could never give it windows other than the two in the outer wall, and these were filled with green and ochre diamonds of stained glass; so where the mosaics were meant to dazzle with Mediterranean light, as they do at Rimini, these could only gloom in the dark. Pibble paced about for a few minutes, until he felt as though the rock were about to fall in and crush him, clenching him in its fist. It was difficult to move with decent slowness to the door. The reek of incense seemed to follow him out.

'Do you like it?' said Nancy, throwing her cigarette into the sea and looking suddenly cheerful.

'Not much, honestly. Do you?'

'I've never been in. But you can give yourself a few marks for good taste, because nobody else likes it either.'

'It's very odd, and that's better than nothing. Do you know how old it is?'

'Victorian. Father Chrysostom lent me a useless old book about the island, written by a schoolmaster before the first war, pages and pages about the temple just down the hill where there's only a bit of pillar standing, and less than half a page about the monastery. He says the Catholicon was enlarged and all the mosaics put in after the English left. You know the English governed the Ionian islands, and Corfu, until eighteen-sixty-something . . .'

'I saw boys playing cricket in Corfu.'

'They do here, too. You must go to the English cemetery – it's a real weepie. What was . . . Oh, yes, my theory is that the monks did still have some pirate treasure which they couldn't let on about while the English were here, being strict with the natives, you know . . . but they blued it on the Catholicon as soon as we'd left. I mean, these pillars – they match, and they're good marble, and we haven't got any marble quarries on the island. If they'd been penny-pinching they'd have used local stone, and bits of the temple, and so on . . .'

'I saw what looked like a bit of classic pillar when I was coming out of the town. Part of the wall of a house.'

'That's right. Anybody uses anything they want for anything here, if it doesn't belong to anyone else. Father Chrysostom pulls down bits of the monastery and rebuilds them just as he fancies. Last spring he . . . Shall we go back?'

As they moved along the arcade Pibble said, 'Was that St. Sporophore's original cave?'

She hesitated, then answered with a rush.

'That's what Father Chrysostom says, but it doesn't mean anything. It takes about a week for people to persuade themselves that something new and horrid is old and holy. A few years ago, Mark Hott told me, the priest down at the church in the town sold their miracle-working icon to an art-dealer, and everybody was furious and there were riots until he came back from Athens with another icon – it looks old too, but Mark says it's a good fake – and that worked some miracles and everybody was happy, and now if you ask they'll tell you it's been here for a thousand years and was an original portrait of the Virgin painted by St. Luke – even people who had their windows smashed in the riots. But I don't see why it shouldn't be St. Sporophore's cave.'

'I'd have expected something smaller,' said Pibble.

She looked at him as though he'd said something odd, then led him through the dark and dazzle of the honeycomb in silence. Pibble mused on the life of the two remaining monks. In a few years – very few, to judge by the blue of their lips – they would both be dead, leaving no memorial except a submerged hill of ouzo bottles below their window. The uselessness of such a life-style oppressed him; it seemed a caricature of his own, with a few minor exaggerations; of most lives, in fact. Nancy oppressed him too. She was like a curious hermophroditic doll, a toy only occasionally loved, but usually left to lie, battered and dirty, in this forgotten corner. To live out one's sappy youth in a hut in a vineyard, and toil at horrible slick icons . . .

The men were quiet in the Refectory. Father Chrysostom and Vangelis were playing dice with moody concentration; Father Polydore was asleep beside them with his head in his hands, as though he had fallen asleep at his prayers. Nancy went over to her desk and swore again, but gaily; the same word sounded perfectly acceptable in this different tone; Pibble went to look.

Evidently Father Polydore had found the inspiration to complete her icon before he passed out, and had done so in brusque, careless brushstrokes, a world away from the genteel inanity of his sober art. Though the blank for the head of the Holy Child had been left in profile, it had been filled in with both eyes visible, and a spare nose.

'Influence of Picasso,' said Pibble.

'Oh, yes,' said Nancy quite seriously. 'The old monkey could draw like a saint if he'd been exposed to decent influences. I couldn't. This is my achievement peak.'

She flicked a disgusted grubby hand at the slippery brushwork of the Virgin's blue headdress.

'I must go now,' said Pibble. 'Thank you for being my guide and showing me everything.'

'Everything worth seeing,' she said.

'There's one thing . . .' he began. She stiffened, but he hesitated and went on, 'I'd rather like to meet some of the people at the South Bay villas – can I just go and knock on the door and say hello?'

'Some of them you could,' she said, relaxing. 'If . . . hang on, tomorrow's the last Saturday of the month, so Randy Wolf will be giving a party. I'll take you, if that's what you really want.'

'If it's not a nuisance.'

'No. It's time I went. I rather rely on them for company when I get sick of Greeks and still feel suicidally lonely. Does Thanatos want to buy them out?'

'Not that I know,' said Pibble. 'My wife has a passion for Greece, and I want to find out what it would be like to retire to a place like this.'

A curious thing about this not very pretty or pleasing girl was that it made him uncomfortable to lie to her. Although she was an adult, and clearly determined to go her own way, there was something uncompleted about her personality – not childish, but as though a growth process had been omitted, in her personality as well as her body. So it felt, after all, like lying to a child.

'I hope you've got something the matter with you,' she said.

'What do you mean?'

She grinned, more like a Dickens urchin than ever.

'You'll see. I'll pick you up at the Helicon Bar, down by the fish quay, about noon. If I'm late, order me a coffee and tell Yanni I'm coming.'

'I don't know your surname.'

'Nor does Yanni.'

'*Andio, Pater. Andio, Kyrie Vangeli,*' said Pibble in a louder voice.

'*Sto kalo,*' said the two dice-players without looking up.

'See you,' said Nancy as she turned to the desk and started to blank out the ruined faces of the Holy Family.

Chapter Three

Most Greek towns, in Pibble's experience, tend to name their
main streets by dates – meaningless to the outsider, but no doubt
celebrating the liberation of the country from the tyranny of
one form of government into the chaos of the next. He had
often wondered how many appointments went astray after the
meeting had been fixed to be at Number 4, February 15th Street,
at 5 on February 14th. But Hyopolis had a proper sense of
history, and so the Hotel Aeschylus stood in the Odos Basilissa
Bictoria.

It stood about fifty yards up the slope from the harbour; two
mosaic medallions adorned its frontage, depicting the Great
Queen and the Great Tragedian staring fixedly away from each
other; poor things, thought Pibble, they have not been introduced.

The foyer was garish, and a juke-box behind the reception
counter played bazouki rock. When he started to ask his question
the manager switched the thing off, so that for a word or two
Pibble found himself speaking in a slow bellow, as if to a deaf
idiot. He started again.

'I am looking for a friend,' he said. 'He is American. He is not
staying in this hotel, but I think he might call here today. His
name is Budweiser, and he cannot walk.'

The manager raised his eyebrows and did the negative click.
Pibble got his Collins Guide out.

'Not necessary,' said the Manager. 'Your friend has not been.
We have one Englishman staying here, and many more come
tomorrow – a party, you know, to paint.'

'Oh, I see. Thank you. In fact Mr Budweiser was going to
introduce me to an Englishman. This might be the one.'

'He comes only this morning,' said the manager. 'In a . . .' he
twiddled a loose-wristed hand above his head to indicate the
rotors of a helicopter.

'That might be him,' said Pibble. The man from the Mafia was
unlikely to be genuinely English, but at least he could save Buck
one piece of checking. 'What's his name?'

The manager riffled a page back in his ledger.

'He is a Mr Vutler,' he said. 'He is in the bar now. O.K.?'

'That's not him,' said Pibble. 'But perhaps he has sent a colleague. I'd better just go and say hello.'

'O.K.,' said the manager and shut the ledger, as though it all sounded a quite likely tale to him.

Pibble pushed through the bead curtains and peered round the bar with deliberate vagueness. There was only one man in the room, who sat like a Greek, with his feet on the rung of a spare chair and his broad back to the wall so that he could watch the passers-by out of the window, but at the slither of the beads he looked round. His face was bland and round and brown, his eyes blue, his hair cropped close. Pibble recognized him at the second glance. He had the reputation of a killer, but nothing had ever been proved. After all, he worked for a very big organization.

There was no knowing from that amiable face whether he recognized Pibble, but it was too late now not to go through with the charade. Pibble walked over to his table.

'Mr. Butler?' he said.

'That's me.'

'I'm Jimmy Pibble. I was expecting to meet a chap called William Thackeray here, but last time I heard from him he said he might have to send a colleague. I thought it might be you.'

'William Makepeace Thackeray?' said Butler with no audible sneer.

'That's him.'

'Never heard of him. But sit down and have a drink and tell me about the place. I've just got here for a short holiday. What'll you have?'

'Coffee.'

Butler shouted an order in quick and excellent Greek.

'You been here long?' he asked.

'This is my third day.'

'Business?'

'Sort of. I retired from my old job in England and . . .'

'Uh huh. I don't know how long I'll be here. Have you heard of anything special I ought to see – not all overrun with tourists – I'm a solitary rubberneck.'

'I'm told the English cemetery is very interesting,' said Pibble. 'I doubt if you'll find any other tourists there. As far as I know you and I are the only English visitors to the island, though there's a charter group of artists coming tomorrow. And there's a few of us who actually live here, mostly in the villas of the South Bay. And there's one girl who lives in a hut on the hill.'

'None of them sound great tomb-haunters,' said Butler. 'O.K., I'll try it tomorrow morning, before the sun gets too hot.'

After that they talked about the weather, spinning the variations out until Pibble had finished his coffee and could go.

Zoe Palangalos's absurd orange helmet burned on the water. It was as unmistakable as a buoy, both in reality and reflection, as she steered a little blue motor-boat down a lane between two lines of yachts. She seemed to be making friends rapidly and happily, to judge by the shouts and the arm-wavings. It amused Pibble that the apparently reptile-chilly George should be married to this coarse, spontaneous creature, but as he trudged along the sandy track that led out of the town to Porphyrocolpos his amusement died and was replaced by vague alarms. O.K., they had convinced themselves notionally but not emotionally that somebody might try to kill Thanatos, and had been going through the necessary steps to protect him without much real conviction – like actors rehearsing a play which will probably never be staged. But now things were different. The Home Office had sent one of their best men from Department J to Hyos – a man who had nearly certainly eliminated more than one of his country's enemies in his time. If it had been the Foreign Office that would have been straightforwardly alarming, for Britain retained a residual interest in the good government of Hog's Cay. But the Home Office. Perhaps Butler had transferred, but it wasn't likely. And why had they hurried him in by the blatant clatter of a helicopter? And why should he want to make an appointment for a long private chat with old Pibble? It would take a few more years before the Mafia actually infiltrated the Home Office, surely. But it was a serious possibility that Butler himself had been bought.

Pibble was very irritable by the time he reached the fence – enough for him to fret at the wait for the telephone call to the house. He inspected the three dogs, which were on parade – two of them looked the part more than their handlers, but the third had a touch of red setter in its ancestry, which gave it a fawning, sentimental look. The fence was as good as could be bought, running along an artificial dip in the land to make it less obtrusive; but Pibble thought a professional, with the right tools, could get through it in twenty minutes without setting off any of the alarms, provided he wasn't interrupted.

'O.K.,' said the guard at last, and motioned him through into unreality of Porphyrocolpos. Four bored horses mooched in a corral. Over the first rise the villa lay, with its white arcades and fretted screens finishing abruptly at the flat roof. It was a sawn-off pleasure dome. Beware, beware his flashing eyes, his floating hair . . .

Her floating hair, actually.

Chapter Four

Buck Budweiser spun his wheelchair over the fine, raked gravel of the courtyard. Tony d'Angniello, her russet hair half-veiling her bare fawn arms, leaned on the balcony above with a stopwatch in her hand and watched the pattern he was making. It was a sunflower pattern, such as a schoolboy doodles on the back of homework books with his first pair of compasses, a basic circle with a series of half-circles curving across it, meeting at the centre and the circumference, to form the petals. Buck's round white face was blobbed with sweat; his big hands grabbed at the wheel-rims to hurtle the chair across each curve; his thin little legs swung out, muscleless, under the centrifugal force until the sudden stop at the outer circle sent them flying forward; the unworn heels of his child-size shoes clattered back into the metal frame of the chair as it twirled for the next curve. Pibble stayed where he was on the edge of the courtyard.

'Hi, fuzz,' called Tony, smiling from her vantage point. Pibble waved back, but said nothing for fear of upsetting Buck's concentration. It was an intensely serious business, a way in which the cripple could get the exercise his body needed by performing an athletic feat up to near-Olympic standards. Pibble was beginning to think Buck the most American American he had met, a particular example of all the generalizations.

The rattle of gravel stopped with a final clack from the dangling shoes. Buck carefully wheeled himself to the corner of the yard, spun round and sat panting and studying the pattern he had made.

'Ninety-eight seconds,' called Tony.

'Third time this morning I broke the hundred, Jim,' said Buck.

'Are you going to try for the ninety now?'

'Uh-uh. Can't be done. Can not be done. I'm going to figure out a new play.'

'I'll give you eight point six for accuracy,' called Tony.

Buck looked disgusted.

'Aw, come on, honey,' he grumbled. 'That's a nine all over. What d'you make it, Jim?'

'You're the Giotto of the wheelchair, Buck. But won't you get suspended by the Discipline Committee for arguing with the referee?'

Buck laughed.

'Thanks, Tony,' he said. 'O.K., Dimitri. *Epharisto*.' His accent was worse than Pibble's.

He dropped a fifty-drachma note on the gravel and trundled himself towards the front door. Tony had already disappeared from the balcony. A gardener appeared from where he had been sitting in the shade of one of the cypress trees, picked up the note and began to rake the gravel.

'How did you make out?' said Buck in a low voice. 'That monastery's some place, huh?'

'Fascinating,' said Pibble, 'but I think we can cross it off our list.'

He followed Buck's chair through the self-opening doors into the cellar-like chill of the hall.

'That's what I said,' said Buck.

'They couldn't use it without the monks' knowledge,' said Pibble. 'And they'd have a tricky couple of miles across the island from anywhere they're likely to be able to take a shot at Thanassi. And supposing the monks *are* bribable, they've got to know that.'

'Yeah. I reckon you're right. Help me up this step, will you?'

'I've done a bit of your job for you,' said Pibble as he tilted the wheelchair up to the different level of the terrace. 'I saw a heli-copter come in this morning, so I called at the Aeschylus to see whether you'd got there on your rounds . . .'

'I had work this morning . . .' explained Buck. Pibble was amused to learn that the threat to Thanatos's life was part of a game – like the wheelchair pattern – compared with real work. Buck certainly had played the game hard yesterday in the Tank, then.

'Of course,' said Pibble. 'Anyway, though I missed you I found the chap who'd come in on the helicopter. He's O.K. And they aren't expecting anybody else there except a charter flight of artists from England tomorrow.'

'Fine,' said Buck as he parked himself in the shade of one of the huge umbrellas. The terrace ran the whole length of the house, to form the roof of both the Tank and the boat-shed, and the sea lapped below its balustrade. With its tables and umbrellas it always looked more like part of an hotel than any private house, and more so than ever now as the white-coated house-servants wheeled out the luncheon trolleys. Buck snapped his fingers at them and called out for a drink. The larger one nodded and glided off.

'Hey!' called Buck, 'I reckon Miss Tony's coming too.'

The man raised a hand to show he'd heard. Pibble fiddled with his chair until his head was in the shade and the rest of him in the sun. Tony, wearing huge round sunglasses, slouched up, laid her fingers like a bishop's blessing on Pibble's balding scalp, and sat in the sun. One of the many pleasant things about her was that she didn't mind being looked at, nor did she mind being ignored. The servant returned with pineapple juice for her, a Daiquiri for Buck and a Guinness for Pibble.

'Can't think how you drink that, this weather,' said Buck.

'Nor can I,' said Pibble. 'But they've got it into their heads it's what I like, and I don't want to worry them by upsetting the system.'

'I'll fix it for you,' said Buck eagerly, as though fixing systems were the finest sport in the world. 'Tell me what you want, and you'll get it.'

'I never know till the time comes, and not always then.'

'Aw hell!' cried Buck and flung himself against the back of his chair, disgusted at this lack of organization in a man's life.

'I found a new method of poisoning someone this morning,' said Pibble, reminded of it by the opacity of Tony's drink. He told them about the samimithi. Buck listened intently at first, as though it were something that might some day come in useful, but became mocking and fidgety when he discovered it was only myth. Tony on the other hand moved from boredom to fasci-nation and was full of questions, soon exhausting Pibble's meagre knowledge and darting off to interrupt the servants in the task of bringing out the banquet which passed for a picnic at Por-phyrocolpos. But as she spoke no Greek, and their English lost its gloss the moment it was called on to do more than answer a guest's ordinary needs, she learnt little more. Pibble was amused to see how her normal lounging posture became athletic and intense as soon as she was really interested in something. Even by the (presumably) high standards of millionaires' mistresses, she was something special – not only beautiful and exotic, but also somehow both childlike and sophisticated. Pibble thought it sur-prising, considering what a ceaseless flicker of flashlights Thanatos moved through in the outer world, that he'd never seen a photograph of her with him. He was sure he'd have remembered her.

A shape moved silently beside him. George Palangalos was now sitting there, as though he had been there all along.

'What amuses Tony?' he asked when Pibble looked round.

Pibble explained about the samimithi again.

'And she believes this?' said George.

'She wants to believe it,' said Buck, 'just because it ain't true.'

Pibble cocked his head.

'These college kids,' said Buck. 'If a thing's real, certain, hard, sharp, always been there, always will – they say it's a dream. And their dreams, that's what's real for them.'

'Tony is not like that,' said George quietly.

'No, I guess not. She's the kind who think that if they bust things up a bit, their dreams will grow on top of the rubble. They got no sense of reality either. No values. You want to know about Tony, Jim . . .'

'Be quiet,' said George, just as quietly but with an emphasis that made Buck blink. He looked at Pibble, then at George.

'O.K.,' he said sulkily. 'But if Jim . . .'

'It's all right,' said Pibble. 'Let's talk about something else. I saw Mrs. Palangalos down in the harbour. She seemed to be making plenty of friends.'

'Zoe is good at that,' said George. 'I am not.'

'You were lucky to find her a boat so quickly,' said Pibble.

'I buy it for her,' said George. 'Easy.'

'What kind?' said Buck.

Pibble was lost in the technical discussion of makes and types of boats. Tony came back to finish her fruit-juice. George made room for a chair beside him, but she settled herself opposite.

'Do you do a lot of sailing?' said Pibble to Buck.

'Not sailing. Power-boats. No-legs like me—' he patted his inadequate thighs '—we get a boost to our ego sitting there with that amount of power under our hunkers. What did Zoe make of Thanassi's boat, George?'

'She says it is beautiful. She says can she have one like it. That I cannot buy so easy.'

'You should see them, Jim. They're a pair, and they're something – all silver and mahogany, made for some duke. Thanassi's rigged them up with modern outboards – I'm taking him out this afternoon, and you can look then. Hi, Dave, what are you drinking?'

Dave Warren came and sat gloomily in the last chair. Despite his gaudy beach shirt he still looked like Mark Antony, but Mark Antony the morning after some Lucullan night. A servant brought him an ice-dewed can of thin American beer, and he sucked pensively at the hole in the lid.

'You told 'em?' he said to George, who shook his head.

'You two missed the excitement, being out,' said Dave. 'We got a wire from Boston, anonymous, just saying "Watch your step".'

'Wow!' said Buck. 'That might be Hochheim. He wouldn't write on Stubbs notepaper.'

'It might be anybody,' said George. 'We are always getting threats.'

'How did you two make out?' said Dave.

'Nothing special,' said Pibble. 'I learnt to pick olives. You may have noticed a helicopter – I checked the passenger. He's O.K.'

Dave's superb head turned to Buck, who seemed to be bursting with news, but it wasn't about any sleuthing.

'I got an idea,' he said. 'Those fishing-boats. You see them going out in the dusk with a train of little lamp-boats behind them. Then they're out all night. 'One of them could lie off from the fleet a bit and pick up a couple of guys from somewhere – Sicily, maybe.

'I don't think so,' said Pibble. 'The contacts between the U.S. and Sicily are still mostly sentimental, with a bit of business added. I should think the Americans would consider Sicilian mafiosi a bit hairy and unreliable when it comes to killing. They'll have the contacts, through the drug trade, to hire the men they want in Marseilles. And I don't think *they'll* go messing about in lamp-boats.'

'It is all a guess about a guess about a guess,' said George with perfect truth.

The whole group stirred, as shrubs in a garden stir at the first breath of evening wind after a still and blazing day. Their movement was subconscious, but an acknowledgment all the same that Thanatos had come out to the terrace, heavy and lowering. Courtiers must have twitched and fidgeted in much the same way at the approach of their absolute monarch, bearing in his person wealth or penury, fame or disgrace.

This monarch was almost naked. Wearing only exiguous shorts he stood for a moment in the sunlight; the brown slab of his torso was marked with a V of thick grey hair running from his navel to his collar-bones – it looked like the marking of some beast. He grunted like a beast, too, and lurched over to the luncheon trolleys, and tore the leg and thigh off a cold roast duck. A servant handed him his silver mug. Chewing his meat he went to his own table in the corner of the terrace and sat down. The convention was that nobody else sat there unless he invited them.

'Get yourself some grub, Jim,' he called. 'I want to talk to you.'

As millionaires go, Thanatos was capable of considerable social tact. He was always anxious that anybody enjoying his wealth really did enjoy it – so, though there was champagne and caviare on the trolleys, there was also beer and corned beef. Pibble took another Guinness and a plate of ham over to the table; Thanassi tossed him a crumpled ball of paper, which he smoothed out and found to be the telegram from Boston; there was nothing to be deduced from it except the obvious, if that.

'I hear you get a lot of threatening letters,' he said.

'Hell, they come and go, but they're all from cranks and nuts – you can smell 'em. I made a few real enemies, too. I suppose there's a couple of them might push me off a cliff if they happened to come up behind me. But they wouldn't *lay* for me. They're too busy.'

He picked the telegram up, rolled it tight, shouted and threw it across the terrace to Warren, who put it in his pocket. Pibble told what he'd found that morning, omitting the fact that he knew who Butler was. He outlined his thoughts about the getaway boat and the possibility of an attack from the sea.

'Dave's radioed my yacht,' said Thanatos. 'She'll be here by nightfall – she's at Patras – and there's enough crew to guard the mouth of the bay.'

'Pibble looked out across the inlet to where the two horns of land came almost together again a mile and a half away; the lower one lay at a safe distance, but the one to his right hulked up, grey and khaki, at the range of a long rifle shot.

'I wonder whether we ought to have a man up there,' he said. 'It's outside the fence, isn't it?'

'You'd have to have an army,' snorted Thanatos. 'It's all scrub, high as your shoulders. And it'd be the hell of a shot, across water. They've got to hit first time. If they just scare me, they've lost me. And if you're expecting me to sit out here in my bullet-proof vest, screw you.'

'Have you really got one?'

'Sure. I've been in some uncivilized parts in my time, Jim. That's why we've got a few guns, too.'

'Well . . . O.K., O.K., I get your point. The other question we haven't talked about is the possibility that somebody inside the fence has been bought. One of us. Or one of the servants.'

'Albert and Serafino are screening the servants. They'll find out. You six? No dice. Dave, George, Buck and the Doctor — they're businessmen. They can count. They're making so much out of me that you'd have to pay them, oh, more than a million bucks to get them to do something legitimate against my interests. And as for rubbing me out . . . Take Buck — he was in Parke Bernet when I found him — put me in the way of a couple of Sisleys and a Vlaminck. I've gone off Vlaminck. At first, I just hired him to take care of some of my art interests; then I found that he's got a gift — he knows what people want. He has this feel for ordinary people's ordinary hankerings. He knows what the mortician's wife from Squaw's Neck, Idaho, hopes to find in fabled Eu-rope. I set him up on his own, as a travel consultant. He does a bit of work for air companies, but mostly it's for me. Even if he hated my guts he'd lose one hell of a packet if I faded out. Look at him. He's as nervy as hell about the business under all that bounce.'

Pibble glanced at the party by the other umbrella. He couldn't see anything different about Buck, but he didn't know him as well as Thanatos. Tony was talking, and George smiling.

'The others are the same,' said Thanatos. 'They get a cut, too. George is a millionaire — dollars, not drachs. Dave will be in a couple of years. Old Doc Trotter will make a mint at Hog's Cay, but not if I'm dead. Then there's the other thing, Jim. You get where I've got by trusting the right guys. You pick 'em, and then you trust 'em. You don't pick many, but when you've picked 'em you stick with 'em. Yeah. It's a relationship. You get a kick out of it, knowing there's so much of you in this guy's hands, and he won't let you down.'

He paused, and again Pibble thought of the strange loyalties of courtiers for their half-holy king.

'That leaves me and Tony,' he said.

'They hadn't time to buy you,' said Thanatos. 'I'm not saying they could, Jim. Just they hadn't time after Hal Adamson's smash-up. Tony – *I* can't buy her, so I reckon they can't either. You like her, Jim?'

'Yes, very much.'

'Me too. First girl in twenty years who's really worked the trick with me. You get me, not just the old here-we-go-again bit, but by Christ this is what I was born for.'

He tossed his bone into the sea. For a moment it was actually buoyed on the surface by the nuzzling of hundreds of little fish who loitered off the terrace waiting for crumbs, then it sank into the calm and brilliant water. The fish were as bad as the people, Pibble thought, all creation waiting to be nourished by a big man's leavings. He wondered, supposing he'd been in the same position as Buck and Dave and the others, whether he wouldn't itch to strike out on his own, bring off some solitary coup, and then swim back to the monster's side, smug in the knowledge that it was possible to survive without him.

'Hi, girl,' called Thanatos in a note of mock warning. 'Lotta calories there!'

Tony d'Agniello had just begun to lick at the vast, many-coloured icecream which was her daily lunch, bending over it with the purring absorption of a cat at its saucer. She looked up, pouted, snatched off the top dollup and slung it at Thanatos like a snowball. It missed and splurged against the balustrade. Thanatos vented his harsh, monotone laugh. One servant came across with a plate and a cloth and wiped the balustrade clean and another appeared with a fresh scoopful of icecream. As Tony returned to licking, Thanatos quietened.

'Great girl,' he said, grinning. 'I'll tell you about her . . .'

'No thanks,' said Pibble quickly.

'Someone else told you? I don't like that.'

'No. All I know is that you began to suggest yesterday that she knew as much about liberation movements as I do about the Mafia, and that you must have a good reason for not wanting the police in on this thing. And she didn't say much in the Tank yesterday, but when she did she hit the jargon and the mood off exactly. Much better than the rest of us.'

'Uh-huh. If you knew, you'd split?'

'It depends what I knew. Supposing that you were to tell me

that she was wanted by the police of a civilized country for a definite crime of some importance – yes. But so long as it's only guesses . . .'

'Stay guessing.'

Pibble felt that he was already slithering into a mess of mixed loyalties, and envied the courtiers whose loyalty lay wholly with their single monarch.

The monarch brooded for a while, gloomily.

'This murder crap,' he said at last, 'what do you *think*!'

'I'm uneasy,' said Pibble. 'Consciously I'm aware that the whole idea is improbable, but that, on the evidence, it's just worth your while taking precautions. Subconsciously I'm more worried. I can't say why. Sometimes I think that it's because there's something phoney about the whole set-up, and sometimes that the set-up's genuine, but whatever's going to happen will happen in a way we haven't thought of.'

'Right. I'll give it two days. Those odds Dave was laying yesterday – that's crap. Life's not like that. I don't come to Hyos to be cooped up in my own yard. I like to sit at tavernas and shout to the fishing-boats. I want to go up the hill and look at those old monks, guess how long they'll hang on. When they go, I got my eye on that monastery for a hotel. That'd be really something, eh, Jim? Tell me about this girl they've got now.'

Pibble, shaken at the vision of that great decaying honeycomb all spruced up and plumbed and glazed and electrified for yelling holidaymakers, told him a few unevocative fragments about Nancy. He didn't say he was meeting her tomorrow. He made no attempt to describe what she was like. Thanatos, who would normally have noticed the deterioration of their intimacy after the first few syllables, was only half listening because his real attention was caught by Tony where she slouched against the balustrade and crumbled bread to toss to the fishes. Suddenly he grunted, lunged out of his chair and strode to her side. He put his arm round her waist, and she acknowledged his coming by kissing his ear before she continued to pamper the already grossly overfed sardines and anchovies. Or red mullet and loup-de-mer, perhaps. Pibble found himself enormously irritated by the foreign-ness of foreign fish. Sexual jealousy, of course. Fish are a famous symbol.

He dozed, dreaming that he was rummaging through a huge

supermarket deep-freeze, all of whose contents had started to thaw, for a packet of fish-fingers still rigid enough to be edible.

A presence woke him. At first it was an unnamable shadow in his dream, and then, though he kept his eyes shut for a time, it was the knowledge that somebody was sitting in the chair beside him. He was tempted to pretend that he was still asleep, but remembered that he hadn't much enjoyed his dream.

The man was Doctor Trotter.

'My thought woke you,' he said.

'Ung?'

'I intruded my thought into your dream. I apologize.'

'That's O.K.'

'I am interested in the theory of knowledge.'

Pibble shook himself into baffled politeness and said, 'I've read Ayer.'

'Ah, yes. Now there you are.'

'Ung?'

'Take Ayer. The question How do we know. It is strictly academic, is it not?'

'I suppose so.'

'Of course it is. All knowledge is relative. My knowledge that I am sitting here beside you is more certain than my knowledge that I sat at this table yesterday, which is in turn more certain than my knowledge that I intruded into your dream or that Caesar crossed the Rubicon. When I say "I know" I am merely betting on very high odds – or odds that seem to me very high – and I was, as it happened, ruminating on the fact that you and Dave both expressed the possibility of a threat to Thanassi's life in terms of odds – very high odds against. It interested me that this was a natural thing to do, but to think in terms of very high odds in favour is less natural. We prefer, unless we are discussing the future, to talk about knowing. That is how my thought intruded on your dream.'

'I see. How did you meet Thanassi?'

'I wrote and asked for an appointment.'

Pibble was astonished. Of all the possible methods of meeting Mr. Thanatos – in a dark wood, in a bramble, on the edge of a grimpen – this was one he had never considered.

'The first Trotter, about a hundred years ago, contrived to be the only man on several islands. The legend – the story – ah, you see what I mean about probability? It is more likely true than Homer, less likely than today's newspaper. What shall we call it? Fifty-fifty? This Trotter persuaded the men of several inhabited islands that a much richer island lay just beyond the horizon. He led them there, leaving all the women behind to till their meagre patches. He had imported a barrel of rat poison from Birmingham, and on this other island he contrived to poison all the men. He sailed home alone and persuaded the women that their husbands' ghosts would haunt them if they did not accept him as a substitute. Thus he repopulated the islands. He exchanged letters with Queen Victoria, but about other matters. He was an old man when he died, and I have seen his silk hat. He created a ruling caste of his offspring, all called Trotter. They are corrupt, but innocently corrupt, as I am also. Would you impute that to environment or heredity?'

'I don't see the connection with Thanassi,' said Pibble.

'Aha! But you would if you had been born a Trotter. Imagine it – a whole archipelago on the wrong side of the blanket! You look at the world sidelong. So among these Trotters there are factions, feuds, piff-paff. My uncles decided that I was to be educated, which is minimally possible on these islands, but when I returned from Oxford those uncles had vanished, and another lot held power. I did not get my share of the byproducts of government, to wit money and power. I was incensed by the injustice of this, but my education enabled me to extrapolate from my own injustice to the injustice the islanders were suffering at the hands of the Trotters. For a while I worked to bring our President to power. He is a very great man, though no relation of mine, and even my cousins could not keep him down. But they crept back and I lost favour – the President is quick to see that he would be tainted should he promote his own friends, so he promotes his enemies. I was incensed all over again, so much so that when I learnt what was planned for Hog's Cay I decided to prevent it. I looked round for a tool, and chose Thanassi. Now the tool uses me. It is odd that none of us would be here, now, if I had not written to him. He makes me afraid, you know?'

'Ung?'

'It is the events always exploding round him. I have sometimes been surprised that television sets do not lose their picture when he comes into the room.'

'I know what you mean.'

In the ruminative pause Pibble shifted himself slightly. The remains of his doze had left him chilly, and the sun had moved while he slept so that most of his body was in shadow. Old blood, he thought. It heats slowly, freezes fast. And in a week's time it will be November.

'I can do it!' shouted Buck's voice, very excitable. 'Leave me be!'

'Are you sure, sir?' said a calmer voice – Alfred, chauffeur and bodyguard.

Buck blasphemed his certainty. Pibble stretched and walked across to the other table where Tony was reading a paperback. All the paraphernalia had been silently cleared away in his sleep, as though he had merely dreamed that luxury, a feast prepared by Ariel.

'What's happening?' he said quietly.

'Buck can't stand to be helped,' said Tony, putting the book down. It was Spanish. The cover was vaguely vorticist, and included a stooped figure and a gun. 'He's going to drive the boat for Thanassi's ski-ing – it won't be warm enough many days longer, I reckon, though the old pig's got a furnace in him. He'd be a good man to share an igloo with.'

Pibble felt strangely trapped. He was obsessed with a notion that she knew what he was thinking – what he was trying not to think – sharing an igloo with her for instance. Anything else he thought of saying – about the book on the table, or his own life, or hers – seemed to lead to dangerous territory. She sat relaxed, and looked at him, but said nothing.

'Oh,' he said at last, 'this might . . . I'm going to a party at the South Bay villas tomorrow, before lunch. I want to check on the people who live there, and the landing places and so on. The girl who's taking me is the one who told me about the samimithi, that lizard. I don't see why you shouldn't come too, if you'd like to, and then you can ask her. We've arranged to meet at the Helicon bar by the fish-quay, at noon – so you can just talk about it there and not come to the party at all, if that's what you want.'

He felt that his voice was hardly his own, some raw boy's, absurdly eager to offer an enticing date to the school beauty. A big motor roared alive, drowning any answer. As it throbbed its way down to a tolerable drumming she rose and walked to the right-hand corner of the terrace. Pibble followed and stood beside her, though there was no question of his arm sidling round her waist, nor of her lips welcoming his almost virginal ear.

Thanatos was already waiting on the slipway that ran all the way down the side of the house and the terrace, projecting far enough into the almost tideless water to allow a fair-sized boat to come alongside. He wore his gold wrap like an emperor's robe and watched Buck manoeuvre the boat in a cunning curve that brought it just to the limit of the slipway, facing towards the bay. Alfred, who had been standing out of sight against the wall beneath them, stepped forward and took the coiled rope out of the stern. Pibble didn't see how Thanatos actually got into the water, because he was staring at the boat.

This was a toy, a dream. Its timber was grained like an antique escritoire, and its fittings twinkled with polish. He deduced that it must be pre-war – anything much later would surely have been made of fibreglass. It was cousin to a vintage Lagonda, except that it had been refitted with a bulging big outboard motor; in fact the commonplace yellow jerrican which rested in the stern provided a very plebeian note amid the sheen.

Thanassi laughed and Pibble looked back at him. He was sitting in the water now, like a man lounging in an armchair, with the tips of his unequal skis projecting from the water in front of him. He was laughing to Tony, laughing like a charioteer in Byzantium under the benches where the official prostitutes sat. Whatever he was shouting was drowned by the sudden bellow of the motor. Then he was being dragged through the water, clumsy only for a moment before he rose on to the skimming skis, kicked the left one off and hurtled away framed between the wings of spray from the boat, gross but triumphant.

'What's this girl like?' said Tony. Pibble was surprised. He had forgotten about Nancy.

'Young,' he said. 'Small, dark, dirty, rude. Interesting. Lives in a hut in a vineyard and makes her living painting icons for an even dirtier monk at the monastery. I liked her.'

'Then I shall. It'll make a change from this scene.'

A tiny gesture of her head indicated the luxurious mansion and terrace, and at the same time allowed her hair (which was so much a part of the unnatural luxury) to shift from one perfection and resettle into another. The noise of the boat, having faded, rose again. Buck had completed a wide half-circle and was heading in towards where they stood, with Thanassi weaving across the wake so that his ski squirted up a twelve-foot arch of spray each time he leaned inward to take the parabolic curve. The extra length of his track meant that he was moving almost twice as fast as the boat.

'Don't you enjoy this kind of life?' said Pibble. 'Then you put on a very good act, if I may say so.'

'I was doing a job,' she said. 'Don't ask me what – it was just a job, and it was worth doing. Then I got ill, and Thanassi said he'd look after me. I needed a man for a bit, yes, but it didn't have to be a rich man – only somebody I clicked with, like I do with Thanassi. If Thanassi were a trucker or a shoe-salesman, I'd still click with him. Move back, or you'll get wet.'

The boat was coming at an angle towards the shore, so as just to clear the tip of the slipway; Buck, hunched at the wheel and grinning, curved his course to run parallel with the terrace, about twenty foot out. Pibble, as he moved daintily back, could see what would happen as Thanatos too, coming at a much sharper angle, cleared the slipway. Pibble climbed on to a chair to watch from a safe distance as the straining shoulders and the red mask hurtled past, fearsomely close to the terrace, yelling with exultation; then the wide plume of water scythed along the terrace edge, drenching the skier's own table, his own umbrella, his own girl.

Pibble tiptoed forward through the swilling brine. Tony was as wet as if she'd been ducked in the sea.

'That must play hell with your hair,' he said.

'The hell with my hair,' she said. 'If that's as far as his sadism goes, I can stand the masochism bit.'

'Are you going back to your job when you're well?'

'Sure – that or one like it. I may have a bit of trouble with the old pig. I don't want to hurt him, but sometimes I guess he's lying to me about what the doctors say. Now I'd better go and change. But that's a date for tomorrow – twelve at the Helicon Bar to learn about lizards.'

'I've got another date before that,' said Pibble. 'You'd better go straight to the Helicon, and if I'm not there ask for Nancy.'

'O.K.'

She slopped off, barefooted. Pibble wondered who she was, and whether he knew her real name – probably not, having been out of touch for over a year. Being ill and convalescing under the care of Thanatos was a convenient metaphor for being wanted and hiding out under his amorous wing. And she paid her debt to him, in the currency he fancied. Pibble wondered whether she was right in believing that she would be able to retain the same relationship with Thanatos if he were nothing but his own personality, without money, without power. The power was part of the personality, surely. Even the physical and sexual vigour at that age must be partly fed by a different sort of potency . . .

He looked out to where the boat was skimming the water with uptilted nose, bouncing slightly as it went; behind it flashed the pale doll, leaning against the pull of the rope and sending his sparkling waterfalls into the sunlight. The boat curved seaward, going very fast, hidden from Pibble by the plume of its own wake, with Thanatos hurtling towards the western headland. It was a beautiful, bright dance. At this range he was no longer gross, but a trained performer playing with veils of water.

Abruptly, as Pibble watched, the dance faltered and the veils died. The doll subsided into the sea. There was something the matter with the boat. Pibble heard a single, wuffling thud just as the crackle of the motor ceased. A black plume rose irregular where the arched white had been – smoke. Buck was pulling himself over the gunwale with his hands, like a man about to be seasick, then tumbling into the water. Pibble couldn't see if he was floating – he didn't even know if he could swim – but Thanatos heaved an arm out of the water, then the other, and it was possible to sense the bulky body surging towards the burning boat. Pibble ran to the side of the terrace above the boathouse and yelled for Alfred, who appeared in shirtsleeves from a door at the lower level and looked enquiringly up.

'The boat's caught fire!' shouted Pibble.

Alfred nodded and ran into the boathouse. Pibble scampered down the marble steps and then down the concrete path to the sea's edge. On this side, between the house and the artificial beach, an inlet had been scooped from the rock so that the water could run at a good depth right in under the terrace, to form an amphibious garage for the rich man's toys. Both the boats and the beach-buggies were kept here. Albert was already in a boat exactly similar to the one Buck had driven; he was kneeling in the stern, fixing feedpipes to another yellow petrol-tank which he had evidently lifted from the row of the things that were stacked along the wall.

'Shall I come, too?' said Pibble.

'If you will, sir. And in that cupboard by you there's a frog-man suit – flippers, skin, goggles, mouthpiece, oxygen-pack. Thank you, sir, yes, that's the lot, and I checked these cylinders yesterday. Will you drive, please, sir, and I will change into this kit.'

He fiddled with the motor for a moment.

'Right. That's the starter, sir. That's the throttle. Clutch-pedal at your foot. Forward and reverse lever. Right, take her out easy, sir.'

The engine banged into life as Pibble pulled the knob; he slid the throttle down, let in the clutch and allowed the craft to chunter out and turn into the artificial inlet. Three seconds after opening the throttle to full he discovered what Buck had meant about having all that power under your hunkers.

'Easy, sir,' yelled Alfred. 'Don't run them down. Left a touch. Slow engine. Neutral. Reverse now – give her full throttle – cut. Left a touch. Beautiful.'

Pibble glanced up. Alfred had stripped to his underpants but still had only encased his legs in the black rubber. His pale but muscular torso rose arrogant in the sunlight as he balanced in the rocking boat and judged the course to where the double-headed creature was floating, one head dark-haired but balding, the other grizzled and close-cropped. As the speedboat drifted to a stop beside them Pibble cut the engine completely. He could hear the dull crackle of the burning boat, though the flames were invisible in the sunlight and there was little smoke now. The whole stern was blackened to cinder – all that glorious wood – and was also sitting lower in the water than before. A big hand gripped the gunwale beside him.

'Going my way?' said Thanatos.

'How's Buck?' said Pibble.

'Passed out, but he's breathing. He may be burnt bad, though. We'll get him in over the stern.'

In fact it was a struggle to get the cripple aboard. He was surprisingly heavy and inert, and the big motor prevented two people reaching him from above. In the end Alfred lugged him up by the shoulders while Thanatos, with one hand on the gunwale, shoved from below. Pibble tidied in the dangling limbs, and then Thanatos heaved himself aboard with a jerk and a grunt like a walrus emerging to its rock. They laid Buck down in the space between the seat and the rear thwart. He was pale, but Pibble could see his lungs moving.

'Pulse not bad, sir,' said Alfred, straightening up. 'If he was badly burnt, his clothes would be singed, and I don't see anything.'

'Great,' said Thanassi. 'We'll get him ashore, and then you can come out and tow the other . . . Hey! Look at that!'

Pibble swung round. The other boat was gone. The flames had burnt through, letting in the water, and the weight of the engine had pulled it under, leaving only a little oil to show where it had been.

'Hell!' said Thanatos. 'Now I don't have a pair.'

'May I buoy the place before we go, sir?' said Alfred. 'I would like to dive for it. I checked that engine . . .'

'Keep down,' said a whispered croak. 'Keep down. Shot at us. Got the tank. Saw the hole. Fire.'

The boat rocked as Thanatos fell to a crouching position over Buck's body and Alfred, still half cased in rubber, flung himself into the driving-seat. The engine bellowed and they were flouncing over the water, weaving irregularly as they went. Pibble, kneeling by the deafening engine, gripped the gunwale and tried to scan the headland – useless. He twisted to see the shore rushing towards them, the white-faced watchers lining the terrace and peering, like aquarium creatures, through the long window of the Tank. The whole boat heaved as Alfred went from full forward speed into reverse. The wash of their coming was still settling on the rocks outside when the boat bumped against the footboards of the boathouse.

'Great steering, Alf,' said Thanatos, heaving out of his hidey-hole. 'You've still got something to beat, Buck, man.'

But Buck had passed out again.

Pibble, trained sleuth, spent the rest of the afternoon and most of the evening patiently quartering the headland in the company of one of the perimeter guards and his dog. The dog was bored, baffled and ultimately unmanageable; it was the red setter/Alsatian cross, so he had many of the right instincts, but he didn't know what trick he was being asked to perform, any more than Pibble did. The three of them picked their way through pathless scrub – myrtle still green and shiny, fierce gorse, grey rock-rose already losing its leafage, and monstrous thistles, yellow now with autumn but barbed with heraldic prickles. The dusty air reeked of sage mixed with a faint animal odour which he took to be drying goat-dung, but he saw no animals – though the dog sometimes tried to streak into the thickest bushes after small prey. Between them, in the six or so steep acres between the shore and the skyline, they found a hundred places from which it was possible for a marksman to sight across the bay. None of them bore a sign of occupation, but the earth was baked hard and all the grass already broken-stemmed. And anyway, they must have missed a hundred other places.

In a way Pibble was relieved. If he had come across a litter of cigarette butts and a cartridge case, that would have been an overwhelming argument for calling in the island police. Thanatos had discussed this briefly with Tony – Tony in fresh clothes and freshly perfect hair, interested and unhysterical. She had agreed with Pibble and George Palangalos that Buck had been mistaken in what he saw: Pibble was almost convinced of this – it seemed incredible to him that a professional gunman should fire a single shot at the difficult target of the swaying skier, and not even attempt the much easier one of Thanatos, five minutes later, standing large and still in the boat. Buck had been furious about this, though more furious at having needed to be rescued. He was adamant that he had heard a sudden clang from the stern, looked round and seen petrol pouring from a small circular hole in the tank, and the whole rear section of the boat exploding into scorching flame. He said that at that instant Thanatos had been directly between the boat and the headland, and how the hell was Jim so sure that it must be a professional when he'd been talking about unreliable hairy Sicilian gunmen at lunch?

'Lay off Jim,' Thanatos had said. 'We've all been guessing, and his guesses sounded good.'

That was the only suggestion that the shooting – if it was not imaginary – was somehow Pibble's fault.

Now, resting for a moment on a bare jut of rock which formed yet another excellent vantage-point, Pibble looked down into the bay to where Dave and Zoe Palangalos were manning the spare boat while Alfred dived for the wreck. If he found it, that would confirm the bullet-hole, or deny it. If it confirmed it, Pibble was determined to go to the police, though still in a chaos of confused emotions about whether to tell them who Tony was. He was fairly sure himself now, having realized that the russet hair was a wig – two wigs – chosen to be as unlike her normal hairstyle as possible. Mooching through the scrub he had tried to picture that flattish, highly intelligent, small-featured face surrounded by dark, short hair. The picture had clicked when he put square-spectacles on it – he must have seen it twenty times in the newspapers, illustrating stories about the heroes of the American left – Anna Laszlo, the Bomber Queen.

From this lonely crag Pibble looked across at the house, wondering whether he would catch a puff of blackish smoke to mark where Thanatos and George were burning a cracked spare tank to show him when he returned. It would be plausibly scorched, fresh dipped in the sea, and Buck would now be sulkily ready to admit that the hole he thought he'd seen could well be a round oil-spot – which Alfred, of course, would confirm had been a feature of the missing tank.

Dusk began to settle. A small red insect bit hideously at his forearm. He heard the motor start in the bay and saw the boat planing back towards the house. If they'd found the burnt tank he would have been able to see it through the binoculars Dave had lent him. They would know that, so there would be no fake tank.

He too called off the search.

Chapter Five

Just where the inland road from the town lifted to tackle the hills there was a patch of beaten earth on which a gang of children were playing cricket. Three very old men were watching them, but Butler was keeping wicket. Pibble saw a child with legs and arms as thin as splints canter towards the crease and bowl a fastish leg-side long-hop with a windmilling action; it was fast enough to scare the little batsman, who dodged but made a half-hearted effort to hook as he did so – more to save face than to score runs; Butler, standing up, took the ball cleanly through the tangle of whirling legs and bat; the child, over-balanced by a bat too large for him, teetered for an instant out of his crease, and Butler had the bails off. The fielders yelled and the old men clapped like Members in the Long Room. Long-off turned and saw Pibble.

'*Englesos?*' he said eagerly.

'*Ney.*'

'*Boleis, Englese?*' said the boy, making a wheeling motion with his arm.

'*Ime poli arheos,*' said Pibble. He stooped his shoulders and hobbled a few paces with the back of his wrist held arthritically to his spine.

'*Kritos, kritos,*' shouted the children.

'They want you to umpire,' called Butler. 'I warn you, there's a lot of local rules to learn.'

'Tell them I'm blind,' said Pibble, shading his eyes and peering at the nearest child. There was a squeal of laughter and several repetitive shouts. Even the Long Room Members cackled.

'They say it doesn't matter,' said Butler. 'All umpires are blind.'

Pibble laughed, pleased with the universality of the joke, and walked up the hill. Butler was a problem. Presumably he had come to that point to see whether Pibble indeed took the road to the cemetery, and had joined the game from the same extrovert high spirits that made him, in his professional field, ruthless. There were a number of possibilities, Pibble thought. The most likely was that he had come to Hyos to find Anna Laszlo – though it was hard to see why an Englishman from the Home

Office should be chosen for that. No, not so hard: Department J might pick up a whisper from their London contacts in the refugee underground – there were quite a few Americans there; they'd merely want to confirm it, before selling the news to the F.B.I. on a quid pro quo basis.

He stopped in the road and scratched irritably at his chin, watching an old woman hoeing a little strip of vineyard. He wondered whether she was older than he was, so bent and yet so dogged. Anna Laszlo's group had certainly claimed responsibility for the Folger Library explosions: how does one balance the destruction of eight First Folio Shakespeares against that of a beautiful and clever girl for whom one feels sudden fierce freshets of half senile passion? And the Pan-Am Building disaster? She had been accused of that – but the left had claimed that the actual deaths were the result of panic and bad handling of the evacuation.

The old woman half straightened and stared at him accusingly, as though it was her that he longed to, er ... He walked on.

The road was a line of brownish-grey dust twisting through an area where the slope had been part-terraced, long ago, and only haphazardly maintained. Some of the patches of earth that thus followed the contours were as neat as an English allotment, growing vegetables as familiar as cauliflowers and as strange as the big radishes whose leaves the islanders esteemed. Pibble would normally have gone and tried to talk to a young man whom he saw tending such a patch about the problems of black-fly and soil and fertilizer and irrigation. His Collins Phrasebook contained a handwritten addendum called 'In the Garden'. But today he had Butler to think about.

Another possibility was that somebody had heard something from the other side about Hog's Cay, and sent out an unofficial bodyguard. It seemed unlikely to Pibble that this man should be playing cricket with kids, rather than making himself known at Porphyrocolpos. More frighteningly likely was that he no longer worked for Department J – that he was the hired killer they had dreamed up in the Tank. That was certainly conceivable – the contact could have been made in the Mafia scare of '67. What was less conceivable was that Butler would have missed his first shot and not fired a second – unless, like the man in the Buchan story – he had brought bullets of the wrong calibre to reload. No, he was a professional, dammit. But just suppose ... was he now going to wipe out the inconvenient Pibble, who had recognized him? Far more likely he would try to spin Pibble some tale which would allow him to get another crack at Thanatos. The only hope was to wait and see.

As the road rose, more of the terraces had been let go, though tethered goats and donkeys grazed them. Away to his left a gang of hired olive-pickers, the poorest people on the island, laboured and shrilled. At each step the sea seemed to become larger and the island smaller – soon he might be able to see Zakinthos, dull on the south-eastern horizon. Just beyond where the road dipped over the first real ridge he found the path he had been told about by Serafino, leading up to his right along the slope and finishing at a small white house that lay in a fold at the foot of the southernmost of the island's two mountains.

He was very hot when he arrived. The path was steeper than it had looked and had been blocked by the cottage's chicken-run, the cottage seemed empty, so there was nothing for it but to pick his way among the flustered fowl expecting all the time to be yelled at, angrily and incomprehensibly, by their hidden owner. Nothing happened. As the cackles died to clucks he sat down on a flat tomb in the shade of a lemon tree and began to read the inscription on the monument opposite. It had been erected to Dorothea, adored wife of Captain Henry Davidson of the 23rd Foot and fifth daughter of Sir Thomas Bartle of Steep in the County of Hampshire, who died in Hyos of the scarlet fever in the thirty-seventh year of her age, leaving, beside her mourning spouse, eight bereaved sons and three weeping daughters. Patience was the chief of her virtues. Erected by general subscription among the regiment which her husband adorned with his valour. Here also were buried Sarah, aged eight; Thos, aged two; and George aged one month, all called to their Maker in the same week by the same fatal agency.

The cemetery, to a man of Pibble's temperament, was inconceivably strange and moving. Under the neat rows of orange and lemon trees the white stones lay cool. The air was full of the sharp scent of citrus, and the glossy dark leaves drank up the sun, so that there was none of the dazzle that seemed to batter one's eyes elsewhere on the island. The cemetery slept in a shallow cup of bare hills, looking out across the cottage tiles to the sea. It would be a good place to die, Pibble thought, supposing Butler were coming up the hill to arrange that.

Or the plausible tale – it was a good place for that, too. No spy was likely to creep unseen down those naked slopes, and the chickens did raucous sentry-go across the official entrance. While he waited Pibble read inscriptions, counted dead daughters, guessed at lives and miseries. All the names were very English. The private soldiers had their smaller stones in a further corner of the grove, and here he was able to work out the home counties of the several regiments which had been stationed on Hyos – the recruiting officer had evidently made a hit in the village of Milverton in Warwickshire, for three young men had emerged from those soggy, reddish fields to lie, before any of them was twenty-five, amid this drought. Perhaps they'd all loved the same girl: more likely, in the late eighteen-thirties, they were yokels out of work because of some upheaval in corn prices. Some of the stones had tilted from the vertical, shifted by roots or the slow settling of the soil, but apart from that the grove was beautifully kept, the brown grass short, and no small scrub growing between the tombs. Pibble was using his penknife to clear lichen from an inscription to the Reverend Tertius Manners when his sentries cackled.

Butler too was hot, and wheezing slightly more than the climb warranted. Pibble watched him pace idly round the perimeter of the trees; then he threaded his way between them and sat with a slight thud on Mr. Manners' tomb.

'Bloody good,' he said. 'No need to talk code. Smoke?'

'No thanks.'

'I rang London about you last night. I was bloody angry when I saw you – I thought they'd got their lines crossed and sent two of us out, though I couldn't think how you'd got the job. But they say you retired a couple of years back.'

'That's right. I told you.'

'But you're working for Thanatos.'

'Just staying with him.'

'They said working.'

'They've got it wrong. I met him last year, and he was kind enough to stand me and Mary, my wife, a free holiday in his hotel at Corfu. He asked me over, on the spur of the moment, for some advice about one of his business enterprises.'

Butler nodded.

'Got himself mixed up with some baddies,' he said. 'Wants to know how far he can go and not get copped.'

'No. The criminals are on the other side. We've been trying to guess what they might do.'

'What did you guess?'

'If you'll tell me why you want to know, I'll tell you, providing it has any bearing on your job.'

Butler, still wheezing slightly, looked at him with his pale small eyes, very bland, very forthright. He had the look of a dog who expects to be loved, and takes it for granted; but Pibble had seen that look before, often, on the faces of criminals – petty fraudsters usually, men of such total egocentricity that they seem to themselves guiltless. A lie on their tongues is as good as the truth, a death at their hands the victim's fault. They look at you like that because they feel they have nothing to hide.

'O.K.,' said Butler suddenly, 'fair enough. I'm here on a bloody stupid exercise. If there's anything in it, Thanatos might be the man I'm looking for, but he'd have had more sense than to cut you in.' He laughed, as though he were slightly embarrassed. 'I mean what I say about it being stupid. I'm hunting the Mafia.'

'For the Home Office?' said Pibble. He had felt every muscle in his body go rigid, but Butler misunderstood the note of surprise.

'I'm on loan, blast it,' he said. 'I'd cleared my desk for another job – I'll tell you about that later – so here I was, a spare bod who spoke good Greek. How much do you remember about the drug trade, opium derivatives in particular?'

'No more than any copper who retired two years back. I did a short course in '65, or '64. And I ran into the results from time to time, naturally.'

'Right, I'll give you another short course. The biggest traffic in drugs is to the U.S.A. Most of the soft drugs come up through Mexico, and most of the hard drugs from Europe and Asia. Heroin is the most important. Just under half the heroin trade in the States is in the hands of the Mafia – it's very big business indeed. The opium poppies are grown in Turkey and Bulgaria. A lot of the crop goes to perfectly legitimate medical needs. We're concerned with the rest. The seed heads are split and the juice collected. That's the raw opium. It's a black or brown tarry substance with a strong characteristic smell – you know it?'

'I think so,' said Pibble. 'It's not like anything else – rich and spicy.'

'Always makes me think of Christmas puddings,' said Butler. 'Anyway, the smell's one of the things that make it difficult to smuggle. Also the bulk, and a tendency to seep. So the trick is to get it to a factory to refine it first into morphine and then into heroin. These are both white, odourless powders with a bitter taste. A given quantity of good opium refines down into about a third of its bulk in powder. Morphine is a great deal more stable than heroin. O.K.? Right, for the last ten years the main factories have been in Marseilles. The Americans tried to get the French to crack down on them, but old de Gaulle dug his toes in. So the factories had an easy time until he went, and then there was trouble. Among other things, the French suddenly got scared about the purity of their own youth, and started to get very tough even with petty operators and transient hippies. The result is that the big organizations have been setting up factory sites elsewhere – and they've learnt their lesson. They aren't all going to the same place, or the same country – a bit here, a bit there, so that if one government gets tough the rest can absorb the trade.'

'Why don't they refine it in the country of origin, and ship it direct?' said Pibble.

'There's a bit of that, but not much. They have problems. In Turkey, for instance, you've got a lot of American influence, but the opium farmers have votes. So the Turks try to keep the Americans happy – show willing – by jumping hard on illicit refiners. They haven't got the votes the farmers have. Now the Greek government – they're very anti-drug, but it's a straggling country, and Greeks have a habit of keeping secrets. An island like this, almost on the route from Turkey and Bulgaria out of the Med – they might try to set up a factory here.'

'But you must have something more than that,' said Pibble. 'There are hundreds of islands – why Hyos? And why the Mafia, and not one of the other big organizations?'

Butler nodded.

'We got a whisper – it came from Montreal – that the Mafia was interested in Hyos.'

'Not a specific connection with the heroin trade?' said Pibble, taking his chance.

'No. Just an interest – but there's only one thing it could mean.'

'Uh-huh,' said Pibble, trying to sound as though he agreed. 'You've got a lot on your plate. I mean, there's over a thousand houses in the town, I should think, and I don't know how many outlying places like this.'

He pointed at the pink tiles of the cottage, baking in the sun below them. Butler dismissed it.

'No good. You need quite a bit of good water and a reliable heat source. I'll fill you in on the process – it's long but not difficult – no fancy equipment or ingredients. You take your opium, mash it up with calcium chloride, and extract it with hot water. All the alkaloids, including the morphine, are dissolved in the water, and the acids precipitate as calcium meconate and you can filter them out. You add sodium sulphite, and then you concentrate your solution down to a syrup . . .'

'Boil it down?'

'No, you'd lose too much of the stuff. The right way is with a vacuum pump.'

'They use a hell of a lot of water,' said Pibble, vaguely remembering gushing taps in the school lab. 'On an island like this . . .'

'You could recirculate that water with an electric pump. Forget it. Next you add sodium acetate, which precipitates a couple of other things you don't want, and you filter them out. You add a little alcohol, then lime and ammonium chloride, and this time it's the morphine which is precipitated. You wash it with benzene, then mix it with boiling water and hydrochloric acid. Morphine hydrochloride crystallises out when it cools. If you want the morphine base you can get that by precipitating it with ammonia. O.K.?'

'It doesn't sound difficult,' said Pibble. 'Only tiresome. Just a lot of boiling and mixing and straining.'

'Right. And waiting about while reactions take place. Now, if you want heroin you treat morphine with sulphuric acid to turn it into the sulphate; you dissolve that in water and treat it with acetic anhydride to acetylate it – that produces a foul vinegary smell – and you've got heroin. Heroin's not very stable, sensitive to light and damp, and liable to go off however carefully you keep it. From a place like this there's strong odds that they'd ship it to the States as morphine and treat it there. Morphine's almost insoluble and very stable.'

'If you cut out the vinegar smell it doesn't give you much to

look for. Sulphuric acid, lime, other common chemicals ...
they're mostly pretty everyday things, even on an island like
this.'

'Yeah, but there's some weak points. Even if they are common
chemicals, you need quite a bit of some of them – enough to need
an explanation for at the harbour. You need a lot of heat in a
reliable form – it'd be three times as easy to do it with electricity as
it would on an open stove. Even the basic kit – retorts and so on –
will sometimes need to be replaced, so you'll have to import.
You've got to smuggle that in too, or account for it at the harbour. It wouldn't be difficult if I could bring the local police in,
but I can't.'

Pibble looked at him, wondering how the local police would
take it if they knew how anxious everyone on the island was not
to secure their services. Butler misinterpreted his glance.

'No offence, old man,' he said after a pause for a wheeze.
'Things are bloody delicate between Athens and Washington
these days, and you know what the Colonels are like. Puritans in
jackboots. If they found out there was a heroin factory in their
back garden they'd smash it up with a will, but they wouldn't be
all that grateful to the guys who told them. And if the guys only
came and hinted that there might be ... well, hoity-toity isn't the
word for their reaction.'

'I see,' said Pibble. 'There was this vague rumour from Montreal, and Washington didn't like the smell of it. So they borrowed you, and if it goes wrong it'll only be London who land in
the shit. Meanwhile, I suppose, the Americans are being kind
enough to shovel some of *our* dirt about, somewhere else, on the
same kind of basis.'

'Right,' said Butler. 'A place called Hog's Cay, I believe. One
of the Southward Islands.'

Pibble almost laughed – the laceration of laughter at what
ceases to amuse.

'How are you tackling it?' he said after a pause.

'I'll get some of the kids on it. You saw me with 'em this
morning – by God, d'you realize they're still playing the pre-
1928 l.b.w. rule? And you should hear them appeal! Where was
I?'

'You were going to tell me how your playmates will help you
spot if anybody's using unusual amounts of electricity.'

'No. I can do the power myself. There's only one potty little office, and I'll get to look at the bills. The kids can check on who's been buying double quantities of paraffin or charcoal. I'll try to buy some opium down in the fish-harbour . . .'

'Would they sell it to you?'

'Yeah. If I choose the right chap, he'll put me in touch.'

Butler spoke with absolute confidence, and Pibble was sure he was right. He had the knack of making strangers believe him.

'Will they have opium to sell?'

'Probably. There's got to be a bit of leakage along the line of an operation like that. The bosses don't like it, but they can't stop it. Everybody takes a cut, and sometimes they take it in kind. If you spot a junkie on Hyos, you're on to something. He'll be getting his highs direct from the factory.'

'What do you want me to do?'

'Check Thanatos over. That I can't do.'

'It would never be worth his while.'

'You've got to check. It's a sort of power, as much as money, for some people. And there's a hell of a lot of money in it. Thirty pounds of snow, a suitcase full, sells for just under a million quid. He's got that yacht, too.'

'Um.'

Pibble felt thoroughly irritated. There was the surface irritation of Butler's assumption that it was somehow an honour to help him by betraying his host. There was the tiresomeness of this seeming confirmation of their mad, bored guess in the Tank – now he would have to believe in it, and not just behave as though he did. Butler's connection with Washington was a threat to Tony, another nudge at Pibble's straining and incompatible loyalties. It would almost help matters if Butler *had* been bought by the opposition, and had told this half-true tale to see how the land lay – if Pibble didn't now come out with *his* side of the story that would be evidence that Thanatos not only knew he had been shot at, but knew why.

'You don't like it?' said Butler suddenly.

'I don't like having my holiday messed up. I don't like being asked to spy on a man who has been good to me. I suppose I'm prepared to put up with both of those, as I like the heroin even less. But I also don't understand why you flew in in such an obvious way; nor why you are telling me all this so openly. That's not like Department J at all – in my day they'd never even tell you whether they liked their tea with one lump or two. Look, when you rang up, they must have told you I didn't really retire – I was politely sacked. If Thanatos is a crook, I could easily be disgruntled enough to give him a hand. I mean, I know some of the people who work for him, and they're his men, body and soul, whatever side of the law he's on.'

Butler laughed.

'That's what they said. They were worried when you became pally with him. They ran a class-four check on you, in fact – I don't know whether you spotted it.'

'No,' said Pibble slowly. Class four – that's the works. Two months of three men's time. Crippens! He felt vaguely elated that anyone had thought him worth it.

'Well, they did,' said Butler, 'and they say you're in the clear and that's good enough for me, these days. You're right, though – it wouldn't have been ten years ago, or even five, but I'm in a hurry. I came on the chopper because I was in a hurry, and I'm baring my breast to you for the same reason. Working in J is just like any sort of police work – you get handed your case and you get on with it. You do the jobs as they come along. But *you* know it isn't like that all the time: when there is a plum coming up, you try and put yourself in line for it. All this summer I've been playing my cards so that I'd have a clean desk just when the M.C.C. tour of the West Indies came up – they like to have one of us hanging around – you never know when politics aren't going to muck up a sporting fixture these days. I was in Australia last winter – Christ, was that a boring tour? But the West Indies is something else, and I'd fixed it for myself. Then the A.D.A. sent for me and said 'Butler, you've got a clean desk. I can spare you to go and sort Hyos out.' Christ I was sick. I said 'What about the West Indies Tour?' and he said 'Clear up this idiot balls in Hyos in five days, and you can have it. Otherwise I'll go myself.' Him! He wouldn't know a Chinaman if he saw one.'

Pibble blinked, wondering how the Yellow Peril had intruded on the sacred turf of Butler's paradise, then remembered that Tony Lock used to bowl Chinamen. No, not Lock . . .

'Were you still serving for the South African tour?' said Butler.

'Just about, but I wasn't involved. The one that was cancelled, you mean?'

'We chickened out,' whispered Butler. 'We let a lot of long-haired louts and yobs scare us. That South African team was as good a side as you'll see in a hundred years. What the hell does it matter who their bloody government is? You go along to the National Gallery and you look at a Velasquez, and what does it matter to you that the man he's painting was a pimply tyrant who burnt his enemies alive? And Graham Pollock's in the Velasquez class, and you can't put *him* in a museum. You've got about five years to watch him at his peak, and we chicken out. Here am I – fifteen years of doing dirty jobs for my country, because it's something I believe in, something I think's worth protecting with every weapon God gave us, and then I watch them chuck it away because a few kids whine at them. My Christ! Now I don't risk anything more than I bloody well have to do to keep my job and earn my pension, and if I see a short cut I take it. The way they treated you, *you* know what it feels like.'

He raised a strangely short arm and snapped off a twig of the lemon tree above their heads. For a moment it looked as if he were going to tear it to bits, leaf by leaf, but suddenly he put it to his nose and sniffed mournfully at the bittersweet scent of its one small blossom. Pibble made a few sympathetic clicks. In its odd way this seemed to him a more reasonable and honest account of one man's patriotism than he'd heard for a long time; if Butler's idea of England – the ideal country for which he was prepared not merely to die but to do dirty jobs – was symbolized by flannel-clad marionettes prancing on green turf, Pibble's own was probably just as parochial – a certain elm at leaf-fall, the attitude of old railway-workers as they bicycled out of the sheds and across the iron swing-bridge . . .

'Five days,' wheezed Butler. 'Are you going to give me a hand, old man?'

'I'll check Porphyrocolpos and the yacht for you,' said Pibble. 'I may tell Thanatos what I'm doing – I haven't really thought it out.'

'I leave it to you,' said Butler dully.

'And I'm going to some sort of party at the South Bay villas this morning. I won't be able to go nosing around, I expect, but I'll let you know if I spot anything odd.'

'Let me know if you don't,' said Butler. 'That'd be something. That sort of crowd, you get everything. Drink, drugs, all the perversions from the little toe to the lughole – and they'll spend their time telling you they've left England because they saw it was going to the dogs. Scum!'

'You can't think of anything else I ought to look for,' said Pibble. 'Apart from the opium smell and the apparatus, I mean.'

'Little mounds of white powder,' said Butler with sudden sarcasm. 'Hell, you won't find anything. The whole thing's a balls-up. No, I don't mean that – there just might be something in it. If you spot a junkie, you're probably on to something. That's all.'

He didn't sound very interested. He was staring moodily at the tomb of Mrs. Davidson.

'Patience was the chief of her virtues,' he snarled. 'That's what they try to tell us. Learn to wait the other chap out, and you'll win. Bollocks. Double-bollocks. I've wasted years waiting, and the best things I've ever done I've pulled off on the instant, by hunch. Like hooking a bouncer. Well, thanks, old man. Sorry to have spouted like this. I don't often get a chance, you know.'

'I'll leave a message at the Aeschylus,' said Pibble. 'If I sign it Jimmy Pibble it's not important. If I sign it James it means I've found something.'

'That'll do.' Butler got up but stood where he was. 'You aren't really too blind to do a stint of umpiring, are you? Those kids!'

'I'm the worst umpire in the world,' said Pibble. 'I'm too easily influenced.'

Butler laughed with mild incredulity and strode off between the tombs. As the clacking of the hens rose Pibble returned to his task of restoring Mr. Manners' virtues to legibility. Butler was out of sight by the time he was clear of the hen-run. The noon sun battered his scalp. It was hard to believe that in three days it would be November. He thought of London – the last plane-leaves shuffling along pavements under a moist chill breeze, the tan greying on the returned holidaymakers. He was bothered by the notion that he had some sort of residual duty to get word to London, to Department J, that their Captain Butler was cracking up.

To whom, he wondered, did he owe such a loyalty? To his elm-tree and railway-workers? To the force which had been his life? No, he decided, it was to two or three men with whom he had worked. They were still on the job, and though none of them was in Department J, or remotely connected with it . . .

And if he told them about Butler, he would have to tell them where Anna Laszlo was hiding. After he had drunk Thanassi

Thanatos's Guinness, guzzled his ham? At this very moment, just over the northern horizon, a dark and silky waiter would be bringing Mary half a bottle of Heidsieck and a little plate of roseate prawns – the sort of automatic luxury which she had never known, and to which she was responding as . . . as a broad bean plant responds to a foliar feed. (Make it a rose-bush, you prosaic elder. But a rose doesn't react with such miraculous speed, nor . . .)

A flicker of pink caught his eye beside the path and was still. He stopped and saw a little lizard, two inches long only, spread-eagled on a whitish stone; it was the colour of smoked salmon, and had the same slightly translucent look; at the ends of its wide-spread claws were tiny pads; a spiny little crest ran down its nape. Pibble stared at it, still as the drooping angel of Mrs. Davidson's monument. It rustled and flicked into a cranny.

Not merely interesting – uncanny. The samimithi. You drink the homely milk out of the familiar cup – an action so ordinary that you never even think of questions about trust or danger – and in the last inch you find this creature. And then you die.

Pure superstition of course.

Chapter Six

He was already late by the time he reached the waterfront. The first thing that struck him was that the charter group of artists had indeed arrived – there they were, dotted along the quay, hunched over splayed easels, frowning as they settled to their first vain effort to capture on canvas the peculiar soul of Mediterranean blue – blue sky, blue water, and in between the blues the yellow-orange plaster, the pinkish tiles and the lounging boats. Pibble picked his way between them, feeling benign. They were no problem. He didn't yet know what to think, but one thing he refused to believe in was a greying matron from Haywards Heath who could hold her own in talk about colour-balance and canvas textures, and on the side was a hatchet-man from the Mafia.

'Jeem! Jeem!' squawked a voice as he passed the posh, expensive bar, the Lord Byron, half-way to his objective. He looked round, baffled, until he saw the startling orange coiffure of Zoe Palangalos. She was waving feverishly at him from a table under the awning, but she looked sulky. George, beside her, wore an uninterpretable expression. Pibble swore and went over.

'Ullo, ullo,' she gasped, like a telephone operator. 'Goodbye.'

Pibble blinked, then saw that she was dressed to travel, and that by her chair was a clutter of carrier-bags and vanity-boxes.

'Are you leaving?' he said. 'Already?'

'Leavink,' she said, pouting. 'An I am not knowink anybody. Comink. Goink.'

'It is not safe,' said George in a low voice. 'I did not mind her playing around in the harbour when I thought the whole idea was rubbish. But now . . . She is too new a wife to lose.'

He patted her hand, but she snatched it away.

'I don't imagine you found anything suspicious in the harbour,' said Pibble, to change the subject. Zoe threw her hands wide, as if to embrace the bay.

'All my friends,' she cried. 'All good men. All bad girls. Is right?'

'Sounds like the Garden of Eden,' said Pibble.

She laughed, partly with pleasure at her own cleverness, as one does when one gets a joke in a foreign language.

'Adamos,' she said, leaning over to pinch George's ear. 'Is always thinkink. Eva is I, is always playink. Jeem, you are my snake, is right?'

'No, I'm just one of the animals, and you can give me a name,' said Pibble. He was embarrassed for George – she was cross at having to go, and was teasing her husband by a blatant display of seductiveness, aimed at any old man who happened to pass by.

'O.K., O.K.,' she fluted. 'You are cold, you are dry. I am namink you Mr. Savra. What is that meanink, George?'

'Lizard,' said George. Pibble blinked with shock.

'Is rude?' asked Zoe. 'Oh, Jeem, I am jokink!'

She leapt to her feet and flung her arms round his neck and kissed his cheek. The scent she was wearing was as strong as catmint, and she pressed deliberately against him so that he could feel the softness of her breasts on his gristly sternum. He made as apologetic a face as he could muster over her shoulder at George, who shrugged, spread his palms and smiled.

'It wasn't rude,' said Pibble. 'It's just that I'd been thinking about lizards. You must be telepathic.'

'What is meanink?' said Zoe, letting go.

George explained in Greek.

'I'm sorry,' said Pibble. 'I'm the rude one, because I've got to go. I'm late already. I'm very sorry that you're off, Zoe. I do hope we'll meet again.

'Ope. Ope,' mocked Zoe. 'Good-bye, Jeem. Watch that George is not talkink to the bad girls.'

'I'll do my best,' said Pibble.

He was cross with himself as he walked on – cross for being disturbed by Zoe's treatment, for letting it bother him at all. Also for thinking about lizards, another famous symbol. He could see the Helicon bar now, a few white tables on the quayside and a faded blue awning; two figures sat at one of the tables. He tried to think about Greek – the hotel manager hadn't known the English for helicopter, Zoe had been baffled by telepathy – it ought to be possible to construct a sentence in English consisting almost wholly of Greek words. Analysing the physiognomy and psychology of synchronous saurians . . . Hell!

He searched the withered landscape of his mind for a more

practical problem to occupy him. Something flicked and was still. Another lizard – a dark one.

Suppose Doctor Trotter had told Thanatos, and then Pibble, five-sixths of the truth. Suppose he had fallen out with his clan over the division of spoils, and gone to Thanatos for revenge, and contrived to manoeuvre himself into a position of power in the future Hog's Cay complex. All that was true, he'd admit. But then suppose that he was planning to use this position in much the way his cousins would have: that he had feelers out to the other side and was offering them most of what they wanted – a depot for the heroin trade in particular – provided he himself got his cut? Was that enough to account for the rumour Butler had brought?

Just possibly. It would have to have been a rapid rumour to have worked so fast, though. Nor could Doc Trotter, however corrupt, have corrupted a bullet-hole into a petrol-tank. He might, then, have got in touch with some other faction of the notoriously riven Mafia. Porphyrocolpos could have an enemy without and within.

Tchah! There was no evidence for it at all.

The Helicon Bar was a whole civilization away from the Lord Byron, and much more Pibble's style. Its orange awning had been patched and repatched, and dimly visible in the reeking cavern behind it a bat-eared girl was cooking something by waving a paper fan at a biscuit-tin full of glowing charcoal. The tables on the quay were immensely heavy and ornate cast-iron, painted so often as almost to obscure the regimental badge embossed on each bowed leg, the stodgy lamb of the 23rd Foot, Captain Davidson's regiment. Pibble bent to examine one, thinking how gratifying it was that this legacy of Imperialism (and probably of some Quartermaster's corruption) should still be finding a use. Then he moved on to where Nancy and Tony sat at the furthest table, deep in talk and drinking tea out of thick tumblers. The proprietor came up as Pibble was pulling back a chair and mumbling unneeded introductions.

'*Thelo mia bira*,' said Pibble.

'The Greeks make the worst beer in the world, and Yannis keeps the worst beer in Greece,' said a voice behind him.

'Then I ought to try it,' said Pibble, looking round.

'Quite right,' said the square young man who had come up

behind him. *'Il s'agit d'arriver a l'inconnu par le dérèglement de tous les sens.* Hi, Nan. *Thio bires, Yanni.'*

He fell into his chair with a thud. He was blond, wore thick glasses, and talked English, French and Greek with an accent that Pibble took for American. The proprietor slid into the dark intestines of his bar.

'Mezethes,' shouted the man after him. 'They don't always bring 'em with beer. My name's Hott, Mark Hott. I'm a painter.'

'I'm Jimmy Pibble. I'm a tourist. I think I've heard of you, haven't I?'

'You from London? I've never shown there.'

'No, but I've seen your pictures in a magazine. White on white?'

'Yeah, that might be me. You don't have to say anything about my work. In fact you better not.'

'Gee,' said Nancy suddenly, 'I just love all that white, Mr. Hott. You're the whitest painter I ever did meet.'

She did the accent very well.

The proprietor came out with the beers and a plate of little fried fish-fragments.

'Screw you,' said Mr. Hott happily to Nancy. 'Who are your friends?'

'I don't know,' said Nancy. 'We caught Mr. Pibble stealing Vangelis's olives yesterday, and he made a date to go with me to Randy Wolf's this morning, to see whether he feels like retiring into that kind of lot. And now he's had the nerve to bring his bodyguard along. She says her name's Tony. You'd better watch your step, Mark – she's tougher than you are.'

Pibble was interested to find Nancy so on-the-spot today. She'd registered Mr. Hott's obvious glances, and she had somehow arrived at this less obvious truth about Tony. Moreover, though not quite clean, she had certainly washed since yesterday. She was wearing one of those Iroquois-looking shifts, more fringe than fabric. Her bare arms were sheathed in thin silver bracelets. Her nose was sharp and her eyes were sharp and her prattle was sharp – he found he liked her less than he had the morose waif in jeans.

Mr. Hott gave Tony a big glad grin. She looked coolly at him, sipped her tea and said nothing. Pibble cleared his throat to describe the pin lizard he had seen, realized that he didn't want this crass newcomer holding forth on the local superstitions which were such close kin with Pibble's own private fantasies, so drank the beer. Mr. Hott's fat, hairy arm swung up suddenly to gesture at the quay. His eyes behind the thick lenses were blood-shot, which made him look more furious than perhaps he felt.

'Look at them,' he growled. 'They paint like they were *knit-ting*.'

It was true. All along the waterfront where the charter artists toiled, the butts of their fifty paintbrushes bobbed and weaved at the canvases with much the motion that the needles used to move in the hands of Mary's mother as she knitted Pibble his ritual, unwearable Christmas jumper.

'Mark's a hard man,' said Nancy. 'He paints with a knife.'

'Keep your ignorance to yourself,' said Mr. Hott. 'I do my preliminary sketches with a brush, just like Breughel, so as even Nan could recognize them as pictures of what I've been looking at. They get a little different when I work them up.'

He was talking to Tony, who had the gift of appearing to take part in a conversation without actually saying anything.

'Canada,' said Pibble suddenly.

'He got it from my Quebec accent when I did my Rimbaud bit,' said Mr. Hott. He was still talking to Tony.

'No,' said Pibble. 'I remembered it from the magazine. You're the one whose pictures keep getting stolen.'

Tony looked at him now, for the first time, from above her tepid, milkless tea which she was sipping as lasciviously as if it were one of the monstrous icecreams that the chef at Por-phyrocolpos concocted for her. The glance implied shared know-ledge and shared caution – that Pibble might remember a series of thefts because he had once been a policeman, but she would say nothing of that, and nor would he of her 'illness'. It was a lot to read into a glance – wishful thinking, Pibble decided, that he could interpret her looks at all.

'Only twice,' said Mr. Hott. 'There's some kind of Hott-addict down there in New York. Four good paintings I lost out of two shows.'

'Lovely publicity,' said Nancy. 'His prices shot sky-high.'

'Yeah, there's that. But these things I did with my guts, and now I don't know what's become of them – don't even know if they're hanging in a good light ... Hey! If we're going to Randy's we gotta be moving – he serves Rumanian Scotch after the first half-hour, and it's twenty minutes' walk – thirty this weather.'

'Tony's brought a beach-buggy,' said Nancy. 'I've never been in one.'

'Thanassi's new toys,' said Tony. 'He brought them this time.'

'Great,' bellowed Mr. Hott. 'Hi! Yanni!'

In fast, horrible Greek he ordered a crate of beer-bottles, paid for them and the drinks, slung the crate on his shoulder and followed Tony up the quay. Even the lip-puckered painters stopped to watch as she went by. She was wearing linen slacks and a plain white blouse, but the moment she had stood up Pibble saw that she was moving not with yesterday's slouch but with a poised sexuality. It made him uncomfortable; it reminded him of Zoe Palangalos. He wondered what had produced the change – not himself, surely. Not virile Mr. Hott, please God: Perhaps it was the tea.

'Is he always like this?' he whispered to Nancy who was trotting bright-eyed at his side.

'Like what? Mark? Oh, yes, only worse. He's a bit subdued today, I should think he was up all night – did you notice his eyes? He goes out night-fishing, and sometimes they don't get back till dawn. Yippee! Look at that!'

The buggy was typical Thanatos, a sawn-off Volkswagen with racing tyres, its bodywork imperial purple picked out here and there with gross gold thetas. It was plushly garish. Nancy nipped into the passenger seat, leaving Pibble and Mr. Hott to cling to the exiguous back seat while Tony took the buggy rollicking over the cobbles. She changed gear as often as possible, roaring the engine as she did so, and as soon as she was out of the town she ignored the road, drummed up a dune and took them slithering down steep sand to the beach, which the set of the tide laid level here for more than a mile. The further end of this wide sweep had been gobbled up by the speculator who built the South Bay villas, but nearer the town it was open sand. A few boys were bathing, and a group of black-clad women were poking along the water's edge with strange-shaped sticks. Tony curved round them, then weaved along the lacy fringe of the sea, playing with the lap of the waves so as to send sheets of water fanning from under her offside wheels. If Thanatos had been ski-ing out there, they could have had a well-matched water-fight. Pibble wondered whether this stink and clamour and show was the normal way to arrive at an expatriates' party.

Nancy and Mr. Hott stood up in their seats and began to yell and wave as they reached the first of the villas. Hott gripped Pibble's shoulder to steady himself and rode the buggy like a charioteer. The villas were all different, though equal in their ugliness and unsuitability, and the fourth was set a little back from the beach so as to allow room for a terrace of brick pillars and vine-shaded walks. The area held a small crowd; as the buggy bellowed nearer head after head turned to watch it. Now they had an audience. Tony stopped the car and switched off, so that Mr. Hott's crude Canadian shouts of fellowship had the air to themselves. He vaulted out of his seat, heaved the beer on to his shoulder and rushed up the slope like a commando on a battle course. People answered his cries with brief, amiable jeers, but continued to watch the strangers. Nancy and Tony followed them up the slope, walking hand in hand like schoolgirls – as though Nancy felt that somehow she had to protect her new friend from the inquisition of all those eyes – for there was no doubt who the eyes were looking at. Pibble wondered if it was the release from Thanatos's grinding personality that had allowed Tony to revert – to bounce like a released spring – from the submissive odalisque to the Bomber Queen. Or had yesterday's melodrama released old impulses from her guerrilla past, stirring her to this potent walk, that wild driving?

Anyway, with such a distraction a couple of paces in front of him, Pibble was able to slip into the party as unnoticeably as a waiter. As the mutter of talk rose again to full throttle, he decided that he was unlikely to be introduced to anybody, and would be lucky even to get a drink. He was surprised when Mr. Hott rushed at him to give him a tall glass of beer, all froth after the bumping across the dunes.

'Come and meet your host,' he shouted. 'Nan's got other things on her mind. Randy's a great guy – he'd better be, because he's my neighbour – but if he goes blank and rushes off to look in a mirror, pay no attention. He's got this satyriasis problem, and he controls it by self-hypnotism ... Hi, Randy, I want you to meet an ex-cop called Jimmy Pibble ...'

During the next hour Pibble was also introduced to Signora Lucci, who hated Greece but was living on Hyos because she'd had the misfortune to be pronounced dead in a Roman hospital, and by the time she had recovered, her death certificate was already passing through the entrails of the Italian bureaucratic system, which meant that she dared not set foot in her homeland for fear that some official would insist on burying her; he met John Bonce of Sheffield, who had suddenly been taken ill in Hong Kong and now continued to exist thanks to a single Chinese kidney; Mrs. Bonce, the surviving member of a pair of Siamese twins, who knew at any instant what her sister was up to in the Great Beyond; Mr. Dokker, a Norwegian, who was engaged in litigation to have his disease, hitherto unknown to medical dictionaries, named after himself and not after the doctor who had diagnosed it; Mlle Guillerand, a novelist allergic to paper, who wrote on silk; old Mrs. McCallender from Wellington, New Zealand, whose companion warned Pibble in a whisper not to mention the name of Sigmund Freud because that would send the old lady into a three-day coma – a neurosis dating back to 1921, when she'd made the journey to Vienna only to be told by Freud that she was not in need of analysis (Mrs. McCallender then talked to Pibble in a manner provocatively designed to bring the conversation round to the potent name); the companion, of course, who had webbed fingers; and a few others whose names and diagnostics didn't register.

He found himself a surprising success with these people, only partly because he was a new face, or rather a new ear. It was when they discovered he was staying at Porphyrocolpos that they became animated. Their dislike and distrust of Thanatos was extraordinary – far more than mere jealousy. He was a new-comer, whereas many of the villa people had lived on Hyos for nearly ten years. He would spoil the island by making it famous. He would bring tourists – he might even build an hotel, and then there would be too much money about and the Hyotes would be spoilt . . .

'It's happening all over the world,' said Mr. Bonce, puffing out his furry cheeks. 'I knocked about a bit before I took ill, and I've seen it again and again. Money's all right in the right hands, but you've got to be careful who gets it or you'll knock the bottom out of a lot of traditions what have kept these people going for generations, you've seen 'em, ways of working the fields, or keeping theirselves amused for an evening. Take fishing – not that I can touch fish these days, more's the pity – you still get bloody good fish on Hyos, fresh every morning from the night-fishing boats – Mark goes out with them – he'll tell you – and they chill what they don't sell here and ship it to the mainland. Any day now they'll find they get a better price there, and you won't be able to buy any fish on Hyos what hasn't been shipped to the mainland and then brought back. And it'll taste like a bloody loofah, too.'

'And the beeootiful little donkeys,' said Signora Lucci. 'When your Thanatos make all the peasants rich, they buy cars, and where then are the donkeys?'

'Has he decided to build a hotel?' said Pibble, treading carefully round an actual lie about his own knowledge. 'Where will he put it?'

'That's what we're waiting for,' said Mr. Bonce. 'We'll fight it, eh, Mark?'

'Fight what?' said Mr. Hott, bringing Pibble another bottle of beer.

'Thanatos building a bloody great hotel behind the beach.'

'He can't do that,' said Mr. Hott. 'That's where they're going to put the aerodrome. Only flat bit of island.'

'What aerodrome?' said Mr. Bonce. Pibble could hear, in those four syllables, property values falling at a thousand drachs a second.

'Over our dead bodies,' hissed Signora Lucci.

'It's all right for you,' said Mr. Hott. 'You can get up and walk about when something has happened over your dead body.'

Signora Lucci laughed, but Pibble thought there was something brutal about Mr. Hott's gross health in this parade of clinical cases. Perhaps his poor eyesight qualified him.

'Hi, Randy,' called Mr. Bonce. 'Mark's got a story about building an aerodrome behind the beach.'

Their host turned, holding a bottle whose label was a maroon and yellow tartan. He was a lean, stooped, likeable-looking man, tanned as brown as the beach.

'It comes every four years,' he said. 'I think I've heard it five times. They won't cut the first sod till 2025.'

He turned away.

'Is he the oldest inhabitant?' asked Pibble.

'I'm the youngest,' said Mr. Bonce, looking half-relieved. 'I bought my house in '68, but they didn't say anything about plans for an aerodrome. These Greeks are all bloody sharks, and the lawyers are the worst.'

'But even the lawyers are being very good under this government,' said Signora Lucci.

'No politics,' said Mr. Hott. 'Come and meet our authoress, Jimmy. Hi, Diane, I want you to meet Jimmy Pibble. This is Diane Guillerand, who has the dirtiest mind between Venice and Beirut.'

'I expect that's where the real competition begins,' said Pibble.

Mr. Hott bellowed meaninglessly, but Mlle Guillerand looked at them with peasant's eyes. She was only in her early twenties, but already as dumpy and sallow as a Normandy matriarch. She was alone when they found her, staring at the beach-buggy standing strident on the classic sands.

'It's more practical than it looks,' said Pibble, wondering whether her gaze meant disgust or envy.

'*Je l'ai déjà vu,*' she said, turning sluggishly towards him. At first her method of conversation was contradiction, but after batting half a dozen of his serves firmly into the net, she introduced a new ploy, a rapid muttered monologue in French, which stopped and waited for an answer at a point which Pibble hadn't even realized was a question. Five minutes' talk with her was a long time, and Mr. Hott left before that. Pibble could usually speak adequate French after a few hours' practice; now it was like walking through deep mud in gumboots, each phrase a squelching effort that threatened to leave all meaning behind in the morass of grammar; he was telling her his adventure in the olive tree when she suddenly shrugged and walked off, leaving him to mouth an unnecessary subjunctive at one of the vine-covered pillars.

He stayed with his back to the party and gazed out over the sea, bored and ashamed. After all, it was his own fault; he had insinuated himself into this farcical community in order to spy on them, to search for assassins and drug-pedlars. There were no assassins here – Mr. Bonce was the latest comer, four years ago. There very well might be addicts in a crowd such as this – Mlle Guillerand had the look and the manner of one – you are always likely to find a bunch of soaks and a few dope-takers in any bored and affluent backwater – but what business was it of his? Yes, yes, the drug trade is an evil thing, and you have a duty to damage it if the chance comes your way. But that was only an excuse – really he was acting for Thanassi.

He looked at the garish vehicle on the sand and thought about his master – there was no other word for the mysterious relationship that Thanatos exacted. He was being asked to behave in a certain way out of *loyalty*. This had happened before: for all his working life he had been loyal to the police force, not merely working intolerable hours but, for instance, several times helping to conceal damaging truths about his colleagues. They would no doubt have done the same for him. Now, ejected from that world, he was ashamed – not for having done what he did, but for having accepted that it was a virtue, unpleasant but admirable, instead of a practical and psychological necessity. Everybody is loyal to something. Take old Butler – his apparent cynicism about his job (supposing he was telling the truth in the cemetery) isn't a failure of loyalty, but a manifestation of loyalty to an idea – arguably, because the idea is abstract, more admirable – or at least more civilized – than a bread-and-butter job-loyalty. What the hell does it matter that the abstract idea is the imagined spirit of King Willow? Or obnoxious Mr. Hott, to judge by his brief outburst over the stolen pictures, was strongly loyal to his art, and so were the charter artists and doddering Father Polydore – and that's only a straight extension of selfishness. In a way, somehow, the loyalty of the courtiers of the Sun King to the monstrous egotist at Porphyrocolpos was more admirable – though, as Thanatos had said, they had nothing to lose by it. There was the same attractive community of people working together for an end as Pibble had known in the police, but far more focussed and comprehensible – he was here because Thanatos needed him here, and that was enough? No. It was just a self-comforting notion. Supposing, by some impossible fluke in the warm wind of love he were able to steal the millionaire's girl from him . . . Yesterday's girl, that is. He was frightened of today's. Now that the wish had become the desire, the impossible the improbable – he smiled sourly at the fancy that it could be his own senescent charms that had caused the change in her; the smile stayed on his face, meaningless as the rictus of some archaic Apollo, as he realized that he had preferred the longing in its wish-form. In its desire-form it shrivelled him with alarm.

'What's so funny?' shouted Mr. Hott in his ear. 'Frightened Diane off, did you? You dirty old man.'

'Bored her off, I'm afraid. Where can I have a pee?'

'Come over to my pad.'

'I ought to be taking Tony home.'

'She ought to be taking you home, you mean. She's lost herself somewhere, man. You've time to come with me and piss some of that beer out. I want to show you my pictures.'

'I won't know anything about them,' said Pibble as they left the alcohol cackle behind and crossed a sad lawn, brown as fudge.

'Sure, sure. But you tell your boss about them and perhaps he'll buy a few to hang in this hotel. They'd look fine up there.'

'Up where?'

'Oh. Any high building. You get a different kind of light once you're properly above ground level. That's why I like selling in Manhattan. Cast your bread upon the waters, that's my motto. I take you round at a party, and you get Thanatos to buy my stuff.'

Mysteriously Pibble found Mr. Hott faintly more likeable for this frank admission that his attentiveness hadn't been friendliness. There are times when one doesn't feel like being claimed as a friend, by anyone, let alone a brawling bear from Canada.

The studio was a surprise. Pibble had expected that Mr. Hott's unnecessary energies would release themselves into flying paint, littered like pigeon-droppings on to every surface. Instead the big shed might have been a laboratory, with a polished cork floor and finically arranged shelves and work-areas. The windows were all thickly shuttered, as though the diurnal motion of the sun had to be kept out, as a disorderly element. Even the necessary shambles of crating up a series of paintings to be shipped off to America had been managed in a tidy fashion, with the off-cuts of timber piled neatly in one corner and all the sawdust and shavings swept up.

As if in defiance of this neat, cool, rational room Mr. Hott lit three josh-sticks and fitted them into holders on the work-bench, before picking out the few uncrated paintings and showing them, without comment, to his visitor. There seemed to be two kinds: the white-on-whites which Pibble remembered from the magazine feature, and a series of gaudy constructions, random bric-a-brac cemented into position on hardboard and then blobbed with smoky stars of yellow sealing-wax. Pibble didn't care for these at all, but he got much more out of the white on whites than he had when he'd read the magazine, partly because he was now able to see how three-dimensional they were, and partly because he was allowed to study the process by which they'd achieved their final, vestal ambiguity. Under the blue lights he traced with fascination the development from a brisk, brilliant sketch of two foreshore cottages; it went through five stages and finished as a six-foot abstract of staring whites. The final stage was more of sculpture than a painting, so deep was its one careful oval incised into the surface, and so far did the one balancing rectangle project.

Mr. Hott pressed a switch behind the easel, and an artificial sun rose, an Anglepoise lamp fixed somehow to an electric motor which drove it in a creeping arc along the upper edge of the painting, so that a bluish shadow appeared inside the circle and another below the rectangle; the shadows began to shift imperceptibly across the plaster surface, just as the natural shadows must have shifted round the cottages of the original sketch as the afternoon leaned towards sunset.

'You ought to supply a little aerosol with it,' said Pibble. 'So that people can make their own clouds.'

Mr. Hott took the idea seriously. He grunted and considered it while he rolled a cigarette with short, efficient fingers, producing a tube almost as smooth and compact as a factory-made article.

'It's an idea,' he said. 'People enjoy a stunt – something they can do themselves. But you have to watch it in case you become too stunty, and then it's just a slice of fashion – this week's trendiest – and next week you're forgotten. I rigged my baby sun as a joke, and then I liked it. Twenty-three minutes after you've set it going, for about eight minutes more – when it's just up *here* – it throws its light flush with this plane, which looks as flat as a wall before and after. But for those eight minutes you see every freckle of the texturing picked out like the craters on the moon. And then it's flat again. But it's still a stunt – I don't reckon I'll show it. Clouds – no. Oh, hell, I'll play around perhaps.'

'Do you sell all the sketches, or do you keep them?'

'I burn them,' said Mr. Hott slowly, passing the tips of his fingers over the surface of one of the intermediate stages. 'They're the sacrifice – I burn 'em, every one. The better I like them, the more important it is to be shot of 'em. You got to keep your weight hard up against the collar of your technique, shoving it all the time as far as it will go. I work in a world where there are bums with money who will swallow anything, just anything, and I know it. I don't give a damn what else I do for money, so long as I can sell my stuff to buyers who know what they're getting and know why it's worth it. Your Thanatos isn't a bum, I've heard. He's bought good stuff, screwing the man down to a fair price, and he's refused to buy big-name rubbish. He's my kind of buyer. I'd like to get him interested.'

'I don't know him very well,' said Pibble. 'But if you like I'll tell Buck Budweiser about you. He used to work for Parke Bernet, and was Mr. Thanatos's art adviser.'

'Good enough. Thanks, man. Now let's go and see what those girls have done with each other.'

He laughed again.

As they walked back towards the beach Pibble had an irritable feeling that there were all sorts of nuances he was failing to catch. Hott's explanation for his friendliness was quite reasonable, but it seemed an extravagant way to behave for a man who expected to sell most of his pictures in New York, at New York prices – but then extravagant behaviour was normal among people who came within the pull of the powerful gravitation centred on Thanatos ...

Nancy had vanished, but Tony was lounging against the beach-buggy, talking to a dark young man. Even from the bank above the foreshore Pibble could see that she had reverted to her stance and mood of yesterday. The play was over.

She drove him back along the official track, sedately enough to allow conversation above the noise of the engine.

'Did you tell Mr. Hott I was an ex-cop?' he asked.

She shook her head.

'He must have known before,' she said. 'He suckered on to us at the bar because of you.'

'Oh, nonsense. It was you he was interested in.'

She shook her head again, making the unreal hair move as though her nature commanded every swag and scroll of it.

'Nope,' she said. 'I know when they mean it.'

As they slowed to enter the town – so white from a distance, so throbbing with colour once you were in it – he found himself watching her dark hand on the gear lever; his eyes travelled up her velvety arm and shoulder and her long neck, half-hidden in hair that was someone else's. Her jaw was firm, but very finely carved – it was hard to imagine it open to scream its anger at National Guardsmen. Or even ...

'Do you chew gum?' he asked.

'Nope. Though when I was a kid . . .'

She slowed, looked at him and stopped the car altogether to look at him more thoroughly. Her large, dark eyes opened wide behind the big lenses of her sunglasses, and then she frowned slightly, as though the question might be a trap.

'Why?' she said.

'I was looking at your jaw,' he said. 'It doesn't seem to have the muscles.'

She laughed and drove on. Pibble almost sighed with relief that he hadn't broken by his idiot question the mood of purring intimacy they had achieved. He had achieved, rather.

'Chewing,' she said suddenly. 'It's a nothing thing. You do it because you do it, and so what? My Poppa was a preacher, you know that?'

'Ung,' said Pibble.

'Thou shalt love the Lord thy God with all thy heart and with all thy soul and with all thy strength. I guess "soul" is the same word as the one they'd have used for "mind". Right?'

'In Latin, certainly,' said Pibble. 'I think they had two different words in Greek – I don't know about Aramaic. Or Hebrew.'

'Shame on you, Jim. Listen. Anything you do – *anything* – if you don't do it with all your heart and all your soul and all your strength, you're betraying yourself. There are things you *got* to do – got to because you morally must, or because society makes you – and even so you do them like that, or you rebel against doing them like that. Big things or little things, it doesn't matter what. That's how you do it.'

'I've watched you eating your icecream,' said Pibble.

'Sure. 'N Thanassi's like that – that's why I get along with him. If he was a starving man in a slum and he found a bit of bone in a trash-can – a bit of ham-bone – he'd gnaw the meat off it with a kinda love. He'd love his hunger, and love the feel of his teeth nicking the stringy shreds out from the gristle.'

'Yes,' said Pibble. She had made this claim before, and again he wondered whether it was true. 'But what's it got to do with chewing-gum?'

She laughed again. She was happy. With his company? Surely not.

'It's a nothing thing, like I said. If I'd a million years to live, I'd run a campaign against gum. And tobacco, maybe. And listen, Jim, I've known guys so far gone on drugs that already they were walking on the cobbles of hell. But drugs aren't a nothing thing, no . . .'

Again Pibble purred in the communicative silence, and again it was Tony who broke it.

'Did Buck see a real bullet-hole?' she said. 'What d'you think?'

'Probably not. A professional assassin would have got him when he was standing up in the boat after we'd fished Buck out. But you have to explain the motor failing and the boat catching fire – Alfred looks after them extremely well – and the telegram from Boston. And I heard a story this morning that the Mafia are interested in Hyos . . .'

'Uh?'

'It's supposed to be confidential, but I'll tell Thanassi and you can listen in.'

'But you think he's in no danger?'

'I didn't say that. I think the odds are that he's in some danger – though I don't know quite what. I still find it difficult to believe that a gunman got as far as the headland, took a shot at him skiing, when he was a difficult target, and failed to take another when he was an easy one.'

'Yeah. It doesn't add up. Jim . . . No. Let it go.'

In those words, as she stopped the buggy at the guarded fence round Thanatos's kingdom, the mood of contact was broken. He wondered what she had been going to ask him for, and whether he would have been able to give it.

'Listen to that!' she said suddenly. 'That's one pig-headed old roughneck. He's got too used to being lucky.'

Above the noise of their own idling engine he heard the sharp tearing noise of the speedboat out on the bay.

Chapter Seven

But it was Dave Warren who was water-skiing. Buck, with obstinate courage, was driving the speedboat again, while Thanassi fretted on the terrace with a little walkie-talkie radio. A screen had been set up between his table and the headland.

'Where you been, Jim?' he said, far from genially. 'We needed you. We got to get a fix on where that boat sank. Go and stand where you were standing yesterday – tell me what you think. Hi, Tony, have a good time?'

Pibble leaned on the balustrade of the terrace and stared at today's scene, trying to superimpose yesterday's fading image on it and see where the pictures failed to match.

'They're too far from the headland,' he said after a while.

'That's what I told Buck. Wassamatter, honey? Off your feed?'

While he talked sharply into his gadget Tony appeared beside Pibble with a plate of ham. He saw that her own icecream was half its usual size.

'I figured you wouldn't want any more beer,' she said.

'That's fine,' said Pibble, and turned to look at the glaring water. Thanassi's low, white cruiser, now anchored in the mouth of the bay, made the perspectives different; moreover it was impossible for the dancers to repeat the moves of yesterday's dance, and even if they had been able to, sending the same veils of spume arching across the same areas of blue, Pibble couldn't have been sure that this was so; the shapes and angles changed so fast that what seemed like a memory of yesterday might be only a memory of five minutes earlier.

'Ask him to go round that circle again,' said Pibble, 'and stop as soon as he's heading away from the shore.'

The boat came round, the plumes of its wake sank, Dave subsided into the water. Everything lay drifting to stillness.

'That's about it,' said Pibble. 'I think the boat was about twenty yards further to the right yesterday, and a little further away from us.'

'Buck says no,' said Thanatos after a further colloquy. 'He says you're likely right about the line from here, but he was never so near the shore. I reckon he'd be a better judge of that.'

Dave was swimming to the boat. He heaved himself aboard, and then there was a further period of adjusting the position, and finally an indecipherable series of movements aboard before the engine rattled again and the boat moved off, leaving a red buoy bobbing where it had been.

'I've got a couple of divers coming tomorrow with a geomagnetometer,' said Thanatos. 'They trail it behind a boat and it picks out metal objects on the sea bed where they cause bumps in the earth's magnetic field. The guy I called isn't sure whether my boat's got enough metal on it to register, but I'd like to give it a try. I want to see that motor.'

'So do I,' said Pibble.

'Yeah. We've got a lot of things here that don't add up. Find anything new this morning, Jim? It'd better be good, sneaking Tony off me for a morning when I'm not allowed to get my exercise ski-ing in my own bay.'

He jumped from the shelter of the screen, scuttled across the terrace like a scout in a Western, grabbed Tony's wrist and hustled her back to cover. She came without resistance, but in a way that reminded Pibble of a child taking part in a game for good manners and not because she wanted to play. Thanassi, in spite of his bad temper, sensed this and let her settle on to the terrace by his legs, with her knees drawn up under her chin.

'I saw Zoe,' said Pibble, 'and she's drawn blank in the harbour. I drew blank at the villas – they've all been here too long, and there aren't any strangers renting any of them. If that was all, I'd have said you were safe to go where you wanted, and that Buck was mistaken about the bullet-hole. But I talked to a man this morning who has been sent out here in a hurry by a branch of British Intelligence. I recognized him yesterday, and made an appointment to meet him today. He says he's here to check on a rumour that the Mafia are interested in Hyos.'

'That's bad,' said Thanatos.

'I think so. If he's telling the truth, he's working on the assumption that they're using the island as a staging-post in the drug trade.'

'Oh, crap!'

'No, Honey,' said Tony suddenly. 'There's a connection there.'

'What do you mean?' said Thanatos, but she shook her head.

'If he's telling the truth, you said, Jim?' asked Thanatos.

'Well, there's another reason why the Americans would be intersted in Hyos, isn't there?'

'Uh huh.' Thanatos didn't look down at Tony, but she frowned.

'On the other hand,' said Pibble, 'this man didn't even ask who was staying at Porphyrocolpos. He simply asked me to look the place over and see whether you were running a morphine factory. The yacht, too.'

'Screwy as hell,' said Thanatos.

'Morphine, not H?' said Tony.

'That's what he said the probabilities were.'

She nodded, as if satisfied.

'There's also the possibility that he's not really working for British Intelligence,' said Pibble. 'He seemed pretty disaffected. Incidentally he told me that in exchange for his coming here the Americans have mounted some kind of operation on Hog's Cay. If that's true, he must at least still have some kind of connection with British Intelligence. But he may just have said it as a throwaway line to see how I reacted, which would give him a line on whether we were on our guard.'

'The guy seems to have been free with his secrets,' said Thanatos, characteristically going to one of the weak points.

'I thought so too. I wondered whether you had the connections to find out whether he was telling the truth about why he's here, or about the Hog's Cay end.'

'Sure, in normal times, ' said Thanatos. 'But I daren't touch them with Tony here.'

'I'm going to hide out for a bit, honey,' said Tony quietly.

'I'll hide you,' said Thanatos.

'By myself. So I can take what action I like without thinking what'll happen to anyone else. You're a great old swine, Thanassi, and I wouldn't want to land you in the dirt.'

'No dirt's deep enough if it's for you, honey.'

He lowered his huge hand to pat her shoulder, but she sidled out from under his touch and he withdrew it.

'Where are you making for?' he growled.

'I got a place, if Alf can run me along the shore a bit, soon as it's dark.'

'Sure. You going to come back, honey?'

She bit her lip, frowning. Pibble could see that in accordance with her doctrines she would tell the truth. She had been Tha-

94

natos's girl, in order to 'recuperate', and she played the part with all her heart and all her mind and all her strength. Now that was over. Pibble got to his feet.

'I'll look round the house and the yacht now, if that's all right,' he said. 'Then I can report back to this man and see if I can find out any more.'

'O.K.,' said Thanatos. 'Tell Serafino. He'll show you round. Dave can call the yacht to send a boat out for you.'

He spoke thickly, as though it were an effort to order his wit and control some coming fury. Pibble nodded and almost scuttered off the terrace, but before he was through the bead curtain he heard Tony beginning to talk in a low, steady voice.

He took his search fairly seriously, using a steel rule which Serafino had found for him to measure rooms with. Sometimes, at the bedroom windows which faced across the bay, he would see the couple still on the terrace. Tony seemed to be doing most of the talking, while Thanatos sat half-slumped, pulling at his lower lip. At one point he saw a servant bring out Thanassi's silver tankard; Serafino saw this too, looked at his watch and made a slight click of disapproval.

The search was not difficult, as the house was straight-forwardly planned. Compared with the curiously painful scene on the terrace it was dull stuff; he found it uncomfortable to intrude on people whom he only knew as obsequious and almost anonymous servants and to find them in a context where they were individuals, sleeping or playing back-gammon or studying for some mysterious examination. In fact their rooms appeared to have more privacy than those in which Thanatos housed his guests; here (perhaps inevitably in the occasional home of a very rich man) there was a sort of depersonalizing luxury which only Buck had been able to make any impression on, thanks to the paraphernalia of crippledom. Even the owner's bedroom, with its gross couch flanked by consoles of switches, might have been that of any rich man who collected erotic Roman mosaics. Tony's room was a shambles: Pibble had seen nothing like it except in burgled flats, where the thieves have emptied every drawer and cupboard on to the floor. Among the litter were several more of the russet wigs, and one with the aggressive Afro hair-do that Anna Laszlo had worn before the Folger Library went up in flames. Afro but not Aphro, he decided. As he measured Dave's ultra-tidy room he found himself thinking about her again: she was nobody's doll; it must be very difficult for the rich not to turn their women into dolls, unless the women can challenge the wealth on equal terms – by being rich too, or by a gift which cannot be bought; hence the perennial popularity of opera singers – a million dollars cannot sweeten a sour note; and Tony had that kind of gift, in her unlikely sphere. Also, no doubt, she gave her elderly Hercules the glory of bedding with an Amazon; to harbour her in his arms was to defy the law of nations – he'd like that. It was not hard, for Pibble of all people, to understand what she meant to Thanatos. But what did *she* get out of the deal, apart from shelter?

He searched carefully, but without real interest, through the house, the outbuildings and finally the yacht. He wanted to be able to tell Butler the truth, because it is simpler than lying. But all the while as he measured and made notes the problem of Tony's love, or lust, or liking for Thanatos teased his mind, sometimes as plain prurient fancies, sometimes as quite presentable questions of psychology, but usually slithering between the two poles.

But when the yacht's own speedboat brought him back across the darkening bay and he climbed up to the terrace, he found the question was now one for the historian. Tony was gone, but Thanatos still sprawled at his table.

'Here, Jim boy,' he shouted as though Pibble were a dog. Like a dog Pibble trotted over.

'What did you find?'

'Nothing, of course,' said Pibble. No need to tell him about the embarrassed lad on the boat, experimenting with pot.

'You call my filing-system nothing?' purred Thanatos. 'You think yourself pretty damned smart to find that, Jim.'

This was true. The big safe with the documents had been carefully made to look like an extension of the lift-shaft. Pibble shrugged.

'You could sell that knowledge, Jim boy.'

'If I knew who to,' said Pibble.

Thanatos, drunker than Pibble had made him, was clearly winding himself up for some act of random menacing aggression. Now he rattled off a list of names, mocking Pibble's ignorance of them.

'If they're crooks you make them sound they'd cheat me,' said Pibble.

'Socrates Agnon, Miami Beach. Stick out for twenty thousand dollars.'

Pibble shrugged again. Thanatos snarled at him.

'You're a loser Jim. You make a trade of it. You want to be cheated, because that makes you an honest man. You wanted my girl, but you wouldn't make a play for her. You were scared, gut-scared, but you told yourself you were acting honourable. Go and get boozed up, loser, and let's see if you've got any guts in you when you're tight. That's an order. And send that nigger out. Tell him I sent for him. Not asked, sent. That's another order. You'll do it, won't you, loser?'

Pibble turned and walked away.

'Answer me, loser,' yelled Thanatos.

He pushed blindly through the bead curtains. A hand caught his elbow, and Dave Warren led him without a word into the big room at the back of the house where all the office work of running a hotel empire was done while Thanatos was at Porphyrocolpos. The other three men were already there.

'Your watch, Doc,' said Dave.

The black man picked up an empty tumbler, smiled without meaning, put a handful of icecubes in it, filled it almost to the brim with vodka and added three drops of Martini.

'Pussyfoot,' said Buck.

Still smiling the same non-smile, Doc Trotter went heavily out.

'You've got to fight back at him, Jim,' said Dave. 'What'll you have? Scotch?'

'Hey! About half that,' said Pibble.

'Knock it back,' said Dave. 'You'll need it.'

'You won't feel a thing,' said Buck. 'It's damned hard to get drunk at all when he's this way. You got so much adrenalin in your blood that you just burn it up.'

'What are the rules?' said Pibble.

'Hit back, hard as you like,' said Warren. 'He'll blast you off the court, even so, but he'll tire quicker.'

'I mean, for instance, do we mention Tony?'

Dave made a face.

'You've got to,' he said. 'Make a rule like that and he'll notice. He's hurt, and he wants you to pick his wound for him.'

'Pain's a way of existing,' said Buck. He knew, of course.

Dave drank, deep and gloomy.

'Jim's an oddball,' said Buck in an inquisitive tone. 'He's not tied to the guy the way we are. I wonder how he'll get at him.'

'I met another oddball this morning,' said Pibble, to change the conversation.

'This guy in the helicopter?' said Dave. 'Thanassi was telling us about him. It doesn't sound good, his rumour about the Mafia.'

'No, I didn't mean him,' said Pibble, irritated by how rapidly he had allowed an official secret to become unclassified gossip. 'Though he's an oddball too – he spends most of his time playing cricket with the boys in the town. But I was talking about a man who lives at the South Bay villas, called Mark Hott, a Canadian, a white on white abstract painter.'

'That guy?' said Buck eagerly. 'What's he doing on Hyos?'

'He lives in one of the South Bay villas. He wants to show you his work so that you can persuade Thanassi to buy a few hundred of them.'

'What's he doing now? Any good?' said Buck, as though this were a perfectly proper suggestion.

'I'm no judge,' said Pibble. 'I'm abstract-blind – like being tone-deaf. But it's gadgety in the kind of way Thanassi likes. And it looks, well, smart.'

'I'll bum out and see him tomorrow.'

'With the hangover you'll have?' asked Dave.

'I got a hollow leg,' said Buck, laughing as he touched his tiny shank.

In ones and twos they took turns with the ogre on the terrace, recuperating in the working-area between whiles. Pibble was on his third huge Scotch – and as Buck had foretold not noticing it – when Dave came back from duty.

'We're changing for dinner,' he said. 'Tuxedos.'

'That is bad,' said George.

'I haven't got the kit,' said Pibble.

'It's in your room. Serafino looked you out something that will fit. Christ, sometimes I could kill that man. Do you know what he said just now . . .'

Chapter Eight

The throb of his hangover was already diminishing when Pibble
left the Aeschylus Hotel, having deposited a note for Butler
making an appointment to meet at the Helicon at six. He had
signed it 'Jimmy Pibble'. But he still had enough of a singing
head to fail to notice that there really was something different
about the town this morning – that the change was not only in
the bloodshot eye of the beholder. The rural differences struck
him first – no old women hoeing among the vines, no parties of
shrilling olive-harvesters, a strange stillness. Then he thought
back and decided that the town too was altered; shops had been
shut, people had seemed older and tidier, the air had smelt less of
fish and more of bread. Now, behind him, a bell began a monot-
onous beat. It was Sunday. All Saints' Day in the West. The feast
of St. Sporophore on Hyos.

Gladly he slowed to the pace of a workless day. Physically he
didn't feel too bad, but morally he felt blasted.

In a year's time, perhaps, he would be able to look back to the
Hallowe'en dinner and be glad to have been there; but now . . .
pictures ran through his mind like fragments of dream in a de-
lirium, repeated themselves, interlocked. J. Pibble strolling into
the never-used dining-room, feeling pleasantly peacockish in the
ridiculous frilled shirt that Serafino had put out for him, to find
Thanatos already eating, still in his slacks and tea-shirt, though
they were now stained with the blotches of a dozen spilt Bloody
Marys. He could feel – no, that must have been much later, after
Thanatos had tossed a decanter of Cheval Blank 1945 through
the window and then began to heckle Pibble for being shocked at
the waste, as if he could discern the difference between decent
wine and Chianti brewed from banana skins – he could feel the
sudden tug that pinned him to the table-edge as the big hand
shot out and ripped one set of ruffles half off his chest, leaving
him to finish his meal with a strip of pale skin exposed, one
nipple and a few grizzled hairs framed by the spoilt finery. It was
odd that the shock of physical assault – the only actual violence
that any of them had experienced during the long night – was
still so strongly palpable when at the time it had seemed so trivial
beside the mental bludgeonings, even in its way a relief from

them. Both Dave and George had ridden the tempest with something like equanimity, except when Thanatos had spent twenty minutes comparing Tony with Zoe, in leisurely, almost dreamy detail. George endured and endured, and then suddenly he was standing over Thanatos's chair, with blotchy patches on his grey face, shouting at him in Greek, while Thanatos sat nodding and smiling like a stage director who has extracted from his performers precisely the effect he wanted. Doc Trotter had wept often, and been too easy meat to please the monster; Buck had shouted and snarled all the time, but seemed only to have been really hurt by sudden random solicitudes, as when Thanatos had insisted that he should sit in a proper chair and that Dave should help him into it.

Of course it had all been a game, a therapeutic game. It had also been an insight into the relationship between a monarch and his court, powerful nobles, each with his own pride, whose lives and fortunes yet depended on one man absolutely. Life with Henry VIII must have had moments like that. And underlying it all, even in Pibble's half-bared breast, there was a steady tide of compassion, sorrow for the great beast wounded and raging in the pit. Pibble had often read about the scared hyaenas round Stalin, but now he understood for the first time how they had mixed their hate and terror with more than mere respect – awe, and a sort of love. Doc Trotter would not have been made to weep by someone he merely hated. And what was it all for? A test of trust: Thanatos pushing his friends to the very limit of their fidelity, not just to prove his power over them, but to prove their loyalty too. They would not follow Tony.

The faint, sage-smelling breeze carried up the hill the far buzz of an engine. He turned and saw, between him and the dunes, one of the ridiculous beach-buggies skimming along the track to the south bay villas; far though it was, Pibble could recognize the driver by the way he sat – eager-beaver Buck, scurrying to start a round of art-wheeling-and-dealing. Pibble hoped that he wouldn't get back to find that miniature sun revolving in his bedroom, though presumably it would not be considered philistine to switch it off at night.

A wave of his hangover washed over him, so that he nearly vomited, and had to sit on a boulder by the path, feverish and sweating. When he started up the path he began to wonder who the private detective had been whom Thanatos had set to report on him almost a year ago, soon after they had first met. Thanatos's mock-genial revelation of how closely he had studied the Pibbles' small lives, of how well he knew Mary's ferocious feuds against random tradesmen, or the four months' money-fret after the mistake over Pibble's pension – this had been momentarily startling, but not really damaging because the man had skimped his job, made mistakes, guessed. (Perhaps Dave was at this moment on the phone to London, sacking him. No – far more likely Thanatos had learnt about Department J's class four check on the Pibbles, and used his influence to get a sight of it. That wasn't particularly reassuring, either.) Thanatos's own guesses at the curiosa of bed and bowels had been more telling. It was not pleasant to have one's introspection done for one by another party, to feel one's mind being drilled without an anaesthetic. His present expedition was one of revenge: he wanted to know something which mattered to Thanatos, but which Thanatos himself didn't know. Pibble was ashamed of this, and tried to persuade himself that it was important that *someone* at Porphyrocolpos should know.

He reached the olive grove where he had first found Father Chrysostom, and turned off between the trees, heading down in the direction from which he thought Vangelis had come. Beyond the grove the ground rose again into an area of small folds and undulations, with many trees obscuring any distant view. He found a small vineyard, but it was neglected and there was no hut in it. By a little copse of ilex and cypress he found a hut, locked, and showing no sign that it had been used for living in. The whole hillside seemed deserted – of course, everyone would be down in the town, the oldsters praying, the young ones sporting on the beach. Even so he still moved carefully, keeping as much as possible in cover, because he would much rather not be noticed snooping. If he was unsure of his own motives, how could he expect anyone else to give him the benefit of the doubt? So he wasted an hour, and found nothing.

Then, over to his left, a strange noise began, a regular clatter accompanied by a regular cry, both noises resonant and uninterpretable. He gave up his search and walked towards them.

As he emerged up a steep slope between clumps of loose scrub he saw Father Chrysostom standing at the monastery door and looking down the path towards the town, making both noises. The clatter came from a heavy old plank which he was beating with a stick, and the cry from his blue lips. He didn't notice Pibble coming up from the side until they were only a few feet apart; then he leaned plank and stick against the wall, smiled with extraordinary welcome – almost relief – and held out his hand to shake.

'*Kaloste, kirie,*' he said. '*Embrose, viazomaste. Argisome.*'

He looked piercingly at Pibble, as though trying to force comprehension into his skull through the eyeballs.

'*Kalos sas vrikame,*' said Pibble blankly. '*Poo ine Nancy?*'

Father Chrysostom clicked a negative, muttered '*Meta, meta,*' and pulled Pibble through the door by the elbow. A minute later he was standing in the refectory while Father Chrysostom draped round him a plain white robe which smelt and felt like a very old horseblanket. Father Polydore, even more elaborately garbed, sat at his work-desk with his head between his hands. But for the stench and weight of his robes and the nausea of his hangover, Pibble might have been quite pleased at this upshot. He had felt inquisitive about the monastery and would have liked time and opportunity to poke round on his own; Nancy had been a very partial guide.

'*Then esthanete kala,*' said Father Chrysostom, working his way into a magnificent chasuble, so moth-eaten that the underlying cloth seemed in places to be held together solely by the gold threadwork. That makes two of us not feeling well, thought Pibble. Gently Father Chrysostom raised Father Polydore from his stool and led him across to Pibble, where he placed the old man's left arm round Pibble's shoulders and Pibble's right round the old man's waist. Then he thrust a smoking censer into Pibble's free hand, picked up a book and a jewelled cross, opened the far door and stalked along the passage, chanting in noble tones. Pibble and Father Polydore shuffled after him; the old man was shivering, and stank. Suddenly, among the booming echoes set off by Father Chrysostom, Pibble detected a faint, quavering buzz, and saw that Father Polydore too was chanting, and by some miracle of memory chanting the same words.

The service in the Catholicon – the big cave-church – was endless but athletic. First of all Father Chrysostom stood before the altar, praying in a rapid mutter; between prayers he would hiss and point, and Pibble would guide his aged burden across to some new station. His head sang. The stink of his robes and of the old man he supported, the reek of the censer, the dank and heavy air, all combined to bring the vomit to his gullet. He swallowed it back, then toted Father Polydore round the whole church in the tracks of Father Chrysostom, praying every few steps to some strange dark saint in a niche; after the first few Pibble knew the words well enough to join in the responses, but despite the comfort of having something to do he was almost fainting before Father Chrysostom flung open the doors and led the miniscule procession out into the hot fresh air.

The religious observances for the day were not yet over, by no means. The monastery turned out to be richly endowed with its peculiar saints, far more than could have been accommodated in the main basilica without overcrowding. No doubt the whole company of them could have danced together on the point of a needle, in the spirit, but their fleshy remains required more room. Besides a number of small chapels the big honeycomb was dotted with individual shrines, usually consisting of no more than a name on the wall with a dark brown icon hanging beside it. But in several places there was more ornamentation, and this was always either a picture or a relief carving of a casket. After a while Pibble decided that at all these places the relics of minor saints had actually been walled into the masonry – here a femur, there a funny-bone – in the belief that their miraculous intervention would, as it were, key the building into the living rock behind, pin it there and prevent it from slithering down the cliff.

They came at last to a place where the miracle had proved insufficient and the winding passage ended in sunlight; two lashed planks spanned the gap to the dark arch where it began again; the hand-rail was of rope and looked grey with rot, but Father Chrysostom muttered a quick, private prayer, crossed himself and marched across the bouncing planks. Pibble hesitated. His head was spinning, and the mess of rocks and tiles and rotten beams below seemed to recede and then climb nearer to him, and then recede again. Father Polydore looked up at him, smiled with sudden sweetness, disengaged himself and darted on to the planks. But half-way across he seemed to lose confidence; he let go of the hand-rail and stood swaying in the slight up-draught; Pibble gave a grunt, dashed forward and caught him by the waist just as he was losing his balance to fall between the walkway and the cliff, hauling him back with his free hand grasping the iron stanchion that supported the rope in the middle. For a moment they stood teetering, with the boards creaking beneath their double weight. Poised thus, Pibble too lost confidence.

Father Chrysostom heard the various noises and turned in the mouth of the dark arch. He looked at them for a moment, then raised his right hand and boomed a polysyllabic blessing. Father Polydore responded in a cracked wheeze and launched himself over the second half of the gulf; Pibble had no recourse but to follow, wondering how many of his sins had now been absolved. He walked carefully across the grey planks, conscious of nothing but the sunlight and the sharp sweet smoke from the censer.

Over here there was only one saintly limb to pray to, walled into a cleft in the rock; but right at the limit of the building they came to a long, irregular room in which lay, neatly on low stone slabs, skeleton after skeleton. Here they used a different form of prayer, which involved only occasional interjections from Father Polydore and no movements from Pibble. He looked out of a slit window at blue sea flecked with gold, and wondered how long the bones had lain there. It was irritating not to know how old anything was – he had always been one of those sightseers who are as much impressed by time as by aesthetic values, so that a shapeless hutch, or the brickwork of a sewer, could give him the authentic thrill provided modern scholarship believed them to be a couple of thousand years old; without that guarantee they were just a hutch and some bricks. It seemed important to know how often this self-same liturgy had been droned in this chamber. Were these the skeletons of hermits who had endured the incredible severities of holy living in the Dark Ages? Or were they simply the results of some medical misjudgment less than a century ago? There was no way of asking.

The return journey along a higher level was less sanctified and so more rapid; and the planks over the gap had a wooden handrail, which made all the difference. They emerged on the flight of steps between the main entrance and the refectory, and here the two monks embarked on what Pibble took at first for a new form of ritual, but soon discovered was a quarrel. Father C spoke mildly but firmly; Father P muttered his disagreement; Father C spoke more loudly; Father P stuck out his lower lip, hunched himself, and said the same words as before; Father C glanced at Pibble and spoke abruptly; Father P simply repeated himself – it was extraordinarily like a liturgy, a litany, with the varying prayers and the unaltering responses. Suddenly Father Chrysostom gave a huge sigh of despair and walked down the stairs without another word. Father Polydore smiled at Pibble.

'Viazomaste,' he said, and set off in the opposite direction. Pibble followed, swinging the censer as little as possible. The dash across the perilous planks had cleared away much of his hangover, but it threatened to return in the claustrophobic corridors. He thought that swinging the censer increased the draught, and hence the burning and the reek. Besides he was, if anything, a very low-church protestant.

This passage was a ramp, sloping irregularly down. They passed the gap in the wall and roof where the builders had been working, and Pibble looked up at the branches of a tree and wondered whether he would ever escape, whether he was now a Greek Orthodox monk for the rest of his meagre days. The ramp sloped down and down until they were well below the level of the cliff-top; from the texture of the floor below his feet Pibble decided that they were walking down what must once have been a sloping ledge on the face of the cliff, though in places it had narrowed to a six-inch toe-hold and had later been artificially widened to form this sloping tunnel. Rock and flagstone and tile were all so worn that they had the texture of boulders in a stream, a ceaseless whispering stream of holy insteps, polishing the rock.

Beyond the broken roof all was darkness; though there were still cells on the right of the passage, they had either been built without windows or had had their windows blocked up, perhaps to encourage an especially severe grade of austerity, depriving their inmates of that last comfort, the Mediterranean sun. This section felt chillier and somehow older than any Pibble had hitherto seen. He peered into musty cells by the light of the lantern which Father Polydore had taken from a shelf and lit with a faltering Greek match.

All of a sudden a raw modern element intruded among the ancient masonry. An arch of bright red brick sustained the left-hand wall where it should not have needed sustaining because it was solid cliff. Father Polydore stopped before the arch, burbled a quick prayer, placed his lantern on a shelf just inside the opening and lurched into the shadows. Pibble followed him.

They walked into a cave. But the cave was a chapel, small as an ordinary living-room, but ornamented with innumerable marbles so that no inch of the real rock showed. Over their heads a mosaic glinted in the yellow light, the fearsome face of Christ in Judgment frowning out of a deep blue dome, a dome which sustained no roof but had been shaped out of the rock. Another mosaic, quainter and duller, covered the apse behind the altar. When Father Polydore settled his lantern up there and began to quaver and lurch his way through the ritual, Pibble was able to look at this picture with as much attention as his sickness and the reek of the incense – much worse in here, and shot through with a strange resinous odour – allowed.

It was extraordinary enough to hold his mind, despite those disadvantages. The Christ was here again, full-length, floating out from a far less intense blue; on His right was the Virgin; on His left a bizarre figure, clearly a man, but with a beak where his nose should have been and all his flesh, except the face covered in fur. No, feathers. Dizzy with the endless ritual and his persistent hangover, Pibble still found it interesting that the Victorian (presumably) monks who had commissioned the decoration of this chapel had chosen a much more primitive style than that of the Catholicon. Primitive was the wrong word, though; the attempt was at a very early, but highly sophisticated style, that of the huge-eyed saints and courtiers in the churches and baptisteries of Ravenna. There was even that startling line of orange tessera to outline the nose. Alas, the result was as insipid as if they hadn't tried at all – just as with English stained-glass windows, where the designer may have had the right ideas, but if the work was done at the wrong period, the glass was inadequate to bring them off. Even so, it seemed surprising that Nancy had thought there was nothing this side of the monastery worth seeing.

Father Polydore swung round, hissed at him, and made a patting motion with his hand. Obediently Pibble knelt, but the movement brought the worst wave of revulsion so far; he shut his eyes and endured the foul air, chill-faced but sweating. Another hiss, and he had to open his eyes to scramble to his feet; as he did so he noticed, piled against the single step of the altar, a little mound of powder as white as salt, looking as though it had fallen there while he knelt.

'Little mounds of white powder,' Butler had said, but satirically. As he followed Father Polydore out of the chapel he realized that it must be something to do with repair-work in the chapel. The arch of brick had looked fairly new, and there was no reason why some repairs to the plaster, unrevealed by the dingy lantern, shouldn't be newer still. And anyway, thank heavens, that was the last of the morning's devotions. Father Polydore led him back to the Refectory.

Father Chrysostom had the ouzo bottle out, and made them great welcome as though they were back from some fraught expedition. As soon as Pibble was clear of the appalling horse-blanket he shook him warmly by the hand and thrust a glass of ouzo at him. There was no remedy but to drink it; as it happened, there was no remedy like it. His mouth and throat scorched, and were clean; his head rang like a gong, and cleared; the rebellion in his gorge was quelled, once and for all. Even the reeking censer began to smell quite pleasant, with none of the chemical-resin odours that had filled the chapel.

'*Poo ine Nancy?*' he said.

Father Chrysostom fetched a scrap of paper and a ballpoint from the cupboard and drew a map, so simple and clear that Pibble at once understood he had been searching the wrong slope of the hill, naïvely assuming that all the Vangelis property would be in one area. He made polite and smiling farewells, but was frowning by the time he climbed the stairs.

The workmen had left their ladders in place, so it was easy to climb back into the monastery, balancing on the wall to heave the lighter ladder over into the passage. Five minutes later he was climbing out again, with a pinch of tasteless and odourless white powder screwed into a fifty-drach note in his pocket, and the resinous smell, uncomplicated by incense, strong in his nostrils. The whole idea was inconceivable – ludicrous. You couldn't imagine a less convenient place for a morphine factory than the Chapel of St. Sporophore. But Father Chrysostom had been anxious to prevent his visit. Tony believed there were drugs of some kind on Hyos, and could only have learnt of them at the South Bay villas. Pibble hadn't noticed her talking to Mlle Guillerand, but . . .

If Father Chrysostom, who liked money, was in on the racket, they'd be able to use the bay below the monastery for shipping in the opium, and not even the local fishermen need know about it. Hell, no amount of small corroborative points could make the main notion any less ludicrous.

The hills were still deserted. Pibble wondered why none of the islanders had attended the service at the monastery, though Father Chrysostom had clearly been expecting a congregation, and in the end had made do with a single heretic. Now the heretic was picking a careful way along the slope above Vangelis's vineyard. He had seen the roof of a hut from a couple of hundred yards away, and so was able to choose a path which kept him just out of sight without having to resort to stooping or crawling. He would prefer not to be seen, but if he was seen he wanted to look as though he didn't mind. In the end he had to cross the ridge and recross further along, so that he could make his final approach between the dark, ordered trunks of yet another olive grove.

The girls were sitting in the sun. He would not have recognized Tony if he hadn't known who she was, though her russet wig was hanging dishevelled by the door. Her scalp was now covered with her own close-shorn dark curls – but it wasn't just that. She sat with her back against the doorpost, cross-legged, her head balanced on the straight column of her neck. Her face as well as her pose had lost its softness, and the noon sun showed up the hollows beneath the cheekbones and the strong muscles round the mouth. He couldn't see Nancy's face because it was hidden in Tony's lap, but her small shoulders shuddered all the time as Tony's dark hand moved across them in slow, tender strokes. Tony stared straight ahead. She looked like a redskin gazing out over lost territories. Beyond the hut a tethered donkey searched for grass.

Suddenly Nancy jerked herself into a sitting position. Her face was grey, her eyes swollen, and her mouth worked all the time.

'I can't!' she shrieked. 'I can't! I can't! Let me go!'

Her head fell forward against Tony's breast and was cradled there. The hill side was so quiet that Pibble could hear the husky comfort of the answer.

'Yes you can, honey. Take it easy. You're not that bad. I've seen it often, often. I brought Ted Follinger through, and he was worse than you. He was bad. He was on H. You'll be better tomorrow, honey. You'll be O.K.'

The cropped head bent, talking now too softly for the words to carry to the olive trees. Slowly the shuddering of Nancy's body quietened until it looked as though she were sleeping, but then her grimy hand and thin arm slid in under Tony's unbuttoned blouse and she pulled herself into a position where they could kiss. After a few seconds Tony raised her head, laughed softly and with beautiful ease and tenderness shifted both bodies into greater comfort.

Pibble moved quietly off, neither stirred nor ashamed of his prying, any more than he would have been if he had been watching the courtship of otters. He had come up wondering how he could protect them from Thanatos, but now he realized that Butler was the greater danger.

He decided to lie to Butler, but show him the powder. At once, if he could find him.

Chapter Nine

'Not H,' said Butler after a sniff and a taste. The slightly prissy way he used the slang was very much part of his personality.

'Thank God,' said Pibble.

For the second time that afternoon Butler looked at him oddly. The first had been while he was still standing by Butler's table in the fig-smelling dining-room of the Aeschylus. Butler had looked up from his work of hacking off the corner of an iron-hard slab of goat cheese and said 'Hello, Jimmy.' 'James,' Pibble had answered and dropped the screwed-up note on the table. Butler had glanced round the empty room and given Pibble a very odd look. And now, as they were sitting over cups of coffee that consisted of a quarter of an inch of tepid ooze on top of an inch of sludge, he did it again before calling for a glass of water.

They sat in silence till it came, then Butler tipped half the powder into the glass and stirred it with his coffee-spoon, watching the liquid cloud and clear again as he stopped stirring and the tiny whirlpool stilled. The powder settled into a white gub at the bottom. Butler dipped his fingers in the liquid and tasted one drop.

'Not horse, not morphine. Almost tasteless – slight flavour of chalk. No sign of a high. I wouldn't have said any of it had dissolved, either. Heroin's highly soluble Not having my lab equipment handy, I'd say it was plaster of paris.'

'So would I,' said Pibble.

'What did "Thank God" mean, then?'

'Just the place I found it. Up in the monastery – and there was a resiny smell I couldn't place, though I don't think it was opium. And I found it in a chapel where one of the monks made a definite attempt to stop me going. It didn't make sense in other ways – I mean the well is some way off and there's no electricity, or any other kit I saw, but . . .'

'Then why this James bit? I was due to meet you at the bar in five hours. Couldn't it have waited?'

'Yes, of course it could. It worried me, though, and I wanted . . .'

Butler was still looking at him oddly.

'I'm sorry,' said Pibble with as much plaintiveness as he dared risk. 'I had a very bad night last night.'

'Gippy tummy?' said Butler with sudden sympathy. 'I'll give you a spot of advice about that. Everyone's dead scared of sea-food, but sea-food can't do you one spot of harm in a place like this. Dammit, the Hyotes *live* on sea-food. They know enough not to gather the sea urchins near the harbour. No, *bean*s is what you have to watch out for. Not decent green beans, but these whitish jobs they give you with everything. They're hell on the intestines, something to do with fermentation processes – you think there's something crooked about the monastery, then?'

'Crooked?'

'Come off it, Jimmy. You've heard the word before – in the course of your career.'

'Sorry. No, not crooked in that sense. It's an extraordinary place, though. It's vast, and it hangs on the cliff like a honey-comb, but there only these two old ouzo priests living there.'

'Come again.'

'Like Graham Greene's whisky priests. I shouldn't think Father Polydore's got more than a couple of months to live, the rate he's soaking the stuff up. They've been very poor, so they haven't had any new recruits, but now some decision in Athens has given them back a lot of land they used to own, and they've nothing to do with the income except repair the place and drink themselves stupid. The set-up's cranky, but not crooked, twisted but not bent . . .'

'Go and write a thesaurus. They've got a harbour?'

'Certainly. Quite a good one in the prevailing winds. But the monks would have to know if it was being used, and I'd have thought the organization you're looking for wouldn't regard two drunk old monks as very reliable conspirators. It's got to be some-thing more professional.'

'Yeah. It's just something Chris said to me . . .'

'Chris?'

'You saw him yesterday, but you mightn't have noticed him. An ugly little runt who bowls a bloody fierce leg break. He said his uncle and aunt weren't going to the special service up at the monastery, which they usually do because they've got land up there. Something unlucky was going on, he said. Just a bit of conversation I couldn't follow up without seeming too interested.'

'Is the uncle called Vangelis?'

'That's him.'

'He's having a row with the monks about the ownership of part of an olive grove.'

'You get around all right, Jimmy. Mind if I call you that? When I checked with London they were a bit funny about you. Chap I talked to, every sentence started off with a pat on the back for you and finished with a but. Anyway, he said you definitely had a sort of a knack.'

'But . . .' said Pibble.

'Yeah. D'you miss all that?'

'I don't miss the work, though it was always interesting or worth doing, and sometimes both. But when I left, after I'd pulled myself together from the shock of being fired, I realized how long I'd been breathing stale air. On the other hand I do miss the people – even the ones I didn't get on with. I think it's natural for a man to belong to an organization, and unnatural to be a lone wolf. It isn't just a loyalty thing – it's something deeper than that.'

'You've been reading *The Naked Ape*. Bloody clever book, eh?'

'As a wagonload of monkeys,' said Pibble. 'But it isn't only belonging I miss – it's being kept, well, *sharp*.'

'In training?'

'Sort of. I'll give you an instance. I was at a party out at the South Bay villas yesterday – by the way I met somebody who might just possibly be a junkie there – and I was talking to a Canadian . . .'

'From Montreal?'

'Didn't ask. Sorry. Where was I? Oh yes, he was talking about the difference between England and America, and he said that England was quite incapable of producing a Ted Follinger. Now, who the hell is Ted Follinger? I know I'd have known a couple of years ago – it rings that kind of bell.'

'Was, not is,' said Butler. 'The cops in New Jersey got him in a shoot-up with the Black Panthers. Last summer. He was wanted before that on a bombing rap. He started with a stretch for rape when he was fifteen . . . Arkansas, I daresay he looked at the lady. They'd have fried him if he'd been five months older. That was ten, eleven years back. No, more like fifteen. He did his rap, and was luckier than a lot of black men who got slung into southern pens those days because he was part of an intake for a showpiece rehabilitation course, and came out with a couple of years' training as a watch-repairer. He went north, fell in with Anna Laszlo and that crowd, made the time-pieces for their bombs for a while. Funny this Canadian of yours should mention him.'

'Oh,' said Pibble, who had been trying to strain a few more drops of coffee out of the sludge to hide his irritation with himself for bringing the name up. After all, there was still a possibility that Butler was here to look for Tony. But he turned out to be interested in a different coincidence.

'Yup,' he said thoughtfully. 'Your Canadian might be from Montreal, where our whisper about the Mafia began. And Follinger tangled with the Mafia: he was all set to become a hero of the Left when they dropped him, bang, and then he was all set to become a bogey of the Right when the cops got him. Thing was, or that's what I heard, that he'd got bored with politics and set out to muscle in on the Mafia's drug interests – and they tipped the cops off where to find him, and maybe sent a man of their own along. He was articulate, so everyone took him for a rebel when all he was was a crook. An articulate bum. What about this junkie of yours?'

Pibble described Mlle Guillerand's appearance and behaviour, telling himself meanwhile that he was at least being half-honest, trying to lead Butler towards his own knowledge of the existence of some kind of hard drugs on the island, without showing him the actual trail he'd followed.

'Dumpy, you said?' said Butler when he'd finished. 'Arms bare?'

'I didn't see any needle pricks.'

'No. But if they've been on it long, you get this wasting. Arms like matchsticks.'

'No. The other way, if anything. Pudgy but unhealthy.'

'Probably just some kind of nut,' said Butler. 'Have you looked over Thanatos's house yet?'

'I did what I could yesterday. I told him what I wanted, and I was given the keys. I measured up the rooms and so on. Unless he's sunk a room into the rock, I don't think there's anything there.'

'I can check on that. He had that place built by imported labour, I'm told, but some of the kids' dads did casual labour on it. How about the yacht?'

'No room for a workshop, but plenty of places to hide parcels of processed stuff if he wanted to. I did find one of the crewmen smoking pot.'

'Throw the little ones back.'

'If I may. There's only one other thing, much vaguer. Suppose there were somebody on the island who was going to run a heroin depot for the Mafia, elsewhere I mean – much nearer America – and he was simply here as part of the process of setting it up. Would that be enough to account for the rumour that reached you?'

Butler looked at him for a long time.

'You've got your eye on somebody?' he said.

'Sort of. He has the contacts, though he claims they are his enemies. He is going to be put in a position where he could do the job.'

'But nothing to do with Hyos, except that he's here at the moment?'

'Yes, and ten days ago no one knew he would be here.'

'I should write him out of your script. He sounds like a very minor character, one of those bloody little pansies who come on in Shakespeare to tell you that the Duke is at hand.'

Pibble blinked. This image of the courtiers surrounding the great man was oddly near his own fancies. No doubt Butler, if he could still do a trick like that, must have been very good at his job once. And he was right about another thing – the very nearness of the great man tended either to drain the character from his attendants, or to force them into eccentric attitudes. Dave Warren was one type, Buck the other. It was hard to tell which way Doctor Trotter would go yet, but it would be a relief to eliminate him from the possibilities – a variable that ceased to be a variable and became zero.

'I expect you're right,' he said.

'O.K. That's all. I've got my in at the electricity company, by the way. One of the kids' uncles runs the place – chief accountant, linesman, repairman, sales executive – and he used to open for the Hyos first eleven. Once took a century off the Mediterranean Fleet. Used to take his fortnight's holiday in England, following Len Hutton round places like Leeds and Bradford. Bet you his missus was sick.'

Pibble laughed as he stood up to go.

'You make good use of your hobby,' he said.

'Keeps me out of trouble,' agreed Butler.

The small, pernickety hunger which sometimes takes over from a hangover was bothering Pibble now. Beer was an essential, even Greek beer, and the little strips of fried squid and octopus that he'd nibbled at the Helicon yesterday would be just right. He walked in that direction.

Today the long, curving quayside was converted into a promenade, thronged with Hyotes, all in their best clothes, walking in families and picking their way politely between the charter-artists. Small groups of younger Greeks stood behind each easel, commenting clear-voiced over the flustered shoulders of the painters, certain that no tourist – at least no tourist who behaved in this fashion – understood Greek. Pibble was delighted to see another nation than the English being insular. The largest and loudest such groups operated towards the further end of the quay, and at first Pibble couldn't see what the attraction was. The painter was a youngish man wearing an old straw hat, and his face was red with more than the heat of the afternoon; but his painting was much like any of the others' – perhaps a little better than most because he was laying the paint on with a certain boldness and spontaneity. Then a voice said something from the middle of the crowd, and a sort of silent snigger rippled all round the artist; the speaker had used Greek, but not with a Greek accent; Pibble knew before he had moved enough to see him that it would be Mark Hott. He commented again, and this time the laugh was audible.

Pibble pushed his way through to him.

'Hello,' he said. 'I owe you a drink.'

'Great,' said Mr. Hott. 'Come along.'

The moment he turned away from his victim the rest of the crowd started to break up. He didn't look back.

'O.K.,' he said, 'you be kind to the animals – you can afford it. But to me they're vermin. Come along – we'll be lucky if we find a table.'

But there were several spare tables under the orange awning, and enough chairs for Mr. Hott to collar one and put his feet on it. Pibble sipped his beer and nibbled the little fishy squares, while Hott growled his tirade against the amateur artist and the problems of educating the public into the new languages that art had found in the last fifty years if the public's eyes were constantly befuddled with degenerate and crass apings of the great impressionists.

'Did Buck Budweiser come out and see you?' said Pibble, not looking at Hott but considering the curious change from yesterday's view, now that the sub-fusc band of the strolling crowd was spread in a diminishing curve across the broader band of the houses.

'Sure – you should've told me he was a cripple. I wasn't ready for that.'

Pibble raised his eyebrows, thinking of the compendium of ailments that enriched the South Bay villas.

'He can look after himself,' he said.

'Sure, sure. He's a great guy once you know him.'

'Was he any use to you?'

'So-so. I didn't sell him anything – it's all earmarked for my winter show, so it's not for sale just now. But he talked the right talk – he'll be a useful contact.'

'I don't think he does any art dealing these days,' said Pibble. 'He's what he calls a travel consultant.'

'Balls. Once you've begun, it's a habit you never kick. Put a guy like that on a desert island and he'll start auctioning oystershells to the turtles at twenty per cent commission. Hi, Nan, I kept a chair for you.'

Little Nancy, wearing sun-bleached jeans and a crudely mended blouse, slumped into the chair and grunted sulkily; without orders the proprietor came out with a glass of tea for her. Hott rolled a couple of his beautifully turned cigarettes and tossed one to Nancy, who sniffed at it ungraciously, stuck it in her mouth and lit up without thanks. Hott went back to his grousing about the charterartists, repeating for her bored benefit the points he'd made for Pibble. As he spoke he emptied the contents of his pocket on to the iron table until he found a pencil and a piece of paper to draw on. Still grumbling, hardly looking at the quay, he started to draw rapidly. Pibble watched him for a bit, not really listening, thinking how thin Nancy's arms were – even for her small body – and that he should have noticed this earlier. He was quite unprepared when Hott shoved his drawing across the table and began to gather his debris back into his pockets.

It was two drawings, one marked Ham and the other Pro. Both were very simplified versions of what Pibble had already seen, the different bands of texture curving and diminishing round the harbour. It was hard to see quite where the two versions differed, except that the central band which was the moving promenaders and the doors of houses and a few parked cars and the despised charterartists themselves seemed to be slightly exaggerated in the Ham version and slightly diminished in the Pro one; but the total difference was immense. Above, a dull and almost uninterpretable series of lines; below, depth and sparkle and the play of light.

'Can I keep this?' said Pibble.

'I haven't signed it,' said Hott with his derisive laugh as he rose to his feet. Nan put out her hand and pushed towards him the unopened packet of cigarettes which he'd left on the table.

'Keep it,' he said. 'It's a present. So long. Be good, kid.'

His hand patted her possessively on the hair as her fingers closed over the packet. She gave a funny little cry, jumped to her feet ran to the edge of the quay and hurled the gift out into the water.

'Girls can't pitch for nuts,' called Hott. 'So long, Jimmy.'

He lumbered away as Nancy came draggingly back to the table and took a few sips of tea. The men at the other tables watched her with dull eyes. Pibble sat, very depressed, looking at the two drawings; when he turned the sheet of paper over he found that it was a receipt for a life-insurance premium from the Ottawa office of Standard Mutual. Not Montreal then. But even so, back to square two. Nancy was an addict, Hott had been expecting her and had brought along a fresh supply disguised as a packet of cigarettes. He went night-fishing, and had a landing-stage by his villa. Joss-sticks burnt in his studio, which would disguise the reek of raw opium. He had all the necessary facilities – and all that meant that Butler's story was true, which in turn meant that there had been no shot at Thanatos. So the question was now not how to preserve his hideous host, but what to tell Butler. There was no link to Hott without mentioning Nancy; if Butler found Nancy he would find Tony; and judging by his readiness with the life and times of Ted Follinger he would know who she was. And why shouldn't he be allowed to? Why shouldn't the whole C.I.A. jump on her with hobnailed boots? Tony d'Agniello might be a harmless odalisque, but didn't Anna Laszlo deserve to suffer? There are no answers to that sort of question. You could say that, pragmatically, as long as she stayed Tony she was harmless, whereas Anna was a focus, either free or on trial, a point of danger. You could add that if she were captured Thanatos would guess who had betrayed him, who had been the lizard lurking in the cup of friendship; and then Pibble would be smashed. You could further mumble that old Pibble was fond of the girl. And then you could look in your diary and work out that by the time these trivia of the conscience had been appeased another cargo of soul-poison would be on its way to Montreal. Hott was shipping an exhibition over next week – it would be something to do with that – perhaps one could sell Butler a hunch about the exhibition, enough to get those fat white slabs of abstract paint sampled and probed . . . Yes, there had been the art thefts, two paintings stolen from successive shows. Ingenious.

'D'you mind if I tell you the story of a film I once saw?' he said.

Nancy groaned.

'If you must. You'll have to buy me a drink, though.'

She called for ouzo in Greek, then turned with lack-lustre eyes to Pibble.

'It won't take long,' he said. 'I can't remember the details, but there was a girl in it who was sheltering someone whom the police were looking for in a general way, and the police wanted to talk to her about something quite different, and one of the policemen – did you know I used to be a policeman? – wanted to warn her but he had to do it in a café where anyone might be listening – you know, warn her that there might be cops coming up the hill to her cottage and just stumbling on this other person who was hiding there. I'm sorry. I've not made it sound very interesting. I was just reminded of it by this bar. It was a French film.'

'I hate French films,' whispered Nancy. 'How did it end?'

'I didn't stay to see.'

She smiled, genuine through the strain.

'It makes a change,' she said.

'What does?'

'Oh, when I first came here I tried to find out something about the Resistance in these islands – my father was in the Resistance – and people used to come to me with the most extraordinary and thrilling stories they'd just remembered. It was only when winter came and I started going to the cinema most weeks that I found where the stories began. I mean, one week there'd be a film about a redskin who rather than be captured dived into the sea and clung to a rock till he drowned, and next week people would start showing me the actual rock where some Hyote had done that very thing. That's what I mean. Your story's the other way round.'

'I see. Let me know if there's anything I can do.'

'You can lend me fifty drachs – I want to buy a bottle of ouzo. Thanks. Did this ... person who was hiding know about the girl and the policeman?'

'I don't think so. They were all – I don't mean the policeman – involved in a sort of eternal triangle situation with someone else. It was that sort of film.'

Her face went very blank as she stood up and leaned with both hands on the rim of the table to look at him. This stance exposed the inner side of her wasted forearms, and they still seemed unscarred – an addict's needle tends to leave a landscape of festering pocks, quite different from the invisible and hygienic results of a hospital hypodermic. Nancy was still sniffing then; perhaps her arms had always been thin; with Tony's help she should pull through. He looked at her face and thought for a moment she was going to spit at him, but then she gave another of her wailing cries and rushed into the taverna like Mrs. Siddons studying at Bedlam to be a madwoman. When she came out, nursing her bottle, she neither looked at him nor gave him his change.

He sat for a long while, slowly drinking beers and nibbling the little morsels of fish. At times he watched the strollers or the boats – a new red power-boat was being incompetently cajoled towards its anchorage by a couple of lubberly but handsome young women who seemed to enjoy being mocked by the other boatmen. At times he brooded dully. His thoughts were not coherent, in fact little more than a Hott-like grumble against the situation in which he found himself. He felt as though he were being pushed around – not deliberately shoved across the board like a counter in backgammon, skipping uncomprehending from peak to peak, sometimes solitary, sometimes in a jostling crowd. No, it was nothing as meaningful as that, more like the motion of a twig in the backwash of a stream below a bridge, round and round and round in the grip of invisible currents. First the threat to Thanatos had been unreal, and then it had been real, and now it was unreal again. First Butler's presence had been a peripheral nuisance, then central, and now peripheral again.

He watched a dark-skinned, plainish girl walking between her wizened parents flash a glance of extraordinary brilliance at a young man strolling in the other direction. The young man spoke a greeting but the parents bowed unsmiling and dragged her on.

That made him think of Tony. Like most men he found the notion of lesbianism sexually stimulating, but the fact of it left him cold. Or was it that Tony was now Anna, and he didn't want Anna – he wanted the luxurious child who ate icecreams? Thanatos, presumably, had room in his soul for both. They made a curious triangle, the gross monarch, his revolutionary mistress and the waif who had drifted between them. He wondered whether Nancy had done this before, whether some of her strain came from a sense of shock. Oh, hell! The problem was going to be how to tell Butler about Hott and get him off the island, without telling him about Nancy and hence Tony.

In an effort to organize his thoughts he found a biro and wrote the possibilities down on a blank space on Hott's receipt. M for murder. H for H. $-H, -M; -H, +M; +H, -M; +H, +M$. He crossed the first two out. H was pretty certainly now plus. He stared at the fourth, then crossed that out. If the Mafia were organizing an H on Hyos, they wouldn't jeopardize it by flooding the island with police investigating an M. That left the third. It also left him no forrarder.

His mind was shying from the problem for the fifth time when a hand touched his arm. He turned to see a simian brown face at shoulder-level, a boy who began to talk to him in rapid demotic. Pibble caught one word the second time round – *astifilakos*, policeman.

'*Ime astilakfilakos*,' he said.

The child frowned and made that negative click and jerk of the head, then tugged at Pibble's sleeve.

'*Ela. Ela*,' he said impatiently.

Pibble paid for his beers and went with the boy, wondering what dim tourist-trap he was being conducted to. But the boy didn't relapse into the confident lounge of the tout who has hooked his sucker; he dodged and scuttered between the strollers so that Pibble had to follow him faster than he wished through the dust and stuffiness of a windless afternoon. They turned up the Odos Basilissa Bictoria, passed the Aeschylus and came to the main square. The boy darted up the steps of what must be the town hall, a stodgily pompous building with windows opaque with old dirt; he led Pibble down a passage, knocked at a door, heard the answering shout, opened the door and motioned Pibble to go in.

Pibble knew where he was before the door had shut behind him with the boy outside. It wasn't merely the wooden counter barring a small area by the door from the rest of the room, nor the dull look of the man behind the desk, nor the uniform cap that hung from the other door. All police stations *feel* alike.

The man said *'Oriste?'* in a bored voice.

'Kserete Anghlika?' said Pibble.

The man became a semitone less bored and called to the next room, a sentence containing the word *Anghliko*. A tenor voice answered and then a slight man, wearing the jacket of his uniform despite the heat, came through the far door.

'Pliss come this way, mister,' he said.

Pibble lifted the flap of the counter and walked through into a stifling small office. The man in uniform was already sitting behind his desk. He spat into his handkerchief and studied the result for a moment before looking up.

'Ullo,' he said. 'Good afternoon.' He studied a phrasebook and added 'What can we do for you?'

'I don't know. A boy, a Greek boy, brought me here and told me to come in. Perhaps it was a joke.'

'Spik slowly, pliss.'

'Pibble did so. The man looked at him, very official.

'Understood. You are friends with Mr. Butler, yes?'

'I know Mr. Butler. I do not know him well. We have talked three times, that is all.'

'Your name, pliss.'

Pibble still carried, from sentimental habit, a few of the unnecessary cards which Mary had given him on his last promotion. The officer looked at it very carefully, then referred to a small dictionary.

'Endaksi. You are colleague to me, yes?'

'I've retired. I'm on holiday.'

'Yes? Where do you stay?'

'At Porphyrocolpos.'

'You are friends with Thanatos?'

This time he had left the final 'yes' off his question, perhaps because of the sheer improbability of the idea. Or perhaps because his English was growing more confident with practice. Anyway, Pibble supplied it.

The officer sat still, turned the card over, turned it back again and looked at Pibble. Then he spun round in his chair and opened a cupboard from which he brought out a bottle of brandy, a soda-siphon and two glasses. He took a clean tissue from a drawer and polished both glasses. Pibble could see that he was thinking all the time.

'Pliss sit,' he said. 'You will have one drink, yes? I am in a . . . difficultness. I will shut the door, pliss.'

Pibble sat on a creaking upright chair, took the unwanted glass when it was handed to him, and waited.

'You speak Greek, no?' said the officer.

'I'm afraid not.'

'Good. My name is Captain Thagoulos. I am chief policeman in Hyos. How do you do? Cheers.'

'Cheers.'

'I go to the ecclesia, the church, this morning. After, I come here. I take one telephone. The man is not Greek, but he talks good Greek. He says Mr. Butler comes to Hyos to play with our little boys. Understood?'

'Yes. Do you know where the call came from. Can you trace a call?'

'Easy . . . easily. It is from Porphyrocolpos.'

Pibble almost did the nose-trick with the dung-smelling local brandy. After that there was no point in trying to hide his surprise.

'Let's talk about that later,' he said. 'What did you do?'

'I send one man to search for this Mr. Butler. He finds him talking with boys. He sees that they are friends, too much friends. Thus he brings Mr. Butler to talk with me. Mr. Butler is not . . . satisfying.'

'Satisfactory.'

'Not satisfactory, no. His story is . . . O.K., but I think it is not satisfactory. He says he is one London businessman; he talks good Greeks; he says he is on short holidays, thus he comes in the helicopter; he plays cricket with the little boys.'

'He likes cricket.'

'So why is he coming to Hyos? He can play cricket in London.'

'Not in October. Too cold and wet.'

'Understood. But I am policeman many years. It is not satisfactory. His room at Hotel Aeschylus is O.K. – no evil books, no evil pictures – but is not satisfactory. Is not the room of the man who comes for holidays. Yes?'

'I know what you mean,' said Pibble. Captain Thagoulos was clearly a good, experienced policeman. Now he opened a drawer and threw a fat yellow volume on the desk. He leafed through the dictionary.

Pibble smiled as he picked up the 1969 *Wisden* and flipped through it.

'I think it's all right,' he said. 'I mean, it is not surprising that Butler brought it.'

'O.K. What does Thanatos want me to do?'

'Thanatos?'

'One man telephones me from Porphyrocolpos. I capture Butler. Now you come.'

'I don't know anything about the telephone call,' Pibble said. 'I did tell the others that I'd seen Butler playing cricket with the boys, because it amused me. I met Butler in the Aeschylus two days ago, and we met again at the English cemetery yesterday. I had quite a long talk with him then. And I had coffee with him after lunch today. I was sitting at the Helicon bar when a boy came and brought me here – that's all I know.'

'Why do you talk with him so much? You have friends at Porphyrocolpos, no?'

'Yes, of course. But I am not used ... accustomed ... to such friends. I liked Butler.'

'You do not like little boys, no?'

'No. Not that way. What would you like me to do?'

'I like *you*. It is Thanatos who likes *me*!'

Captain Thagoulos suddenly frowned and riffled through his dictionary to peer despairingly at a page in the L's.

' "Like" means a lot of different things,' said Pibble. 'Anyway, the hell with Thanatos. You're sure it wasn't a Greek who spoke to you.'

'He speaks good ... well. But if he is Greek, he ... pretends he is not. Why?'

'A Greek might not have understood what I said. And he might object to an Englishman playing with Hyote boys for reasons of morality.'

'Yes?'

'I don't know. I think you've made a mistake. Can't you just let Butler go and tell him that?'

'No. No. I cannot. We are a very pure country. I have a very pure island. I do not wish Athinai to say I permit that rich Englishmen play with my little boys.'

'I'm sure that part's a mistake. He just has this passion for cricket.'

Thagoulos simply looked at Pibble, not even mockingly.

'Are you going to prosecute him? Have you got any evidence?'

'The evidence of boys?' A movement of the Captain's shoulders implied that you might just as well pick straws to decide guilt or innocence. 'No, Mr. Rivvley. I wish that Butler leaves my island. But I wish that he leaves easy . . . easily. No policeman to push him on the boat, yes?'

'O.K. I'll talk to him. Is he at the hotel?'

'Come this way, pliss.'

Cells too are much the same anywhere, allowing for such trivial variations as the difference between glare and gloom in the corridor, and the residual odour of wine-vomit as opposed to beer-vomit. They are all places where time goes by, unmeaning.

Butler was sitting, perfectly patient and calm, on the single chair.

'I leave you,' said Captain Thagoulos. 'The door to stay open.'

'Thank you,' said Pibble to the spruce back.

'Hello, old man,' said Butler. 'What brought you along?'

'A boy fetched me. He had a face like a monkey.'

'Chris. What's the line out there?'

Pibble looked meaningly at the door.

'We're not wired for sound,' said Butler. 'They claim that they've got a buggery charge against me.'

'The Captain told me. They haven't got any evidence and I don't think they're aiming to fake it. Did you ask to see the British Consul?'

'Nearest one's at Corfu. No point in bringing him in if the thing would clear itself up without. Does me no good at the office.'

'Would you be prepared to cut your holiday short and go home now?'

'I'd prefer to stay on a couple more days.'

'No go. I think if they had they'd *put* you on a ship; but of course they'd rather you went of your own accord.'

'Hell! If it comes to that ... Thing is, I particularly don't want to blot my copybook with this West Indian deal just coming up – and the office happen to know I'm, er, that way inclined. That's how they like it, matter of fact – no domestic entanglements. But they'd be distinctly shirty if they heard I'd been thrown out of Greece for buggery. Not that I've ever gone for small boys. I hope you don't mind my saying so, old man, but policemen are more my line.'

'Shut up!' said Pibble, furious. It was astonishing how the old gibe still stung. But when he looked at Butler he saw that he might not have been joking: that note of irony in his voice which had bothered Pibble at times might not be irony at all, only a schoolboy tone of voice, acquired to conceal awkwardness, now a habit.

'I think I can help you keep your office sweet,' he said. 'You remember that deal in Montreal you were talking about? I've just realized I know exactly the contact you need.'

'Come off it.'

'No, I'm sure. This chap'll do the trick for you all right.'

'Thanatos put you on to him?'

'No. I don't think he's got any contacts in Montreal. Look, if I tell Captain Thagoulos that you're ready to pack and go without a fuss, I think he'll let you out at once. Then I can give you the details while you're packing. It's an hour and a half till the ferry leaves.'

'I'm in your hands.'

'I don't know whether that part was a new idea,' said Pibble, sitting on the bed and watching the finicky accuracy with which Butler folded every garment and put it into a prepared place in his suitcase. 'I mean, smuggling heroin disguised as abstract sculpture. He had two paintings stolen each time out of a whole show, so if the customs just tested a sample they'd have a good chance of missing them.'

'Why bother to have them stolen? Couldn't some rich guy just come along and buy them?'

'Well, some other rich guy might have got there first, and to prevent that you'd have to have the gallery's complicity. And it broke the trail, I suppose – no receipts or fake documents. And the cops would be looking for professional art thieves. I don't know how much morphine he could get into one of those paintings.'

'How much do they weigh?'

'The big ones – half a hundredweight or more.'

'They'd be about seventy-five per cent plaster – say fifteen pounds of drug to a picture.'

'It doesn't sound much.'

'It's a lot. But it's not as much as I'm looking for. Perhaps his bosses are trying to get him to expand. How'd he take that?'

'I don't think he'd like it. In fact, I suspect he may be trying to get out. There's been a curious side-effect to the whole operation, which is that the thefts from his shows produced a lot of publicity, which raised the prices of his pictures to a point where he could live off them. I wouldn't be at all surprised if he was trying to duck out. How would the Mafia take that?'

'They wouldn't like it.'

'I mean what would they do? Rough him up?'

'Not at once. They'd offer to let him buy himself out, and set a price much higher than he could possibly pay. That'd be a start. Anyway, if you're right, we can do quite a neat job. The Canadians can pick this lot up – make it look like a fluke – and then tell Athens where it came from. Athens can jump on Hott then, without thinking that they're obeying big brother over the Atlantic. I wish you could give me a bit more, though. It's pretty thin so far. If you've sold me a bum steer about Montreal, and the office learns why I left Hyos, I won't be getting much of a sniff at my pension rights. They're bastards about that sort of thing.'

'Do you mind if I talk about X?'

'It's your alphabet – do what you like with it.'

'The first time I met X he was sulky and rude and rather difficult. He's young, and his arms are very thin, and he looked dirty. He'd been given a drink of ouzo but I saw him pour it away surreptitiously, though he told me he liked the taste. Then the two of us went for a walk, and I went into a church to look round, but he stayed outside. When I came out he was suddenly much perkier. Then I met him down in the town, next day, and he was very bright – sharp – quite different. And he'd tried to clean himself up a bit. Then I saw him later with a girl, out up the hill. They didn't know I was watching them. He kept shouting "I can't, I can't." The girl tried to comfort him, and told him about somebody she'd helped who'd been on H.'

'Uh-huh,' said Butler. 'That sounds like something.'

'Wait. Last time I saw him was an hour ago, at a bar. I was with Hott when X arrived. He looked as though he'd been expecting to find Hott there. He also looked pretty sick. Hott found an excuse to take all the contents out of his pockets, and then put everything back except a fresh packet of cigarettes, which he offered to X. X jumped up and threw the packet in the harbour.'

'You can't smoke morphine, you know.' The ironic note in Butler's voice was very strong, but probably still unintentional.

'I know. Hott rolls his cigarettes, very tidily. So he'd have no need of a packet. I thought it might be an unobtrusive way of passing morphine on – X does smoke, by the way. Anyway, Hott didn't seem at all surprised, and when he'd gone X borrowed some money off me to buy a bottle of ouzo, so he's back on that now. I talked to him in an elusive way about lying low for a bit, and he got what I was talking about.'

'Right,' said Butler. 'Let's add up. Hott goes night-fishing, so he's got the opportunity to get the opium in. Joss-sticks in his studio would hide the smell. His studio is windowless and well kitted out. He is geared to ship his pictures to the U.S. If I've got my chemistry right, he could precipitate morphine base out of an aqueous salt with ammonia – that's almost insoluble in water, so he could mix it with plaster of paris, which isn't very soluble either. There'd be very little reaction. Any good chemist could separate it all out at the far end. Yeah, it would work, but . . .'

He paused, thinking.

'. . . but it won't wash,' he said.

'What do you mean?'

'It's all so fancy. Joss-sticks! Stealing pictures! Asking an ex-cop into the place where he does the work! Passing the stuff in fag-packets, to some nut!'

'Yes, he's a show-off. The very first words he said to me were a quotation from Rimbaud about disordering the senses, which I think were part of something about experimenting with hash and absinthe.'

'You think that's Mafia style?'

'No, I don't. Besides, there's one or two other things you've left out. The most important is that the quantities he'd be able to get into two pictures being quite a lot too small.'

'Yeah.'

'Well, what I think is this. He's an amateur. He's set this up by himself, or perhaps with one or two other amateurs. Hyos isn't a very likely place to start a fair-sized operation, but he chose it because he was already living here. Now his system seems to be working, and he's getting the stuff into the States on a fairly reliable basis, and so he's attracted the attention of the big boys. They want to take over. That's how the rumour got about that the Mafia are interested in Hyos.'

'Uh-huh. You may be right. Amateurs will try anything, and sometimes it works. We'll let Canada check it out.'

'I feel fairly confident.'

'Bully for you. I take it this X is a girl.'

'If you say so.'

'Thing is, there's no real percentage in his flogging the stuff on the island, especially to someone who doesn't carry the price of a bottle of ouzo; but it's a way of making an independent dolly dependent, and he sounds the type. You want to look after her?'

'If it doesn't muck things up for you.'

'She's going to have a hell of a time getting off – she'll be lucky if she's through it in a couple of months . . .'

'Isn't morphine easier than heroin?'

'Not that I know of. Athens is going to move before then, and Thagoulos will give all Hott's buddies a proper going-over. He's pretty certain to spot her, wouldn't you think?'

'I don't know.'

'Otherwise she'd do bloody well to skip for a couple of months. Athens is damned nasty about this sort of thing.'

'It doesn't queer your pitch, leaving X out?'

'Far from it. She's a British citizen, I take it?'

'Perhaps.'

'Well then, if Athens picks her up, that's a hell of a lot of trouble for the F.O. And if it gets back to the F.O. that Athens was acting on a tip from us, that's a hell of a lot of trouble for Department J. That's why it's so neat letting Canada handle Hott – keeps *our* noses clean.'

Everything was so neat, thought Pibble, moodily watching the military back on its way up the gangplank of the ferry-boat. Butler disposed of, pressure off Tony, Nancy left out of the reckoning with Hott, Mafia's interest in Hyos accounted for.

Neatness is all, he thought, turning away and nodding to Thagoulos where he stood in the shadow of the Customs shed. What we need now, he thought, as he started back along the dusty road to Porphyrocoplos through the yellow slant light of evening, is for Alfred to have found the speedboat and fished out the motor and found out what made it burst into flames. Then we can all relax in a totally neat world.

Alfred had done his stuff. The motor lay on the terrace. There were two bullet-holes in the petrol tank that stood beside it – a neat round for entry and a torn gash for exit.

Chapter Ten

I' the how-dumb-deid o' the cauld hairst night . . .

It was a clue. No one would write a line like that just for its own sake. It must be an anagram of something . . . Behind the hill . . . only one *l*. Too difficult to remember all the letters with a half-drowsing mind . . . hairst . . . R.I.'s hat . . . his rat . . . boring . . .

I' the how-dumb-died o' the cauld hairst night . . . dammit, nicht . . .

In the dead silence of the cold harvest night Pibble twitched himself over on his too-luxurious mattress and tried to trick his mind away from the misdealings of the day into the preferable ambiguities of sleep. But it wasn't even a hairst nicht. All is safely gathered in by the first of November . . . unless you count the olives, still ripening on the trees for drunk monks to clamber up and gather, looking like great apes as they did so. Primates of Constantinople . . .

'Crap! Crap! Crap!' That had been Thanatos, yelling at the mauve Ionian dusk and bringing to an end the footling and amateurish discussions of ballistics.

I' the . . . hoots! Wull ye no gang awa fra a mon's thochts, Mr. MacDiarmid, forbye?

The alternative is to lie on one's back and positively resist sleep, by coherent thought. To enumerate, pressing thumb against successive fingertips, all the things that are wrong about the set-up as seen from Porphyrocolpos.

First, the failure of the gunman on the headland to fire his second shot. The psychology of professional gunmen had also been argued inconclusively back and forth in the gathering dusk. Pibble still didn't believe any of the theories that accounted for it.

Second, the telephone call. No one admitted to that. No one was interested in it. It was conceivable that one of the courtiers had attempted to please the monarch by removing Butler, as a potential threat to Tony. And it is part of a courtier's loyalty to do the necessary crooked deed in such a way that the monarch remains untainted. Besides, it involved the police, and Thanatos wouldn't like that. Or, as George said, a mistake might have been made in tracing the call. Why the hell should anyone at Porphyrocolpos want to remove Butler, unless someone there *was* the Mafia's man, deep in the morphine trade? Wait. Buck had shown a sudden eagerness to meet Hott, had driven out to see him, hangover and all. And Hott had good as asked to meet Buck – and then been implausibly surprised to find him a cripple. If he'd wanted to see him, either above or below board, why shouldn't he make contact direct? Just the fancy footwork of the amateur again, probably. Mlle Guillerand said she had already seen the beach-buggy, and the buggies were new toys. So perhaps Buck had been out to the South Bay villas before, when he should have been checking hotels. Yes, Hott had known about Thanatos's plans for the monastery; he'd known Pibble was an ex-cop; according to Tony he'd been more interested in Pibble than her. He'd wanted to check on this possible new danger, and wanted to provide an excuse for more meetings with Buck. So the telephone call had been made by Buck.

No. Buck's accent was worse than Pibble's. So someone else at Porphyrocolpos was in the ring. In that case, they must all be.

Inconceivable. Rubbish. Airy nothings. A mere construction.

And another thing – if Hott was just shipping a load off, he must have got his raw materials in long ago, so there'd be no need to go night-fishing for fresh supplies, and get his eyes redrimmed with lack of sleep. No, perhaps he'd be starting afresh, at once; presumably the opium harvest was over, and it was sense to lay the stuff in at once. Forget it.

He found his thumb pressing so hard against his middle finger that he might have been trying to squash some nasty bug there. With an effort he shifted the pointer on.

And anyway, though it was untidy and unaesthetic to assume that a mess of unrelated skulduggery was in progress on small Hyos – Anna Laszlo and Butler and Hott and the mystery marksman – it was one degree more credible than the notion of a single intricate pattern relating them all. Suppose Hott were the mystery marksman ... with glasses that thick? Things happen round a figure like Thanatos; he not only made events of his own will, but he attracted them involuntarily. He threshed; whirlpools eddied round him; weaker creatures were sucked in, threshing too, as Pibble now threshed on his bed. Suppose ... suppose that the marksman had intended to miss, then? To scare? To mew Thanatos up in his plush prison for a while? Bloody fine shot. Buck collaborates with Hott. Together they're a damn fine shot.

There was something there, but sleep took him before he could interpret it. The hypnagogic picture that slid before his eyes was the image of St. Sporophore, beaked and feathered, holding in his hand a stick of yellow sealing-wax. Automatically he moved his thumb to his little finger, as if to count the absurd saint as yet another unresolved fraction of the puzzle.

Dozing through lurching images and half-dreams he kept his hand under the obsessive tension until its discomfort woke him. It was night still, but might soon become dawn. With his left hand he felt for his right to discover what this strange, numb grip was clutching. It turned out to be the knowledge that St. Sporophore had committed a miracle, puncturing a petrol tank with a shot fired at another time.

Wide-eyed in the dark he thought about it, then switched on his bedside light and dressed.

The corridor was fully lit. As he walked towards the stairhead a voice hissed at him. He looked up and found himself covered by a squat machine-gun, confidently handled by Serafino who had been standing sentry in the niche outside Thanatos's bedroom.

'Where you go?'

'Outside. Up the hill. There's something I want to check on.'

'Must wait until day. Mr. Palangalos orders.'

'O.K.'

Pibble went back to his room and thought about it some more. Then he picked up the telephone, looked at the extension sheet and pressed the numbered button. The far bell rang only once.

'*Oriste,*' said the calm voice.

'This is Jimmy Pibble. I want to go and check on something out on the island, but Serafino says I must wait till daylight. It'll be much more difficult then.'

'Something important?'

'I hope so. If I'm right it'll explain all the bits that don't make sense, and tell us who fired the bullet.'

'O.K., I will tell Serafino.'

'You wouldn't like to come too? I might need somebody who spoke good Greek. It won't be dangerous.'

'How far?'

'About three miles. I don't want to make a noise, so I'd rather not take a car.'

'O.K. I will come to your room.'

'We'll need a torch.'

'It will soon be light.'

'We'll still need a torch.'

'O.K.'

A large moon was loafing down the western sky, giving enough light for easy walking. The sentinel hound sniffed them at the fence. They didn't speak until they were out of earshot from the gate.

'Wait,' said George. 'I must know more. Where are we going?'

'To the monastery. I want to get there before the monks are about.'

For the first time George seemed at all surprised.

'What can you find there?'

'I hope to find a reason why someone in Porphyrocolpos arranged an apparent shooting, so that Thanassi would stay inside the fence for a while.'

'Am I this someone?'

'No. At least, that first day, you were very much against the idea that anyone would try and shoot Thanassi.'

'I still am. But someone did, though you said an *apparent* shooting. I have thought of Buck twisting in his seat and shooting the holes with a pistol, and then setting fire to the petrol that leaked out. But even he could not achieve that, though he's great with his hands. He would have to be so quick, and still steer normally, and not be seen by Thanassi, and dispose of the pistol, and even then he could not be sure that the boat would sink and the tank not be found with the holes showing that the bullet travelled in the wrong direction.'

'They went in the right direction.'

'They were bullet-holes?'

'Let's go and see whether I'm right about the monastery. Then we'll have a reason. Everything else is just an amateurish bag of tricks, a sort of showing off.'

'O.K. I do not enjoy walking. You carry the torch and I will take the pistol.'

'Pistol?'

George took it from his pocket, a middling-sized automatic, its metal too dark to glint in the moon. Pibble laughed.

'I don't think we'll need that,' he said.

'Who knows?'

As they walked on Pibble saw that he still held the weapon ready in his hand, only putting it away as they walked through the town. Two dogs yelped at them as they entered and another as they left. Already the sky was greying, and they met an old man leading a donkey laden with empty baskets down to the harbour. George began to pant as they climbed the hill, and stopped to rest where the terraces between the olives gave him a convenient wall to sit on. Now it was more day than night, just, with the beginnings of sunrise stretching a pale streak of pink along the eastern sky; but the sea was still heavy-hued, as if it had been dyed with darkness, and across it the fishing-boats crawled home trailing their strings of lamp-boats, each showing still its paraffin spark.

'Ah,' said George, 'it is a long time since I have seen this. You work, you make yourself rich, you take risks, you begin to need doctors and cupboards full of little pills, and you forget . . .'

'We ought to get on,' said Pibble. 'We've got to get there before the workmen.'

George smiled, still looking at the sea.

'The day after Sunday the workmen will not be early at their work. You are taking me to see Tony?'

'No. Not that I know of.'

'O.K.'

'Hadn't you better put that gun away, just in case we meet somebody?'

George smiled and shook his head. It was a good gun, made for use and not for show. Pibble started impatiently up the track, irritated with himself for his inability to enjoy this one hour before the dew was gone, when the moisture seemed to suck out of leaf and soil the fresh smells which would soon fade into the general dusty drought of noon.

'You think there is a traitor at Porphyrocolpos?' said George from behind his shoulder.

'No. At least, not the sort of traitor we've been looking for.

Like Thanassi says, you're all tied to him much too tightly for it to be worth your while to betray him, in that kind of way. But he's such a powerful personality that some of you must itch sometimes to be your own men, and do something to prove it. I think that's what's happened this time.'

'It is possible. I do not feel such longings, but I am a dull Greek. If Thanassi makes a lot of money, I make a little, and that is good enough for me.'

'How did you meet him?'

'Wait for me. I cannot talk to your back. I was a *kamaryeris*, a bell-hop, at his first big hotel, in Cyprus. There was a suicide, a French film star, and the hotel manager was not very sensible. It could have been very bad publicity, with talk of the Thanatos organization failing to act in time, then trying to conceal; but I gave evidence to the police and to the magistrate. I gave the right evidence. Thanassi helped me after that, so here I am, walking up this hill before breakfast in tight shoes, to look for a traitor.'

Yes, thought Pibble. He could see young George, pale-skinned and slight but with just the same black eyes, sticking to his story. There are some witnesses whom no policeman on earth can shake. They seem invulnerable.

It was full day by the time he turned aside from the path. George immediately dropped behind. Once, when Pibble looked back to check his bearings, he saw that the pistol was half up and that George was looking left and right among the bushes and tree-trunks, like a jungle patrol. So it seemed tactful for Pibble to go up the ladder first and heave the spare ladder over single-handed, and then to descend to the passage alone. For a few seconds George stayed on the wall, looking dubiously down into the darkness below him.

'Will you shine the torch, please, so that I can see?' he said, or rather ordered. 'Also hold the ladder?'

Pibble obeyed, holding the torch to illuminate himself more than anything else. He also stood so as to present the best possible target. George came very slowly down the ladder with his back to the rungs; the third eye of the pistol pointed steadily at Pibble all the time, while the other two darted to either side, ready for ambushes. Pibble couldn't see, against the glare of the brightening sky, whether the safety-catch was on or not.

As soon as George reached the bottom he took the torch and

shone it up and down the corridor, probing the empty shadows. Then he grunted and handed it back to Pibble, who led the way down the slope. As they passed each cell he allowed time for a brief check that it too was empty, though he tried to behave as though his own interest in these bleak and boring cubes was real but academic. Their understanding – his and George's – seemed perfect. *Probably* Pibble was acting from good motives, but it was sensible for George to act as though he might not be, and equally sensible for Pibble not to take offence. Certainly George's vigilance didn't relax; even when they reached the chapel he took the torch and explored for several cells further down the corridor, leaving Pibble alone in the almost-dark.

Faint glints of gold came from the halo of the Christ in the dome as the torch wavered back up the corridor. Pibble stood, sniffing the strong odour that permeated the place, recognizing it for what it was now that the smoke from the censer no longer muddled his nostrils. It was nothing as natural as pine resin, no, far too chemical for that.

'What is the smell?' said George in his passionless voice.

'Glue. A modern impact adhesive, like you stick formica on with. Anyway, I'm pretty sure. Have a look at the dome.'

The torch-beam swung upwards. In its direct light the face of Judgment frowned down, terrific. They could see every stone that made up the enormous lozenge-shaped eyes and the implacable lips. Pibble was amazed that he had ever thought it Victorian. George muttered to himself in Greek what sounded like a prayer.

'It is genuine?' he said suddenly.

'I don't know. If it isn't, we're back to square one. Now have a look at the apse behind the altar.'

The beam swung down.

'It is rubbish, that,' said George at once. 'Modern rubbish.'

He was right. It wasn't even mosaic, just paint on a roughish surface perfunctorily imitating the mottled pointillism of tesserae. But in the strong beam of the torch it was possible to see that it had been done with a certain dash, a touch of caricature, as though the artist were amused by his own swift expertise and knew he could afford to take risks because his work was never going to be seen by any eyes except those of elderly, ouzo-riddled monks, or by any light except that of the dim lantern they used. But he must have worked hard at it, and at the later processes, night after night. No wonder his eyes had been rimmed with red.

'Shine it down here,' said Pibble. 'Behind the altar.'

But first the light swung away to search the sides of the chapel for hidden enemies. When at last it lit the place where the painting ended at a pillar, Pibble knelt and worked his fingers in behind the surface. It was slightly resilient, not like old plaster on linen; it was cardboard. Fully confident now he gripped it and pulled it forward to clear the pillar so that he could begin to slide the whole thing sideways along the apse. It came stiffly, without the floppiness you'd have expected of unsupported cardboard – probably they'd nailed a few battens behind it to steady it. It was light but awkward.

'Can you take the other side?' he said. 'I want to get it right out of the way and see how far they've got.'

George hesitated for a moment before laying the pistol and torch on the altar and taking the far edge. Backing and filling they manoeuvred the whole false apse down into the body of the chapel, where it stood like part of a stage set. Eagerly Pibble started for the altar, but George gripped him by the elbow and he stopped – he mustn't seem to be rushing for the pistol when it was the torch he wanted. He managed to stand still, though the lust to see made every muscle in him shiver. George picked up the pistol before shining the torch on the apse.

'Ah,' he said, wholly unastonished. 'What does it mean?'

It had been made by the same workmen as the Christ in the dome. Once again every tile glowed or sparkled. The blue of the background seemed to comprise innumerable receding deeps, in front of which the three figures floated – the passionless Christ, the suffering Virgin, and the saint whose emotions were concealed by his beak and feathers, but who no longer seemed a ridiculous figure. The curious distancing of the great mosaic made him also majestic. His feet were missing where a big triangle, comprising almost a quarter of the whole work, had been removed from the lower right-hand corner.

'I wonder if they can put it back,' said Pibble.

'What is it? Who are they? Is it genuine?'

'I think it must be genuine or they wouldn't be stealing it. Do you know Ravenna?'

'No.'

'There are some tremendous mosaics there, in this style, and it's only just across the Adriatic. They were done in the time of Justinian, in the sixth century, when this monastery might have started to get rich by collaborating with pirates. The monks might have hired workmen from Ravenna, I suppose – or it might have been a common style at the time. I don't think anyone knows about that, because all the early mosaics in the Eastern Empire were smashed by the Iconoclasts. You only find them in Italy now.'

'But why in this little hole? Why not in the Catholicon?'

'My guess is that this was St. Sporophore's own cave. The passage down to it looks as if it might have been a cliff edge – I don't know whether you noticed. I expect they bricked it up to hide it from the Iconoclasts – I've read that there were monasteries where every monk died defending their pictures. Something like that could have happened here, and when new monks came back they didn't know about it. I don't know how Father Chrysostom found it. Perhaps the wall collapsed – you can see that the arch is new. Anyway, he wouldn't have known what it was worth – it wouldn't be until someone came up who knew about the art world, and realized that here was an entirely unknown mosaic of a sort which doesn't exist in any museum in the world. I've no idea what it's worth if you could get it to America – a million quid?'

'Buck,' said George softly.

'Yes, I mean, no one else could have arranged for the boat to catch fire without risking Buck's life, and I don't think we've got a murderer on our hands.'

'But he could never do the work. Who is helping him? Dave?'

'No. Somebody at the South Bay villas, I think. A very competent chap.'

'How is it done?'

'I'm not sure of the details, but I've watched workmen restoring painted plasterwork – I think they'd have to start by making some sort of matrix out of plaster – I found some plaster on the floor – to set the tiles at their proper angles when they put it together; and then they'd take it section by section, glueing the tiles to fine canvas and then sawing away behind them. You'd have to use a soluble glue.'

'I found a pile of workman's materials in a cell down the passage,' said George. He no longer sounded very interested, but

Pibble said 'Let's see,' and groped off down the passage. George followed, silent-footed.

The cell smelt less unused than some of the others they'd explored. Old cement sacks covered a shapeless pile of oddments in the far corner, not looking like anything special; but the kit underneath them was new and neatly stacked. A roll of fine canvas, two pressure lanterns, a roll of India paper wrapped in polythene, several big tubes of Evostik, bags of plaster of paris, buckets, trowels, some odd-shaped saws, and two crates. The first was full of carefully wrapped flattish objects; Pibble undid the wrappings of one and found a slightly curved white irregular slab, about nine inches by fifteen, whose concave surface was rough from the trowel and numbered '12' and whose convex surface was rough in a different way, with the exact impression of two hundred tessarae.

'Yes, that's part of the matrix,' he said as he wrapped it up and put it back.

The second crate was less than half full of different-feeling flattish objects, also wrapped. Pibble grunted with the surprising weight of the one he lifted out; it was more awkward to handle because of its slight flexibility; he unwrapped it with almost holy care. It turned out to be a numbered sheet of the canvas, a little larger than the piece of matrix; glued to its surface was a meaningless pattern of glass cuboids, which showed only a glint or two of their brilliance through the mortar powder.

'That's the mosaic,' he said, staring. 'I should think each bit corresponds to a different bit of the matrix. It must be pretty alarming getting them off. You see, they could build the matrix to its proper shape when they set it up, and strengthen it, and then get each section of the canvas into place and push new mortar through from behind. If they were patient enough they could get every tile at exactly the same angle and position that it held here.'

'They would smuggle it?'

'Buck's helper is an artist, who produces white abstract shapes. I don't think he'd have much trouble passing the matrix off as the same sort of thing, and these other bits as a new departure.'

'And the monks know what he is doing?'

'I think one of them does. I came to the service here yesterday, and he tried to prevent the other monk bringing me down this way. And I've a notion that some of the islanders know something's up. I heard a rumour that the reason why no one except I came to the service was that they say something unlucky is happening in the monastery.'

'It is likely. You can never guess what a Greek peasant knows. Who is Buck's helper? What is his name?'

Pibble hesitated. He didn't want to complicate Butler's task, but it would look pointed if he refused to answer.

'Mark Hott,' he said. 'Do you remember, the night before last, I told Buck that an artist had asked to meet him? That's the man. In fact they'd already met, but they wanted an excuse to see each other more often. Buck came up here, on Thanassi's instructions, before the rest of you arrived, and I think he must have found the mosaic then. They had to remove it before Thanassi saw it, but they couldn't start till they got him safely cooped up at Porphyrocolpos. Buck wasn't keen on my coming up here, that first morning, though he was keen enough on the notion of bumping Thanassi off. And Hott's eyes are red with working on it all night. Oh, yes, and I saw some yellow sealing-wax in his studio.'

'Sealing-wax?' said George. Pibble could almost feel the careful brain working it out, neither amazed nor angry. He got it right.

'They shoot holes in the petrol tank in Mr. Hott's studio, is that it? And then they plug them with the wax. And Buck chooses his time and starts a fire in the back of the boat to melt the wax. How?'

'I think he'd have a flask of petrol hidden somewhere. He insisted on getting the boat out himself; I heard him being very angry with Alfred about it. And the beach-buggies are kept with the boats, and there's a row of the cans there too. As soon as he was clear of the shore he'd pour his flask over Thanassi's robe and throw it back into the corner by the tank. Then all he's got to do is toss a cigarette back there at the right moment.'

'Too clever.'

'Yes, not a professional job. But it worked, except that he didn't expect the boat to sink.'

'Why did he bother?' said George. 'Thanassi was inside the fence anyway.'

'Yes, but only for a couple of days. I remember he sounded put out when I said it needn't be longer than that. He managed to have the telegram sent from Boston somehow, as a stop-gap measure . . .'

'Easy, if he knows someone there,' said George. 'Only a telephone call.'

'It can be traced.'

'Not so easy. We are always telephoning all over the world.'

'I suppose we're too late to stop the bodyguards coming,' said Pibble.

George shrugged, as though so small an expense didn't matter.

'They are late already,' he said. 'They probably will not come, or come to the wrong island. So now Thanassi is free, huh?'

'I think so. We're reasonably sure that there are no professional assassins on the island. We can account for the shooting. I should think Buck or Hott arranged to have that telegram sent from Boston. I think you probably heard about the man who came from London looking for a Mafia drug-factory – that's all part of another problem, though I still don't know why anyone should have rung up from Porphyrocolpos to get him thrown out.'

'That was I,' said George, matter-of-factly, after a slight pause.

'Oh. Why?'

'I thought he had come to look for Tony. Do not tell Thanassi.'

Pibble blinked. So now George, and presumably the other courtiers, knew that he knew who Tony was, and didn't mind declaring their knowledge. They had assumed that he too was now drawn into their network of personal loyalty, overriding all other loyalties.

'O.K.', he said, half accepting the role. 'That tidies pretty well everything up. There was simply too much going on.'

'It is like that, round Thanassi.'

'I know. I know.'

'What do we do now?'

'Put the screen back, then go and persuade Buck to tell Thanassi what he's been up to.'

'O.K.'

But as they walked up the sloping paving they saw a light which should not have been there glowing yellow and erratic under the arch. George switched his torch off. Damn, thought Pibble – it depends which one it is. Then Father Polydore staggered out, lantern held high, and peered up and down the corridor. The only hope was that his mazed old eyes wouldn't spot them. They did.

'*Kleftes!*' cried Father Polydore, tottering towards them and shrilling comminations. Pibble saw George switch the gun to his left hand while he crossed himself with his right. But all the while the barrel pointed steadily at the old monk's heart. Either Father Polydore didn't notice it or he was too enraged for fear.

'Try telling him I'm a policeman,' said Pibble. 'He's the innocent one, I think.'

George put the pistol in his pocket, waited for a gap between curses and then spoke firmly to the old man. Father Polydore blinked and, still mumbling the wrath of Heaven down, raised his lantern to peer at the intruders.

'*Anglikos!*' he said with sudden pleasure. '*Kalos orisate, kirie.*'

'*Kalos sas vrikame, pater,*' said Pibble.

Father Polydore clawed Pibble by the sleeve and dragged him back to the chapel, pouring out plaintive incomprehensibilities. It took some time for George, despite the infrangible glossy patience of the trained hotelier, to calm him. Together they moved the false apse back into position and waited while Father Polydore said the morning office. He seemed perfectly content now that the mocking caricature covered the austere riches of the mosaic. As Nancy had said, *a* picture, any picture, was good enough for faith – perhaps the worse the better. Great art might actually impede belief, focusing the mind on itself, where characterless cliché was, as it were, transparent. In that case Nancy and Father Polydore were performing a truer service to the buyers off their slick production line than if they had been painting icons of any real merit.

'We must go back,' whispered George behind the droning syllables. Pibble was sure that Father Polydore was saying the office twice, or had somehow switched to a prayer near the beginning and was following the whole thing through again; but he shook his head.

'We can't. We've got to talk to Father Chrysostom, the one who's in it – though he'll have arranged things so that no one can prove he is. If Father Polydore tells him we've been here, the whole show might get out of control. He might even try to do away with the old boy.'

'It is no concern of ours. Probably the mosaic belongs to the monks, and they are perfectly entitled to sell it. It is only being removed in secret because of a disagreement between them.'

'You may be right. But I bet they haven't got a licence to export it, and if Athens learns that one of Thanassi's friends has been in on that there'll be trouble. And Thanassi wants this place for a hotel, too. How do you think he'd . . .'

For the first time Pibble saw a real emotion in George's dark eyes, and it was fury. But it went as quickly as it had come.

'O.K., but there is much to do,' he said.

Father Polydore turned from the altar with that look of abstract serenity which is the property of the almost senile. George crossed himself. The lantern was extinguished and returned to its niche and they went up the corridor by torchlight until the hole in the roof made it unnecessary. Pibble, despite his insistence on seeing this artificial mystery through, was in an almost frivolous mood, the burden of other people's sins had slipped from his shoulders, and he felt pleased with himself. Pleased at having sorted the problem out, and even pleased by such trivia as his having understood Father Polydore's first shout of *'Kleftes!'* Thieves! In the Collins phrasebook the word came in a single sentence with 'Help!' and 'Fire!' under the heading 'General Difficulties'. Pibble sometimes had wondered why the word for 'Rape!' had been omitted from the catalogue of tourist calamity, especially as the book had been printed before the chaste rule of the Colonels began.

And now, as he helped Father Polydore down the erratic stairs to the Refectory, he wondered whether the old man had already forgotten the whole drama of the missing mosaic. If you are

    (*a*) superstitious
    (*b*) on the verge of senility
    (*c*) riddled with ouzo
    (*d*) a bit simple-minded anyway

then there must be multiple opportunities for the confusion of fact and fantasy. It would be difficult for even the most rigorous philosopher to build a theory of knowledge on your perceptions, in which dream and belief and fact and oblivion ceaselessly shaded and faded into each other, so that the fake mosaic could become the real one, with a corner missing, and then shift back into the fake one without your having to postulate two separate phenomena to account for the diverse appearances. It was wasted speculation; Father Polydore took a deep breath at the door of the Refectory, squared his frail shoulders and lurched into the room bawling that the monastery had been robbed.

Father Chrysostom was there, but so were Tony and Nancy. At the sight of the girls responsibility leapt back and squatted on Pibble's neck. George the impassive was also perceptibly shaken; no doubt he could accept a monk who robbed his own monastery, but was shocked to see him consorting with women. Tony wore her wig, but perfunctorily so that it was obviously a wig, with the long coils tucked inside her shirt. She was no less the warrior queen as she stared half-sideways at George advancing smiling to greet her. Nancy was at her easel, grey and sweating, but before he could greet her Pibble found himself clutched again by the sleeve and pulled to where Father Chrysostom now stood frowning at the High Table.

Dialogue ensued, ardent but meaningless.

'*Then sas katalaveno*,' said Pibble, several times. Neither monk believed him. An Englishman who can intrude into holy places, desecrating shrines, should at least be able to defend his actions in the language of the country.

'George!' called Pibble, also several times. 'George!'

At length he had to shake himself free of Father Polydore to fetch his unwilling interpreter. George was arguing with Tony, low-voiced but intense. In the few steps that it took Pibble to cross the room Pibble saw something which his own unlikely longings had made him blind to. It was obvious in tone and stance, in gesture and expression. George, too, was besotted. Pibble, now almost cured, was so overwhelmed with sympathy that he hesitated before waking his friend from the impossible dream.

'George,' he said. 'Sorry to interrupt.'

With an effort George retracted his emotions into their carapace.

'For God's sake come and sort this out,' said Pibble. 'Tell them we know who's been taking the thing, and that we'll make them put it back. Ask Father Chrysostom if he wants us to call the police in – he'll say not yet. Don't let on that we think he's in it.'

George flickered a smile at Tony and moved up the room to where Father Chrysostom was already fetching the bottle, glasses and sponge-sealed pitcher out of his cupboard. With a shock Pibble remembered that Nancy nearly certainly knew what had been going on; cautiously he turned to see how she'd reacted. She seemed not even to have heard. As he watched her she lifted her brush from the wood, waited while a long shudder shook the whole curve of her back, and then returned to the blue draperies of the Virgin.

'She's not so good today,' said Tony, low-voiced at his shoulder. 'I brought her down this early to work. Work cures all, my Poppa used to say.'

'Come and look at the view,' said Pibble.

They leaned out over the sill, with the pillar between them. The early morning sun lit the man-made cliffs opposite, but still shone at too low an angle to reach the water, which lay calm and green-purple beneath them. In this light it was easy to see the whole of the monks' submarine midden. It appeared to be composed almost exclusively of bottles.

'It's morphine she's been on?' said Pibble. But Tony shook her head.

'Just grass. Hash.'

'But . . .'

'Yeah. I know. You wouldn't think it could do that to somebody. But Nan's so small, and she's got personality problems. A great big balanced bear like Mark can smoke as much as he likes, and he'll be O.K. But that kind never figure there's anyone different to them – kids with no resistance in them, body or spirit. They think they're being just friendly, but they can do a hell of a lot of harm.'

'I thought . . .'

'What she's got now is plain hangover,' said Tony. 'So've I. We drank a bottle of ouzo last night. Say, that's foul stuff.'

Pibble sighed. It was no business of his if Nancy had lied to Tony, and Tony, lost in love, chose to disbelieve plain evidence.

'Look,' he said slowly. 'There's trouble coming. A lot of people, including Nan, are going to be questioned by the local police. Unless she's behaving in a fairly rational way, she's bound to be spotted. The people in Athens are very tough on any kind of drug-taking, so I think you ought to try and get her out of Greece in the next week or so.'

She gave him one of her solemn, intense stares.

'Thanks,' she said. 'You'll tell Mark?'

'No, I don't think so. If they learn that the word's been passed round, there'll be real trouble. They might even try and come after you, I think Mark can take care of himself.'

'I guess so,' she said. 'He's a tough bastard. Also, he treated Nan wrong. Yeah, I'll let it happen.'

In the long pause Pibble found himself wondering how this terrifying girl could have so subdued her personality to attract his timid, elderly lusts. He wondered too whether Thanatos preferred her armed or submissive. She seemed to divine his thought.

'How's my old swine?' she said, withdrawing herself into the room.

'He's not so good, either,' said Pibble, following. 'He took it very hard. I think you must have meant more to him than ... than just another beautiful girl.'

'I'm sorry.'

The shrug of her shoulders was not dismissive. It implied affection and sympathy for the old swine. And farewell, and a deliberate putting-out-of-mind.

'Better not tell him you've seen me,' she said.

'But George ...'

Tony made a slight face, glanced at the suave back of George cajoling and blackmailing Father Chrysostom, and shook her head.

'What are you going to do?' said Pibble. 'I mean, after you've got Nancy through.'

'Go home. Start work.'

'With her?'

'Yeah. She's interested. She's lived her life in places where nothing happens.'

'Won't you have trouble getting her in? And yourself?'

'Up from Mexico. I've got trouble, I know. I *am* trouble. Both sides will want to see me in the big trial scene. Have you noticed how liberation movements are getting less mileage out of their martyrs? So what do they do? They find a very American solution – they throw in more martyrs ... You don't like it?'

'I like you. But I can't imagine a situation in which your kind of random violence is morally justified. I'm sorry. I'll have to let them know you're coming. And Nancy.'

'You would, too. I'll tell you something about your kind – you think you've got a monopoly of duty. When *we* die, when we are tortured, when we stick out life-sentences in the pen – that's not duty.'

She spoke seriously, without contempt, her voice gentle and

low – an excellent thing in woman. But Pibble felt as though he had been scythed down by her bladed wheels.

'You'll still go, even if they know you're coming?' he said.

'Uh-huh. But I'll tell you another thing. Violence was last year's scene.'

'What will this year's be?'

'I don't know. We all keep saying we've got to show that we can build, but I reckon Middle America will like that even less than the bombs. Maybe they'll let us show that we can suffer.'

'Nancy too?'

'If she wants it. She . . . you know something? She was reared in a home, but she knew who her father was. He was a writer. He didn't even know she existed. She only saw him once, in a bookstore, where he was signing his books . . .'

'Nancy told me he was in the Resistance.'

'Yeah – Yugoslavia. Then he settled down to be a sex 'n' violence man. She went to this bookstore to look at him, and she bought one of the books. She showed it to me and guess what. She's been through every line of that book with a brush and indian ink. Now the only words you can read are the signature. And she keeps it by her bed – like that.'

'Poor girl. Yes. I see. Did you tell Thanassi you were leaving him?'

'Uh-huh.'

'And for whom?'

'Love that grammar. Of course, I spelled it out.'

'I wonder if he understood,' said Pibble, wondering if *he* did, either.

'Ask him.'

Even in that near-whisper Tony could make reproof wince. She was going to say something more, but broke off to run to Nancy, who now stood swaying at her workbench. Tony laced her arm round her waist, led her to the window and helped her to lean far out, stroking her shoulder-blades between the retchings. When Pibble turned back to the room, squeamish and weary, he saw that the art-fraud conference was breaking up amid expressions of mutual distrust and esteem. George drained the last of his ouzo and extracted a perfunctory blessing from Father Chrysostom before coming impatiently down the room. Seeing what the girls were doing he stood and fidgeted.

'All fixed?' said Pibble.

'O.K. The Mosaic will be restored. Then Athens will be told of its existence. Thanassi will make a donation to ensure its proper upkeep. If the criminals make restitution the police need not be informed.'

'Well done. That sounds all right.'

George didn't even hear him. As soon as Tony turned from the window he darted in front of her, totally ignoring Nancy. Tony looked at him with an odd expression combining tenseness with boredom.

'Please,' he said, 'do not be angry. I see you are right. It is best for you to keep away for a few days.'

'I was planning to,' said Tony, suddenly dismissive. As she turned to Pibble he was wondering whether he was going to get similar treatment, but she smiled.

'Bye, Jim. I'll let you know what this year's scene will be, and then you can do your duty. Right?'

'I expect so.' He started to smile in a fatherly way at Nancy, who had the purged and saintly look of any child fresh from vomiting; then he remembered about the blacked-out volume and the deficiencies of fatherliness, so he swivelled and said his guidebook good-byes to the monks.

'What does she mean about next year's scene?' said George as they came through the gate of the monastery into the already desiccating morning.

'Oh, nothing to do with any of this.'

George frowned and swallowed his inquisitiveness. Pibble wondered whether it was worse being successful but not attractive than it was being neither. There was something of the half-man about George, the hotel servant, bred to behave with insensate politeness, to lie with tough discretion about the suicides of film stars, to be all things to all men – how could he ever now become anything special to one woman? And for the woman he wanted to be Tony? It was a measure of his passion that he had let his mask slip so during the scene in the Refectory. Poor old George. But though Pibble genuinely did feel a certain sympathy for his companion, he found that what he was really thinking was poor old Zoe.

The ripping noise of a hard-driven engine came from below them, sorting through rapid gear-changes on the erratic slopes.

'This'll be Buck,' said Pibble. 'I think we'd better let him know. I don't think he'll be difficult – it's been a sort of game – but if he's got Mark Hott with him you may need that pistol.'

'Idiots,' said George quietly, and stepped away from the track.

Buck was alone. Pibble was tensed to jump for his life as the purple buggy hurled up at him, but Buck lugged at the hand-brake and halted it in the last possible instant.

'Strong nerves!' he shouted above the idling motor. 'Where've you been? Where's old George? Serafino said you left together.'

Pibble nodded to where George was standing between two gorse bushes with his right hand in his jacket pocket, and then walked round to Buck's side of the buggy.

'Great!' said Buck. 'Thanassi was fretting. I'll run you home.'

'We've been looking at mosaics,' said Pibble quietly.

'Mosaics, huh?'

'Yes. Now we ought to go down to Mark Hott's to see if he's got any of that yellow sealing-wax left. But George wants to get home.'

Buck blinked once, like a boxer taking an unexpectedly hard punch, and turned to see how George was reacting. But George had composed himself to his usual cold calm so Buck turned back to Pibble's more interpretable features. Then he flung back his head and shouted with unembarrassed laughter.

Chapter Eleven

Astonishingly Thanatos laughed too, a long weeping cackle, nearer the edge of hysteria than Pibble had ever imagined he could come.

'That makes two good losers,' said Dave with extreme sourness; but Thanatos and Buck only laughed again, Buck grinning and bouncing in his wheelchair, the practical joker whose wits have been enough to bewilder a group of clever men with proper legs.

'That first morning was some giggle,' he said. 'I didn't need to do a thing, not after Jim had come up with the idea of bumping you off – only keep bringing the rest of 'em back to the point when they shied away. George didn't like that at all, did you, pal?'

'I knew it was nonsense,' said George, smiling the smile of the courtier who smiles because the king smiles, and with no pleasure of his own. Pibble, just beginning to be able to read the emotions behind the mask, decided that George was irritated by the whole episode, and bored with the recapitulation of its details, just as he would have been bored but polite if he'd had to listen to two moderate golfers recounting the ups and downs of some close, inept contest; but at the same time he was glad it was over, because now sane business life could begin again and distract him, perhaps, from fretting after Tony.

Doc Trotter, by contrast, was mystified but fascinated. He could not begin to understand how an adult could behave in this fashion; the idea of deliberately stepping out of the comfort of Thanatos's shadow into the blaze of the competitive world was for him an inconceivable motive. His bloodshot heavy eyes wheeled from face to face, as if hoping that one of them would suddenly reveal that this post mortem on Buck's hoax was itself a further leg-pull, designed to baffle innocent black men.

And Dave was furious. He'd already been furious when the beach-buggy had come churning into the courtyard; he'd had a teleprinter message clenched in his fist and had thrust it at George before he was out of his seat. George had read it and passed it to Pibble, saying 'At least that need not now disturb us.'

Between the gibberish of transmission instructions, Pibble had read 'GUARDS DISPATCHED AS REQUESTED BUT REPORT HITCH AT FRONTIER STOP ENTRY REFUSED STOP CUSTOMS SEARCH DISCOVERED SPECIALIST EQUIPMENT STOP PROPOSING DISPATCH FRESH PARTY WITH PERMITTED ARMS ONLY.'

'Goddammit!' Dave had shouted, 'what kind of boneheads did they send, trying to get through all in one party?'

'Playing stud on the ammunition boxes,' said Buck, reading the message over Pibble's shoulder.

'I'll have their balls,' said Dave.

'Forget it,' said George. 'It is of no consequence. There has been no attempt on Thanassi's life, no shot fired at him. Jim will explain. Cancel this second party of guards, Dave.'

It had taken Dave some time to begin to understand Pibble's explanation, even with the grinning corroboration of the culprit, and then he had become really angry. And now he was angrier still when he discovered that Thanatos wasn't. Watching him, Pibble wondered how much of this rage was fuelled by his own repressed desire to do some similar thing, to be his own man, to act and conquer outside Caesar's provinces. He sucked his lips in and gulped saliva; he didn't touch his drink; he began sentences and cut them short; finally he strode to the terrace edge, drank his whole glass at one draught and stood staring out to sea.

Slowly the mood of the little court changed, responsive to the ruler's mood. Only Buck failed to realize that he was no longer the all-licensed fool, and what weather was now coming.

'We've got to get Tony back now,' said Thanatos. 'No reason for her staying out – think you can find her, Jim?'

Something rang hollow under his confidence. Pibble shook his head.

'Ah, come on, Jim. Call yourself a detective?'

'Not that sort of detective.'

Thanatos realized how ill-chosen the words were before Pibble did. He glared up, made as if to hurl himself out of his chair with his usual crude energy, then sank back as if he had been pushed in the chest by an invisible hand.

'You know where she is,' he said. There was no need for Pibble to answer because it wasn't a question.

'She can bring the other girl,' said Thanatos. 'They can have rooms right away from mine – one room, if that's how they fancy it. We're broadminded in Porphyrocolpos, provided nobody tells those oafs in Athens. You tell her that, Jim.'

'I don't think I can help you.'

'I don't think I can help you,' mocked Thanatos. 'Christ, you're a prissy old maid. Ah, go and knit yourself a coffin. Never met any lesbians before? Didn't know they existed?'

'Hey,' said Buck, 'do you know the one about the butch usherette at the girlie show? There was this . . .'

Thanatos gave a jerk of his head and George rose quickly from his seat, tilted the wheelchair back so that the brakes on the little front wheels wouldn't bite, and whisked Buck into the house like a waiter hurrying off with the fruit-trolley. When he came back his mouth was working down and sideways as though he were chewing on something.

'Do not send for Tony, my friend,' he said. 'Let us settle these . . .'

'Screw you,' said Thanatos.

'No. What you said to Jim, about this other girl, are you serious?'

'Yeah. She spelled it out.'

'But then . . . how could she . . .'

It was distressing to watch George. In most ways he was a very conventional man; up in the Refectory he had been so obsessed by his own yearnings that he had never noticed the relationship between the girls. Now, in his shock, he was asking the unaskable – if that was Tony's nature, how could she have borne to be complaisant, let alone apparently delighted, with a gross herd bull like Thanatos?

"Screw you,' said the bull. 'We got along.'

With an effort George settled his features into blankness.

'Perhaps if you leave her alone the madness will work itself out,' he said. Thanatos ignored him.

'You'll tell her what I say, Jim?'

'If I see her.'

'O.K. When are you leaving?'

'Tomorrow, if that's all right. There's a ferry in the afternoon. I don't want to leave Mary alone longer than I can help.'

'She's all right, pal. I told my manager there to find her a handsome fisherman.'

'That was friendly.'

'Christ, maybe I should have too, for real. Sometimes I don't know what to make of you, Jim. Now I'm going to ski. Then there's work to do – we'll clear a couple of hours in the afternoon to go up to the monastery and see what all the fuss was about. Buck's going to laugh a mite less when he finds he's got to pay to put it back. And Christ, I'll sting him for that boat of mine. One of a pair, that was, belonged to the Duke of Westminster, unique. Hey, Buck . . .'

The trip to the monastery was surprisingly enjoyable. George had sent a message to warn the monks that they were coming, and that Thanatos might be shocked, and therefore less generous with his donations, if he found the sacred edifice littered with women. Father Chrysostom greeted them with grave pomp, speaking to the millionaire on equal terms – or more than equal, like God receiving Mammon. Doc Trotter bought an icon from Father Polydore, who sloughed his senility to demand six times the price he would have asked from an ordinary tourist. Two bottles of ouzo were drunk.

They had left Buck behind, sulking now; so it fell to Pibble to expound what he thought was the technique for removing the tesserae from the wall and reassembling them in whatever American museum was expecting to announce next year its unique new treasure of unknown provenance. No, Buck wouldn't have had time to find a certain buyer; but he knew that world well enough to be confident. While Father Chrysostom stood suave and smiling in the shadows of the chapel, Thanatos stared at the two Christs, fidgeted with the torches to achieve the maximum play of light from innumerable titled facets, and ran caressing fingers over the tesserae. For the first time for three days he seemed himself again, sucking the world into the whirlpool of his own enjoyment.

'Yeah, yeah,' he said. 'I know a bit about mosaics – I have some in my room, which Buck found for me. He'd know how to do it. This kind would be easier than Roman ones – look at these bloody great gaps between the tiles.'

'But what is it worth?' said Doc Trotter, is his solemn, furry voice, fretting perhaps at the knowledge that Father Polydore had overcharged him for his icon.

'A million bucks?' guessed Dave.

'Crap,' said Thanassi without turning from his study of the Virgin. 'You'd get any price you wanted. There isn't a museum in the world that wouldn't try to raise the dough, once it was cleared through customs. What about that, Jim?'

'Hott's got a boat which he could bring round to the harbour here. He'd have lowered it down and taken it round to his own place, then just crated it up as part of his exhibition. He's shipped exhibitions in before, and . . .'

'Bloody convenient,' said Thanatos. 'Finding a guy who could do all the work, and had all the kit, and could fake it up as modern art.'

'Yes,' said Pibble. 'But put it the other way round – I don't expect he would have tried if he hadn't got someone like that to bring it off.'

Thanatos grunted. Pibble hoped he was too absorbed in his appreciation of the mosaic to notice the wariness of some of the answers. There was a lot it was sensible to keep quiet about: Hott's need (if Butler was right) of a big lump sum to buy himself out of his Mafia concession; Nancy's lie, the first time he met her, about the existence of the chapel; and had Hott continued to supply her with morphine because he might need her to manage the boat while he lowered the mosaic down? There was no question of Father Chrysostom touching any aspect of the theft except the final pay-off.

'Like it, Doc?' said Thanatos suddenly.

Doc Trotter sighed, a strange deep whistle that was almost a groan.

'How can I tell? I must be educated to appreciate such things. I must be shown. I must see other things of the same kind, and learn the relationships. How can this happen if the only examples are in places which I never visit? Ravenne? And now Hyos? It would be better in a museum.'

Thanatos's cackle crackled, and from dark cells down the corridor the echo crackled back.

'O.K., O.K.,' he cried, 'so we'll bring the people to it. I was going to wait until these two old soaks were dead, but now I reckon I've got them fixed. They'll be an asset, and we'll hire a few more, too. We'll keep a section of the place going as a monastery – this, and the Catholicon and a batch of cells – and the rest of it we'll do up with plumbing and lifts and a five-star restaurant. We'll make it like Mount Athos, on wheels.'

'A two-sex Mount Athos?' asked Dave, nodding to where Father Chrysostom stood gravely contemplating his feathered patron.

'I've got them fixed,' said Thanatos again. 'He was in this, up to the neck, and we can prove it, eh, Jim?'

'I expect so,' said Pibble dully. Thanatos slapped him on the back.

'Ah, cheer up, you old misery! Now let's go home and do a bit of ski-ing. I don't trust this weather to last.'

'There's a pile of work waiting,' said Dave.

'How much?'

'You won't get through it in eight hours.'

'Right, we'll stay sober this evening and do half of it. Then we'll tackle the other half tomorrow morning. We gotta keep the afternoon clear, Dave, so we can have a bit of a drink before we see old Jim on to the ferry.'

'Carry him up the gangway?'

'Right. Jim, you'll find Tony and tell her what I said?'

'I'll tell her if I see her.'

'Do that.'

Pibble hung about the monastery after the others had left, strangely cheerless. For a while he explored the enormous honeycomb, finding little that differed from any other part of the building. Then at the extreme end of the corridors beyond the Chapel of St. Sporophore he found a broken wall which allowed him to scramble out on to an area of tumbled rock, inaccessible by other means, with cliff above and cliff below. Here he sat for a good hour, enjoying the milder vigour of the sun as it sloped towards setting. He tried to work out why he so disliked Thanatos's plans or the monastery. They would mean that the place became alive again, and that the mosaic would be seen and enjoyed by people, many more of whom (probably) would really appreciate it than the monks ever had, even when the cells were all filled with them. But, despite all rational arguments, he found himself thinking that he would prefer the whole place to decay, to slide into the sea, than thus to be artificially preserved. He wondered whether he could do anything to forestall the change, even if it meant betraying Thanatos . . .

A patch of colour on another rock, less than six feet away, caught the corner of his eye. Knowing that there was only one thing of that precise hue, he moved his head round with painstaking slowness to stare at it.

This samimithi was twice the size of the one he had seen on the path down from the cemetery. Spread on the rock, it relished the same sun as old Pibble. He could see the minute palpitation of its breathing, and the jerky flicker of its gold eye. It was not really translucent; only its colour was so much fleshier than flesh that it seemed that some of it must come from inside the surface, a radiation, a sort of warning. Pibble wondered whether it glowed at all in the dark – it looked as though it might. As he watched, the crest on its nape rose, webbed with skin between the spines; a gill-like area behind its jaw-bone puffed out to double the size of its mask; the creature gave a shrill, shivering rattle which lasted for an incredible time – more than a minute – and then the spine and the gills subsided and it lay still again.

Pibble released his breath slowly, as though he were himself an animal in danger. It had been a performance, anthropomorphically speaking, of extraordinary malevolence. No wonder the samimithi accumulated superstitions – if you found one of those things drowned in the cup you had been drinking from, flabby with death and the glow of the skin fading and the gold eye glazed, you'd have every right to feel frightened, and betrayed by the friendly and innocent milk that had hidden the corpse … It was curious that what he had at first thought of as a sex-symbol should now have become an image of betrayal. Or perhaps they were the same thing.

Well, he would do what Thanatos wanted. Forget about the monastery, find Tony and give her the message. Sex and betrayal could be left to someone else.

At the sound of his little snort of self-disgust the samimithi flicked out of sight.

The sun had set before he reached Vangelis's vineyard. In the dusk he walked noisily between the yellowing rows of vines, scuffing the shaly soil so that it rattled and coughing once or twice. Tony came to meet him with her finger to her lips.

'She's asleep,' she whispered.

They moved further away from the hut and Pibble gave her his message as impersonally as he was able.

'Tell him no,' said Tony. 'Tell him thank you, but no.'

'All right.'

'Nothing happens twice. Will he understand that?'

'I doubt it.'

'Look, when an American chooses to live my kind of life, she sacrifices all kinds of things. Like they say, you are born to the American dream; you decide with your head that it's a bad dream, and that you must fight it. But you still want it – you want it without the guilt. The old swine gave me that, to be that other Anna, dreaming the dream. And that was fine. I let myself go. Like I told you, if you do anything you do it with all yourself. Thanassi understands that, because that's how *he* lives. But then I woke up. No, it wasn't because I met Nan . . .'

'I thought it was the shooting.'

'No, not that. When Thanassi put me into his game, in the Tank, then. Oh, I tried to go back to sleep again, the way you do, but it wasn't for real any more. Then I met Nan. Then it looked as though the pigs – sorry, the cops – were on to me. Then I was awake. You tell him all that. *You* understand, huh?'

'I suppose so.'

The funny thing was that even without her wig she was back to being the other Tony as she explained this. Not Thanatos's luxurious girl, but the earnest and half-innocent child who had pestered the servants about the samimithi; again it was her way of what she called 'doing it with all yourself'. She made her case well as she could, and part of her case was also to make herself attractive to old Pibble at the same time.

'I'd better say goodbye,' he said. 'I'm leaving tomorrow afternoon.'

'Oh. Well. Huh. Well, so long.'

'Say good-bye to Nancy for me. How is she?'

'Picking up. I've been letting her get pretty drunk between whiles, but she'll be able to lay off that in a week. She's had an easy ride, compared to some.'

'Good. Well, I hope you'll be happy.'

He couldn't avoid giving her this last blessing in the tones of one's embarrassed good wishes to a colleague who has taken it into his head to marry a tart. Tony reverted to Anna.

'It doesn't matter, that,' she said.

'I hope it anyway,' said Pibble with much more feeling.

'Thanks. So long.'

He went back down the hill.

Pibble was getting into his pyjamas when Thanatos sent for him, so he went down to the work-room dishevelled and cross. Alfred was at the teleprinter, Dave writing out messages for him in longhand, George working with one hand on a calculator which he didn't even glance at as he flipped through a type-written report, extracting the seam of figures from the spoil of words. Thanatos sprawled on a low chair in the middle of the room surrounded by piles of paper, and didn't look up as Pibble spoke.

'O.K.,' he said at last. 'I've done with her. Thanks, Jim.'

But they all knew it was a lie.

That was probably the reason why Pibble's farewell party at the Lord Byron, the expensive bar by the ferry terminal, was not a success. Thanatos said almost nothing; Buck maintained his peculiar brand of joshing bonhomie through yawns and glowers; Dave was interested in the red power-boat which Pibble had seen before, and managed to work up an argument with George about its probable price and performance, but Thanatos refused to be drawn into anything except grunts and snorts, all derisive. But most of the time he sat silent, tilting back in his chair, sweating rivulets and looking bulkier than ever because of the bullet-proof vest which he had insisted on wearing in mockery of his courtiers' useless solicitudes.

Life of a sort arrived in the shape of Mark Hott, who came striding between the charterartists, deliberately jostling a couple of easels, and plunged up to their table. Pibble saw Alfred move forward from the beach-buggies, ready to act as a chucker-out.

'Hi, Buck,' said Hott. 'Hi, Jim. Mind if I join you? Thought I'd better come and kinda apologize.'

'Siddown,' mumbled Thanatos.

'My labour force,' explained Buck with a giggle.

Hott dragged a chair across and called for beer into the dark cave beyond the awning.

'How's the painting?' said Buck.

'All packed up and ready to go.'

'Then you will be able to supervise the restoration of the mosaic?' asked George. 'That is good.'

'Me? Sorry, pal, but I'm wanted in Canada.'

(And that was true.)

'You are in a weak position,' said George. 'If the mosaic is not restored by the time the authorities in Athens are told of its existence – and soon they must be told – they will want to know how it was damaged.'

'That's Buck's lookout,' said Hott without interest.

'It depends what they are told, sir. We are not without influence in Athens.'

Hott swung his thick-lensed stare round to check with Thanatos, who answered him with a snort of enraged contempt. They were two of a kind, Pibble thought, but not of a kind that get along well together, more like the tusked wild swine which will fight any other male off its own territory. He listened for a moment as George continued to press Hott with business details. He had no wish to be drawn in, and was happy to be distracted by a big motor booming on the water. The red power-boat was moving now, with half the harbour shouting advice to its bosomy crew. When he turned back to the table Hott was drawing.

'You have hurt your arm,' observed Doc Trotter.

'Girl bit it,' said Hott, not ceasing to glance from his glaring host to his sketch and back. Pibble could see on the top of the working forearm a few drops of red, which he had taken for spilt drink, or paint.

'They spotted you over here,' said Hott. 'Me, I can't see that far. I asked them to come along and introduce me, but they went all coy, and one of them bit me.'

'Where?' said Thanatos, addressing him directly for the first time.

'Helicon Bar,' said Hott and pointed.

Thanatos stood up like a puppet jerked out of collapse by a twitch of strings. Before anyone else was on his feet he was blundering through the first cluster of charterartists.

'Some guy,' said Hott as everyone rose. Pibble looked at his watch – there was still half an hour to the ferry. George was counting notes on to the table to pay for the drinks. When he had achieved the exact sum he sighed, shrugged, and added another hundred-drach note, a ludicrous over-tip. The others had already left, Dave wheeling Buck.

'I'll just tell Alfred where we're going,' said Pibble.

'O.K.,' said George, without looking up. He seemed deeply depressed – harrowed in advance, Pibble decided, by the scene that was about to take place at the Helicon. Pibble turned away and left him to his griefs.

As he repassed the Lord Byron he was amused to see what the girls on the red power-boat had been up to. One was now sunning herself on the cabin roof while the other had nudged the boat in a deliberately purposeless fashion towards the ferry terminal and the Lord Byron. And now their prey had leaped to his feet and gone. It was astonishing, he thought, how fast the word got round that a man like Thanatos is in the market for a new companion. Poor thing, this one would not do, no matter how languidly she displayed her wares. She was well-proportioned but ordinary, like ten thousand other anemones of the Mediterranean littoral, looking so soft and harmless despite being mostly stomach. Even George, despite his troubles, had noticed their unambiguous approach; Pibble saw him frown at them like a grandfather and shake his head before following the trail of courtiers after the vanished monarch. It seemed kinder to leave him to himself, so Pibble stooped to examine Hott's unfinished sketch of Thanatos Furens. Disappointingly it was O.K., but nothing special.

Even before he reached the Helicon Pibble could see that Thanatos was alive once more, as he had been up in the monastery. Alive, but not boisterous. There was something about his pose that suggested an angler playing a big fish on tackle too fine for it. Evidently he had decided to try Nancy first; she was still the starved waif, but perhaps a crust less starved than yesterday, and having tasted Hott she looked ready to take a bite out of Thanatos also. Tony was wary but in control of herself and the situation, while the nobles of the court were all vicariously on edge for their king. Only Hott seemed wholly relaxed.

One table was already full by the time Pibble arrived, so he joined George and Doc Trotter at the neighbouring one. Poor George had seated himself as far as possible from Tony, but was still able to torture himself with looking at her. Dave finished his hellos to Tony and joined the outcasts, making the whole party into a loose figure-of-eight, an amoeba on the point of fission. The conversation in their half was meaningless; they might just as well have been muttering 'rhubarb, rhubarb'; the curious contest at the other table was what mattered, its contestants so ill-matched and its judge so biassed. In fact they talked about golf architecture – George being a large-green man, Dave a table-topper while the doctor gargled for some intermediate area. Pibble would have liked to switch the talk to something he could take part in, such as the antics of the girls in the red power-boat, now once more aimlessly homing in on them.

After all, it was *his* farewell party. But perhaps the rich might feel that their own tendency to attract parasites was not a subject for polite conversation; and it would only be another vulture at poor George's liver. So he stopped even pretending to listen to his own table and simply watched the faces at the other. Vainly he tried to imagine what it must be like to be Nancy, suddenly faced by this gross rival in love, this all-time father figure; it seemed inconceivable that she should not detest him, yet now he had made her smile, and Tony laugh. He tilted his chair, hooking his foot under the heavy iron table to prevent himself from toppling right over, looking gross and totally relaxed. Only if you knew him well could you see how wary he was. In fact a curious tension seemed to emanate not only from him, but from the group at the table where Pibble sat . . .

Never mind that. Nancy looked much better today, a living proof of Tony's will-power. Hott rolled one of his slick cigarettes and offered it to Tony, who looked at him guardedly and shook her head without smiling. So she still thought . . .

Not thought, *knew*. And Nancy *was* better. And Hott rolled and smoked pot, using joss-sticks to conceal the smell of them in his studio. And naturally enough put them into a cigarette packet before passing them to his girl – his ex-girl. And Nancy hadn't lit her fag in the Refectory that first day, and had thrown it away half-smoked the moment Pibble had come out of the Catholicon.

Like slates ripped off a roof by a freak wind, a whole area of Pibble's assumptions were whisked away, leaving the intellectual edifice naked to the light of reason. Hott had never been mad enough to try and steal a mosaic on an island where he was already making handsome money by processing opium into morphine, because the morphine factory was an illusion. And the smuggling of the stuff disguised as abstract art had been an illusion. And the theft of the pictures only less of an illusion by being, as Nancy had hinted, a publicity stunt.

So that was that. Pibble felt a real aesthetic satisfaction at having eliminated this unnecessary complication, and produced the theft of the mosaic and the decoying of Thanatos away from the monastery as a single, tidy, and contained event. Pity about Canadian customs, waiting to probe and analyse Hott's new show, in vain. That was an untidy strand, and poor old Butler would probably get into hot water over it . . .

Butler . . .

He had come to Hyos because there'd been a rumour that the Mafia was interested in the island, and they'd thought it must be for the drugs.

But there were no drugs.

Therefore the Mafia interest, if it existed, was in something else.

A flood of alarmed illumination streamed through the stripped roof of Pibble's mind, like a baleful sunrise. Involuntarily he glanced across the table at George's saurian face, only to see it launched away from him as George flung himself sprawling across the cobbles. Then the noise began.

In a whirling world Pibble seemed to see in the same instant, as if through a fish-eye lens, the beauty on the cabin roof scrambling away, the masked face behind the gun muzzle at the window below where she'd lain, Thanatos hurled backwards out of his tilting chair with the table crashing behind him, Tony on her feet and yelling as she dragged Nancy away, Hott's yellow shirt turning crimson on the ground – and then, close up, the grey-purple cobbles where his own muscles had thrown him unwilled, while the second burst of bullets clanged into the iron table-top and winced, singing, into the dark taverna.

The yammer paused and began again before the juddering of it was out of his head. Something not quite solid flipped against his leg. White crumbs of plaster suddenly flecked the cobbles. The firing stopped and a deeper note took over. For several seconds he crouched, thinking it was another sort of gun, then recognized the note and raised his head in time to see the power-boat weaving away across the harbour, tilting to skim the water while its ridged wake bounced the other boats about.

Thanatos was on his back behind the fallen table which had screened him from all but the first burst; from a muddle of torn flesh in the left side of his neck blood pumped in sudden pulses. So he was still alive. Pibble wrenched the shirt open, only to find the bloodied khaki furrows of the bullet-proof waistcoat covering the whole torso – no time to get him out of that. He hunkered round until he could slide his hand into the bloodslimed collar-opening and with a fierce contortion dig his thumb into the flesh of the neck just above the collar-bone where the common carotid ought to be. The blood still welled, and he pressed harder. It stopped its jerking flow.

Either he had plugged that leak, or the heart was done with pumping and Thanatos was dead.

A shadow covered him; he looked up and saw Nancy, with spread nostrils and huge eyes, bending over the body. Her tongue licked thin along her lips.

'Sit down, baby,' said Tony and eased her away. Then she was kneeling beside Pibble.

'Dead?' she said.

'Not yet. Get a sharp knife out of the taverna and cut him out of his shirt, then see if you can get his waistcoat off. I can't hold the artery much longer at this angle.'

She was gone, leaving him alone in the precise, intent world of his own urgency, a sphere of concentration outside which the screams and shouts of the Greeks fluctuated with a remote meaninglessness. A pair of smart black shoes and dark trousers strutted into the sphere and a man's voice shouted in Greek. Pibble simply shook his head.

But that small action, like the shake of a kaleidoscope, resettled the pointless mess of the last two minutes and made interpretable shapes. The gunman was on the red power-boat. He came from Sicily – Marseilles – didn't matter. He'd brought two women, accomplices and bait and camouflage, to manage the boat while he hid, and make it look harmless and ineffectual, and provide a reason for trying to get within range of Thanassi when he came down to the harbour. And the boat had not appeared until Zoe had left. And George had known that the bodyguards had gone astray, and had cancelled . . .

Tony was suddenly kneeling beside him, working quickly at the sleeve with the bitter-sharp little knife that is used for boning raw fish.

'Where's Trotter?' said Pibble. 'He's a doctor – he'd be better at this than me.'

'Philosophy, philosophy,' said the Negro's voice, between sobs. 'What can I do?'

'Keep these damned people away. See that somebody goes for the police. Get Alfred.'

'George is dead, George is dead,' cried someone in a wailing chant.

'Come on, Dave,' said Doc Trotter resolutely. 'Help me keep those good folk at bay.'

The clamour outside the sphere lessened a little. The smart

shoes moved reluctantly away. Tony had the shirt off, and was wrapping it round the mangled and bleeding arm. Pibble managed to achieve a new posture that allowed her to get at the zip of the waistcoat.

'He might be O.K.,' he said, grunting with the strain of his attitude. 'He was tilting his chair and that first blast knocked him over, and then the table screened him. It depends how quick we can get him to hospital.'

'Is there one?'

'I don't know. Ease that flap back if you can. That's better.'

'Christ! Alf's got bandages in the buggy – a whole first-aid kit.'

'Doc! Doc! Get this chap to stand clear!'

And then, at last, above the shrilling and muttering of the crowd, the buggy's harsh engine and Alfred cursing his way through.

Alfred took charge, and Tony moved out of the sphere. He was firm and skilful, contriving with his inadequate kit a jury-rig under which the battered hulk might just possibly sail safe to port. But it was twenty minutes before Pibble could stand, numb with cramp and tension and reeling with shock, to find himself in a circus. Thagoulos was the ringmaster, and the thrilled sightseers made the ring. Buck, white and weeping, a distorted clown, sat in a gleaming piece of gymnast's apparatus; two assistants trundled on a more deliberately comic machine, a hand ambulance so old that it had probably been built to wheel the dead children of the 23rd Foot up to the British Cemetery.

Thanatos groaned, a windy, despairing note, as they lifted him on to it. Blankets covered the bodies of George Palangalos and Mark Hott, who could afford to wait. A helicopter clattered down above the ferry quay. Inside the taverna the bat-eared girl whooped and whooped with unstoppable hysterics. The ferryboat was gone.

Pibble wiped the blood off the glass of his watch to look at the time. But there was no question of his leaving for at least another day. He sat down at one of the taverna tables and began to arrange the muddle of knowledge and guesswork in his mind, ready for questioning.

Chapter Twelve

The interpreter was another kind of lizard – the brown, dry scaly sort that live remote from men and look wise and wary. He was, in fact, a very old and distinguished British archaeologist whom Captain Thagoulos had whisked over from Zakynthos, where he now lived, to help with the preliminary investigations. He was called Sir Thopas Jones, a name which Pibble's unreliable memory associated with a long-exploded theory about the Etruscans. Now he sat in the sultry office, bright-eyed but dry-voiced, and interpreted Captain Thagoulos's questions into careful English, and Pibble's replies into equally careful Greek. Captain Thagoulos finished reading aloud from a typed report in front of him. Sir Thopas spoke.

'The gist of that is that the doctors have no idea whether your friend will live or die; if he lives, they have no idea what sort of mental and physical condition he'll be in – that is to say whether he will make any real recovery. They don't even know whether they're going to amputate his arm.'

Pibble sighed, and felt bleak. No more water-skiing. No more exultation.

Captain Thagoulos put the report back in the file on his desk and picked out of it a small rectangle of cardboard. He flicked it with a fingernail as he spoke.

'The Captain,' said Sir Thopas, 'is under the impression that you told him last time you met that you were an active policeman. He has since been in touch with London and learnt that you left the force under, well, not exactly *dubious* circumstances, but . . .'

'I told him I'd retired,' said Pibble firmly. 'He may not have understood.'

'O.K., O.K.,' said Captain Thagoulos, waving his hand forgivingly. He then spoke to Sir Thopas at some length, and while he did so Pibble considered his own situation. Thagoulos was a good and careful policeman. He wouldn't bring up a point like that, and then dismiss it, except as a deliberate warning. From now on nobody was going to get away with anything. And Pibble, after a shocked, dazed night in grieving Porphyrocolpos, had still not decided what to do – about Buck and the mosaic, about Nancy and the pot, about Tony and the bombs.

'The Captain is appealing to you,' said Sir Thopas suddenly. 'He says that you will understand, having been a policeman. Hyos is a small island, and now the eyes of the world are on it. There will be senior policemen arriving from Athens this afternoon, and it is important to him to know as much as possible about the reason for these murders. He is anxious to be able to present Athens with a clear and coherent picture of what has been going on in his bailiwick. He is under the impression that you know considerably more than you have yet told him.'

Damn the man's impressions, thought Pibble. He was too sharp.

'No,' he said, 'that's not true. I mean, of course I know more than I told him, but with one exception – about a man called Butler – I did tell him everything I then knew which was relevant. I've worked out a lot of other things since. I'll begin at the beginning. First . . . do you think you can explain to him what a war game is?'

'Game?' said Captain Thagoulos. 'Cricket?'

Sir Thopas explained until Captain Thagoulos held up his hand and said, 'Understood.'

Pibble went into Thanassi's war game in some detail, giving the roles that all the participants had played. Captain Thagoulos made notes, but sighed and made a negative click of disbelief when Pibble explained how he had represented the Mafia.

'I was a stop-gap,' said Pibble. 'There was a chap called Hal Adamson who was supposed to take the part, but he had a last-minute accident in Minneapolis. I think it might just be worth sending a wire to find out whether there was anything fishy about the accident. I mean, he's apparently some sort of an expert on the Mafia, and it's possible that he was deliberately delayed.'

Captain Thagoulos made another note as Sir Thopas translated, then held up his hand for silence as Pibble began to speak again. He made Pibble write Adamson's name down for him.

'You can get the other details – address and so on – from Dave Warren at Porphyrocolpos,' said Pibble.

Again the negative click, and a brief remark.

'Apparently you have implied that somebody at Porphyrocolpos is not to be trusted,' said Sir Thopas. 'I don't follow that.'

'If Mr. Adamson's accident wasn't an accident,' said Pibble, 'somebody must have told the Mafia where he was going, and why. But it's all right – that man's dead.'

Captain Thagoulos frowned, wrote on the pad which bore Adamson's name, called one of his bleary-eyed assistants in, and gave him the paper with brisk orders. The man went out, then Pibble carried on with his tale, until he was interrupted again.

'Why didn't you consult the island police about this assassination threat?' interpreted Sir Thopas.

'Because nobody really believed it. It seemed just worth while taking our own precautions, and Thanatos is rich enough to send for professional bodyguards and regard them as a minor precaution. But although he has a lot of influence at Athens he doesn't like using it for things like this; it was probably only a silly scare.'

The half-truth sounded weak. He still hadn't decided what to do or say about Tony. Meanwhile there was also the problem of Buck and the mosaic. The odds were that Dave Warren or Doc Trotter would come out with that. So . . .

'Now we come to a major complication,' he said. 'One of the people at Porphyrocolpos wanted to keep Thanatos inside the fence for his own reasons, so at the war game he supported the idea of an assassination attempt very strongly, and then faked a shooting attempt which sank a boat which was towing Mr. Thanatos while he was ski-ing.'

Thagoulos's eyebrows asked the obvious question.

'I'd rather you asked Dave Warren about that,' said Pibble. 'The thing is, it's something over which Mr. Thanatos *would* be prepared to use his influence at Athens, supposing he recovers. If I were you I'd move very carefully.'

Captain Thagoulos listened to the translation and suddenly looked very tired. When he spat into his handkerchief he inspected the sputum with no real interest. Presumably he had been up all night, helping a bewildered and panicking headquarters in Athens to organize the pursuit of the killers.

'Now I think I'd better account for Mr. Butler's arrival,' said Pibble. 'I couldn't tell you at the time, but he was in fact an active policeman – not quite a secret policeman, but that sort of thing. London had heard a rumour that the Mafia was interested in Hyos – it's all right; they thought it was nonsense too, but they thought they'd send a man to check, rather than bother Athens with a mare's nest . . .'

Captain Thagoulos looked not at all appeased by this explanation, and his pencil dug deep into his pad as he made the necessary notes. Pibble thought he did well to be angry.

'Naturally,' he continued, 'we were alarmed when we learnt this. I tried to persuade Mr. Thanatos to consult you, but he wouldn't. Butler's idea was that if the Mafia did have an interest in Hyos, it was as a staging-post for the heroin trade. I agreed to tell him if I found anything which was an indication one way or the other, but I didn't tell him about the possibility of a murder attempt. Again, this was because Thanatos was anxious not to complicate his deal with the government of the Southward Islands more than he had to. Despite the rumour which Butler's bosses had heard, he still thought the notion of killing him was nonsense.'

Captain Thagoulos listened to the interpretation without full attention; he seemed to have accepted the idea that Thanatos was outside the law – at least for the moment.

'The next thing that happened,' said Pibble, 'was that George Palangalos rang you up from Porphyrocolpos and told you that Butler was playing with Hyote boys.'

'Palangalos,' said Captain Thagoulos, and added a sentence in Greek.

'He is your traitor?' interpreted Sir Thopas. 'The least likely person?'

Pibble ignored the donnish gloss. Poor George – he had been the only possible person, once one had realized what passions churned beneath the still exterior.

'Yes,' he said. 'He wanted Butler out of the way, in case he should spot the men the Mafia sent. At first he denied having made the call – and so did everyone else of course – but he told me yesterday morning that he'd done it.'

Thagoulos asked a question.

'Why did he tell you? What reason did he give?' said Sir Thopas.

'He told me because I'd worked out about this other thing I was telling you about – the man who wanted to keep Thanatos at Porphyrocolpos – and was taking George to show him. If that was cleared up, George didn't want any other unexplained mysteries lying around. The reason he gave for the call was the one he'd given on the telephone, that he didn't approve of rich foreigners seducing Greek boys.'

Thagoulos nodded. Pibble realized that he'd now passed his last chance to tell him who Tony really was, without having to admit to lies and half-truths. So now he would never tell – and if next year, somewhere on the other side of the world, the torn bodies of the half-innocent sprawled on a sidewalk . . .

'Have you any other evidence than the telephone call to involve Palangalos?' said Sir Thopas. Pibble hadn't even heard the original question in Greek. He pulled himself together.

'Nothing absolutely direct and concrete, but I'm fairly sure I'm right. First, Palangalos had been the strongest opponent in the war game of the idea of an assassination; then, when we agreed to try to check the island, he arranged for his wife to do the harbour. But as soon as the fake shooting occurred he used that as an excuse to send her out of danger. The assassin's boat arrived next day. Then, when I took George out to look at this red herring I was telling you about, he kept me covered with a pistol most of the time – why should he do that if he was really convinced that the threat to Thanatos was imaginary? And why should *he* be in danger? Next, when we got back from this expedition we were told by Dave Warren that the guards we had sent for had been searched at the frontier and refused entry because they were carrying illicit weapons. George immediately cancelled the order for a fresh lot of guards to be summoned . . .'

Captain Thagoulos held up his hand before Pibble could take over from Sir Thopas's fluent Greek. He asked a brief question.

'You think the customs were, um, tipped off?' said Sir Thopas.

'I certainly think it would be worth checking,' said Pibble, 'though I doubt if you'll find a direct connection with George. He was a careful man. Where was I? Oh, yes, when we went to the harbour yesterday afternoon at first we were sitting outside the Lord Byron, but then we moved down the quay to the Olympia. I'd noticed the girls' boat edging towards us, and I thought it was just that they wanted to attract Thanatos's attention. There was one sunning herself provocatively on the roof. But we moved off to the Olympia before they got near enough for shooting. I went off to see about my baggage at the ferry terminal, and when I came back I noticed George shaking his head at them. At the time I thought he disapproved of the girls' behaviour, but now I think it more likely that he was trying to persuade them not to make the attempt. Last of all, just before the shooting started, I saw him throw himself flat on the quay — he knew what was coming. And then, of course, they shot him on purpose. They fired a separate burst at him. I felt his body knock against my leg. He had served his purpose.'

Captain Thagoulos sat looking at his notes for a while, sorting them out in his mind.

'Where did the girls come from?' said Pibble. 'I imagine they checked in with you when they arrived.'

'The documents are from Brindisi. The Italian police are already looking for them.'

'I can't imagine they'll find them alive,' said Pibble. 'My bet is that they'll have been shot and dumped overboard as soon as the boat was clear away.'

'Dear me.'

That was Sir Thopas's own comment. Pibble looked at him and saw that the old man was for the first time visibly distressed. It took him several seconds to translate Captain Thagoulos's sudden question.

'Why should Palangalos do this? He's known to be a close associate of Thanatos — his right-hand man.'

'There was a girl at Porphyrocolpos called Tony d'Agniello . . .'

'One harlot,' said Thagoulos, without waiting for the translation.

'No,' said Pibble. 'She was Thanatos's mistress, but he didn't give her money. In fact I'm convinced he loved her and she was fond of him. She's very attractive indeed, and George wanted her, though he had recently married a new wife. It took me some time to realize how obsessed he was with her . . .'

Pibble paused for the translation, swallowing his own obsessions.

'A *crime passionnel*,' commented Sir Thopas.

'Not wholly,' said Pibble. 'It's rather difficult for anyone who hasn't experienced it to realize the intensity of the loyalty which someone like Thanatos demands from his followers. At times he deliberately tests that loyalty to breaking-point — I saw this happen a couple of nights ago. But when the loyalty really does break, it goes with a vengeance. Literally, in this case. George was not an attractive man, cold and reserved and rather ugly. In some ways he was rich and successful, but he owed all that to Thanatos – it wasn't his own, so to speak. I think even Zoe, his new wife, he really owed to Thanatos, because I doubt if she'd have married him if he hadn't been rich and successful. But Thanatos himself could have what he wanted, and it was his own thing. For instance Tony, though she left him a couple of days ago, told me that she'd have got along with him – and by implication been his mistress – even if he'd been poor. I don't think George could ever have commanded that sort of response. So, though he was genuinely obsessed with Tony, there were deeper impulses at work. I mean, if she hadn't been there I think he'd still have broken with Thanatos in the near future, though perhaps not so violently.'

Thagoulos frowned as he listened to the translation, then spoke.

'Apparently the girl was present at the shooting,' said Sir Thopas. 'She was questioned with the rest of you last night, but didn't say she'd left Porphyrocolpos. Do you know where she is?'

'Staying with a girl called Nancy in a hut on the hill by the monastery. The hut belongs to a man called Vangelis.'

Captain Thagoulos nodded and commented.

'He says this Nancy is a half-wit,' said Sir Thopas. 'Of course the Greeks have their own ideas about the degrees of lunacy.'

'She is a bit unbalanced,' said Pibble. 'When the Captain questions Miss d'Agniello, he might bring up another point which has a bearing. Yesterday morning George and I met her, and George had an argument with her. I didn't hear it all, but my impression was that at first he was asking her to come back to Porphyrocolpos, because he couldn't bear not to have her about; but then he realized that if she stayed away then Thanatos was more likely to get frustrated enough to leave the safety of his own grounds and go somewhere where he could be shot at.'

Captain Thagoulos made a final note, drew a line under it, then sat silently gazing at Pibble. After a while he leafed through the file and removed a telegraph form which he read carefully through, frowning and consulting his dictionary a couple of times. At last he took from a drawer the necessary kit to roll a cigarette and started carefully on that job. Watching him tease the treacly-looking tobacco into shape, Pibble thought of Hott's neat, stubby fingers doing the same job. Hott was dead. Would he have been alive if Pibble had read the signs more accurately? No, he would still have drifted up against Thanatos's magnetic bulk at the lethal moment. Pibble had made no difference. Hott had been a large life, and he was obliterated. Thanassi, a larger life still, hovered on the grey frontier. And George. It was lucky that there hadn't been more – in some ways the ruthless indiscriminacy of the shooting had been the worst thing of all. They didn't care who died, provided their enemies were among them.

'I think you are one friend,' said Captain Thagoulos suddenly, and passed the telegram across the desk. It was addressed to Pibble at Porphyrocolpos, and had been sent from London Airport.

'YOUR MONTREAL CONTACT CHECKED LAST YEAR AND FOUND OK STOP THINK AGAIN STOP AM PROCEEDING BARBADOS PRONTO BUT GROUNDED HERE BY BOMB SCARE ON PLANE STOP KEEP STRAIGHT BAT MESSAGE ENDS.'

There was no signature.

Pibble sighed. The bomb scare would have been a hoax, of course, but in his mind's eye he saw the wreckage scattered over eighty fields, bright torn chunks of metal, smoking segments of engine, unrecognizable lumps of rag and meat which had once been people, the stretchermen trudging about, the useless ambulances, the gathering gawpers kept back by police. He also saw Nancy's tongue licking thin along her lips as she stared at the mashed body on the quay.

'There's one other thing I ought to tell you,' he said. 'Though it doesn't concern this case directly. The girl who calls herself Tony d'Agniello . . .'

He explained in an emotionless voice. When he'd finished he sat in silence while Thagoulos made a fresh set of notes, but all the time he seemed to hear a shrill hissing note in his ears. Thagoulos put his pencil down and took out the brandy, glasses, and a jug covered with a needlework square. Sir Thopas smiled when this caught his eye; he studied the design for a moment, then turned to Pibble.

'There's a curious legend on a number of Greek islands, he said conversationally, as the brandy bottle glugged. 'I don't know whether you've come across it. It's about a species of lizard called the samimithi . . .'

Fiction

GENERAL

☐ The House of Women	Chaim Bermant	£1.95
☐ The Patriarch	Chaim Bermant	£2.25
☐ The Rat Race	Alfred Bester	£1.95
☐ Midwinter	John Buchan	£1.50
☐ A Prince of the Captivity	John Buchan	£1.50
☐ The Priestess of Henge	David Burnett	£2.50
☐ Tangled Dynasty	Jean Chapman	£1.75
☐ The Other Woman	Colette	£1.95
☐ Retreat From Love	Colette	£1.60
☐ An Infinity of Mirrors	Richard Condon	£1.95
☐ Arigato	Richard Condon	£1.95
☐ Prizzi's Honour	Richard Condon	£1.75
☐ A Trembling Upon Rome	Richard Condon	£1.95
☐ The Whisper of the Axe	Richard Condon	£1.75
☐ Love and Work	Gwyneth Cravens	£1.95
☐ King Hereafter	Dorothy Dunnett	£2.95
☐ Pope Joan	Lawrence Durrell	£1.35
☐ The Country of Her Dreams	Janice Elliott	£1.35
☐ Magic	Janice Elliott	£1.95
☐ Secret Places	Janice Elliott	£1.75
☐ Letter to a Child Never Born	Oriana Fallaci	£1.25
☐ A Man	Oriana Fallaci	£2.50
☐ Rich Little Poor Girl	Terence Feely	£1.75
☐ Marital Rites	Margaret Forster	£1.50
☐ The Seduction of Mrs Pendlebury	Margaret Forster	£1.95
☐ Abingdons	Michael French	£2.25
☐ Rhythms	Michael French	£2.25
☐ Who Was Sylvia?	Judy Gardiner	£1.50
☐ Grimalkin's Tales	Gardiner, Ronson, Whitelaw	£1.60
☐ Lost and Found	Julian Gloag	£1.95
☐ A Sea-Change	Lois Gould	£1.50
☐ La Presidenta	Lois Gould	£2.25
☐ A Kind of War	Pamela Haines	£1.95
☐ Tea at Gunters	Pamela Haines	£1.75
☐ Black Summer	Julian Hale	£1.75
☐ A Rustle in the Grass	Robin Hawdon	£1.95
☐ Riviera	Robert Sydney Hopkins	£1.95
☐ Duncton Wood	William Horwood	£2.75
☐ The Stonor Eagles	William Horwood	£2.50
☐ The Man Who Lived at the Ritz	A. E. Hotchner	£1.65
☐ A Bonfire	Pamela Hansford Johnson	£1.50
☐ The Good Listener	Pamela Hansford Johnson	£1.50
☐ The Honours Board	Pamela Hansford Johnson	£1.50
☐ The Unspeakable Skipton	Pamela Hansford Johnson	£1.50
☐ In the Heat of the Summer	John Katzenbach	£1.95
☐ Starrs	Warren Leslie	£2.50
☐ Kine	A. R. Lloyd	£1.50
☐ The Factory	Jack Lynn	£1.95
☐ Christmas Pudding	Nancy Mitford	£1.50
☐ Highland Fling	Nancy Mitford	£1.50
☐ Pigeon Pie	Nancy Mitford	£1.75
☐ The Sun Rises	Christopher Nicole	£2.50

Fiction

HORROR/OCCULT/NASTY

☐ Death Walkers	Gary Brandner	£1.75
☐ Hellborn	Gary Brandner	£1.75
☐ The Howling	Gary Brandner	£1.75
☐ Return of the Howling	Gary Brandner	£1.75
☐ Tribe of the Dead	Gary Brandner	£1.75
☐ The Sanctuary	Glenn Chandler	£1.50
☐ The Tribe	Glenn Chandler	£1.10
☐ The Black Castle	Leslie Daniels	£1.25
☐ The Big Goodnight	Judy Gardiner	£1.25
☐ Rattlers	Joseph L. Gilmore	£1.60
☐ The Nestling	Charles L. Grant	£1.95
☐ Night Songs	Charles L. Grant	£1.95
☐ Slime	John Halkin	£1.75
☐ Slither	John Halkin	£1.60
☐ The Unholy	John Halkin	£1.25
☐ The Skull	Shaun Hutson	£1.25
☐ Pestilence	Edward Jarvis	£1.60
☐ The Beast Within	Edward Levy	£1.25
☐ Night Killers	Richard Lewis	£1.25
☐ Spiders	Richard Lewis	£1.75
☐ The Web	Richard Lewis	£1.75
☐ Nightmare	Lewis Mallory	£1.75
☐ Bloodthirst	Mark Ronson	£1.60
☐ Ghoul	Mark Ronson	£1.75
☐ Ogre	Mark Ronson	£1.75
☐ Deathbell	Guy N. Smith	£1.75
☐ Doomflight	Guy N. Smith	£1.25
☐ Manitou Doll	Guy N. Smith	£1.25
☐ Satan's Snowdrop	Guy N. Smith	£1.00
☐ The Understudy	Margaret Tabor	£1.95
☐ The Beast of Kane	Cliff Twemlow	£1.50
☐ The Pike	Cliff Twemlow	£1.25

Fiction

SCIENCE FICTION

☐ More Things in Heaven	John Brunner	£1.50
☐ Chessboard Planet	Henry Kuttner	£1.75
☐ The Proud Robot	Henry Kuttner	£1.50
☐ Death's Master	Tanith Lee	£1.50
☐ The Dancers of Arun	Elizabeth A. Lynn	£1.50
☐ The Northern Girl	Elizabeth A. Lynn	£1.50
☐ Balance of Power	Brian M. Stableford	£1.75

ADVENTURE/SUSPENSE

☐ The Corner Men	John Gardner	£1.75
☐ Death of a Friend	Richard Harris	£1.95
☐ The Flowers of the Forest	Joseph Hone	£1.75
☐ Styx	Christopher Hyde	£1.50
☐ Temple Kent	D. G. Devon	£1.95
☐ Confess, Fletch	Gregory Mcdonald	£1.50
☐ Fletch	Gregory Mcdonald	£1.50
☐ Fletch and the Widow Bradley	Gregory Mcdonald	£1.50
☐ Flynn	Gregory Mcdonald	£1.75
☐ The Buck Passes Flynn	Gregory Mcdonald	£1.60
☐ The Specialist	Jasper Smith	£1.75

WESTERNS

Blade Series – Matt Chisholm

☐ No. 5 The Colorado Virgins	85p
☐ No. 6 The Mexican Proposition	85p
☐ No. 11 The Navaho Trail	95p

McAllister Series – Matt Chisholm

☐ No. 3 McAllister Never Surrenders	95p
☐ No. 4 McAllister and the Cheyenne Death	95p
☐ No. 8 McAllister – Fire Brand	£1.25

Fiction

CRIME

☐ The Cool Cottontail	John Ball	£1.00
☐ Five Pieces of Jade	John Ball	£1.50
☐ Johnny Get Your Gun	John Ball	£1.00
☐ Then Came Violence	John Ball	£1.50
☐ The Widow's Cruise	Nicholas Blake	£1.25
☐ The Worm of Death	Nicholas Blake	95p
☐ The Long Divorce	Edmund Crispin	£1.50
☐ Love Lies Bleeding	Edmund Crispin	£1.75
☐ The Case of the Sliding Pool	E. V. Cunningham	£1.75
☐ Hindsight	Peter Dickinson	£1.75
☐ King and Joker	Peter Dickinson	£1.25
☐ The Last House Party	Peter Dickinson	£1.75
☐ A Pride of Heroes	Peter Dickinson	£1.50
☐ The Seals	Peter Dickinson	£1.50
☐ Gondola Scam	Jonathan Gash	£1.75
☐ The Sleepers of Erin	Jonathan Gash	£1.75
☐ The Black Seraphim	Michael Gilbert	£1.75
☐ Blood and Judgment	Michael Gilbert	£1.10
☐ Close Quarters	Michael Gilbert	£1.10
☐ The Etruscan Net	Michael Gilbert	£1.25
☐ The Final Throw	Michael Gilbert	£1.75
☐ The Night of the Twelfth	Michael Gilbert	£1.25
☐ The Blunderer	Patricia Highsmith	£1.50
☐ A Game for the Living	Patricia Highsmith	£1.50
☐ Those Who Walk Away	Patricia Highsmith	£1.50
☐ The Tremor of Forgery	Patricia Highsmith	£1.50
☐ The Two Faces of January	Patricia Highsmith	£1.50
☐ Silence Observed	Michael Innes	£1.00
☐ Go West, Inspector Ghote	H. R. F. Keating	£1.50
☐ Inspector Ghote Draws a Line	H. R. F. Keating	£1.50
☐ Inspector Ghote Plays a Joker	H. R. F. Keating	£1.50
☐ The Murder of the Maharajah	H. R. F. Keating	£1.50
☐ The Perfect Murder	H. R. F. Keating	£1.50

NAME..

ADDRESS...

....

Write to Hamlyn Paperbacks Cash Sales, PO Box 11, Falmouth, Cornwall TR10 9EN.

Please indicate order and enclose remittance to the value of cover price plus:

U.K. CUSTOMERS: Please allow 55p for the first book, 22p for the second book and 14p for each additional book ordered to a maximum charge of £1.75.

B.F.P.O. & EIRE: Please allow 55p for the first book, 22p for the second book plus 14p per copy for the next seven books, thereafter 8p per book.

OVERSEAS CUSTOMERS: Please allow £1.00 for the first book plus 25p per copy for each additional book.

Whilst every effort is made to keep prices low it is sometimes necessary to increase cover prices and also postage and packing rates at short notice. Hamlyn Paperbacks reserve the right to show new retail prices on covers which may differ from those previously advertised in the text or elsewhere.